Two Faces of a Patriot

May 2020

The Library of Congress Cataloging-in-Publication data is available upon request.

ISBN 978-1-7346201-0-8 (hardcover)
ISBN 978-1-7346201-1-5 (quality paperback)

www.twofacesofapatriot.com

Printed in the United States of America

Two Faces of a Patriot

Norm Novitsky
John Truman Wolfe

IC Liberty Publishing
2020

Prologue

Bathing in peace and tranquility with the Gods is coming to an end. My penance for silence, and what I didn't do, I must pay for, by birth on Earth, which is seven sunsets from tomorrow.

My warm soul chills ever so slightly. The blue sky that had warmed my spirit since I left Earth now slowly turns darker and darker and will be a black shadow over me seven sunsets from tomorrow.

I have birth but I am powerless to choose where and to whom. My memories fade as I struggle feverishly to hold on to them, and who I was. How can I better my path this time if I don't remember how to unlock the prison of past responsibility?

Will I be able to change? Will I be able to make a difference, for the good this time? Will I be able to live this new life righteously and not give in to darkness and evil as I did in my previous life? A path that haunted the deepest caverns of my soul.

Chapter One – Surveillance
October 1, 2025, Thousand Oaks, California

When Ashley Lawford bolted through the screening portal at the entrance to Barack Obama High School, red strobe lights flared and a security alarm erupted into an ear-splitting alert.

It was so shrill that Jonathon Carr, who had entered right in front of her, dropped to one knee, threw his hands over his ears, and squeezed his eyes shut as if blocking his sight would turn the screeching off.

Ashley remained standing but was also covering her ears when the team of flak-jacketed DAA agents, guns drawn, faces hidden behind black-visored helmets, charged at her screaming, "On the floor! Get on the floor. Face down. Now! Now! Now!"

Ashley turned toward the men. "I just forgot—" was all she managed to get out before she was tased, crumpled to the floor, and started flopping around in the hallway like a freshly caught tuna.

Ashley, having stayed up all night studying for her sexual diversity exam, had left home burnt and bleary-eyed and had forgotten to take her meds. She instantly realized what had triggered the alarm when she'd bolted through the screening area, late for class. She had tried to tell the DAA goons as they approached her but time was not on her side.

According to the school behaviorist, Ashley suffered from Conduct Disorder, a disease of the mind that manifested as disobedience and non-compliance with authority. It was manageable with psychotropic medication.

By the time she recovered, one of the DAA agents had her pinned to the floor with his knee in her back and the rim of his palm around her neck. He retracted his visor and smiled as he pawed through the leather pouch that had been Velcroed to her syntho-leather pants.

"Get off me, you pervert!" she yelled.

The DAA agent pulled out his stun device and tased her again, this time just a few inches from her body. She went back into spastic mode.

On the 17th of September, 2024 the Department of Homeland Security expanded its jurisdiction over American education.

Dissident Activity Administration, as it was called, was justified on the grounds students were being radicalized in schools that placed undue emphasis on the American Revolution and the Declaration of Independence. Analogies were made to the radicalization of young Muslims reading the Quran in madrassas before the Iranian Revolutionary Guard invaded Saudi Arabia and became the dominant force in the Middle East.

All DAA suspects were categorized by the Homeland Security Domestic Terrorism Division.

In a massive expansion of the agency's authority, teams of DAA screeners, long since dubbed Pervert Patrols or just Pervs by the students, were deployed to hundreds of high schools and colleges around the country, classified as at-risk breeding grounds for domestic terrorism.

Despite the fact he lived with his parents on the edge of what many would call an upper middle-class neighborhood, Jonathon Carr, an academically talented student, was still referred to as a "street kid." His broken nose, the product of an after-school fight with a kid three years his senior, gave him a rakish rather than pugilistic appearance. The other kid was left with a whopping shiner, a split lip and two broken ribs.

Jonathon would have wound up in juvie had he not made it to high school, where his penchant for physical combat was channeled to the wresting team. When it came to the opposite sex, Jonathon was a hopeless romantic and was in love as only a fourteen-year-old boy can be. Rays

For Jonathon, Ashley Lawford hung the moon. His plans were to marry her when they graduated from high school and have a passionate marital relationship. The plan had one minor drawback. Jonathon wasn't sure she knew he existed. From the first day he noticed her he tried to work up the courage to ask her to hang out, but like many fourteen -year-old boys the thought of rejection, of her saying no, was too much to deal with and prevented him from even speaking with her.

Ashley had wild, green eyes, lustrous black hair that she usually wore in a pony-tail, and at fifteen, a rapidly developing body, after which Jonathon lusted with poorly-concealed longing. She was smart and rebellious, but in an upbeat sort of way. And while Jonathon had yet to discuss the matter with her, he knew Ashley would be his wife.

Seeing her comatose on the hard tile floor, with the DAA agent's knee pressed into her spine, triggered something in Jonathon which, in another day, would have been called chivalry but today was foolish gallantry.

At five feet, seven inches and one hundred thirty pounds he was bigger than most kids in his sophomore class. He rose to his feet, ran directly at the DAA agent, aimed his kick at the back of the kneeling agent's head, and yelled, "Get off of her, you asshole!"

At the precise moment Jonathon kicked, the DAA agent quickly turned and bolted to his feet. Jonathon's kick bounced off of the agent's Kevlar vest with a dull thud. Jonathon fell backward, hit the wall and landed on his butt, dizzy from the blow.

The agent, NBA tall, stood to his full height, saw Jonathon wobbling, trying to get up off of the floor, and went for his stun device.

"Robinson, put the fucking toy away and bring the girl over here."

"What about the kid?"

"Leave him alone. Let's go."

Jonathon, with the wind knocked out of him, sat on the floor with his back to the wall, watching Ashley and the pervs. The big guard pried her mouth open and put a pill in it. She spit it out. He took hold of both her shoulders and held her immobile. The other guard put the nozzle of an air gun on her upper right arm and pulled the trigger.

"Ouch! Shit!" Ashley cried out.

There was bedlam in the hallways, students rushing to get to class, others turning and yelling perverts, while being ushered to their classrooms by teachers and hall security.

Ashley got up, saw Jonathon down the hall and began walking toward him. The guard who had injected her smiled as he watched her. Jonathon managed to stand stably this time, brushed himself off and gave the guards his best "fuck you" look. The guard turned away and Jonathon's "fuck you" finger went up.

The perv's didn't react, just smiled as if they had already won.

Ashley said as she approached, "I was pretty out of it, but I heard you screaming at those assholes."

"I, eh . . . yeah," Jonathon said, but wanted to say I could have beat the crap out of that goon for what he was doing to you, yet couldn't get the words out.

"Did you try to jump them?"

Ashley stood two feet in front of him. Dirt from the floor smudged across her exquisite cheek. He could see the temporary defeat in her eyes but also her demeanor recomposed. At that moment he wanted to reach out and comfort her with a tender hug, reassuring her all will be ok but checked the impulse and brushed it away.

"I– they . . ." His mind raced, trying to find something, anything, to say.

Ashley glanced up at the digital chronometer on the wall and back at Jonathon. Her attention shifted momentarily to his mop of curly, blond hair, and she smiled. She seemed to make up her mind about something and leaned in closer. She smelled of coconut and almonds. "Listen," she whispered, "I've gotta run but they shot me up with the real junk just now. I can't stand to have that crap in my body. Will you help me get it out? It takes two people when they inject it."

Roughly half of the students at O had been labeled with one mental disorder or another, which were managed by a litany of mind-bending molecules.

All students on meds were tracked electronically for their own safety and that of the community. Once diagnosed, they were injected with nano-plants, microscopic implants driven into the upper arm with a high-powered air gun.

The implants stayed with them for life, as did the diagnosis… and the loss of their right to ever own a firearm.

The implanted students were monitored by the global positioning systems controlled by the United States Air Force, using vehicles and drones.

He ran his hand through his curls wondering what if they got caught, the danger, the consequences. But it was Ashley and he would do anything for her. "Eh, sure, but I don't . . . I'm not sure how to do that."

"I'll show you. We just can't get caught."

"No. Right."

"Can you meet me at the beginning of the lunch period?"

"Where?"

"Behind the bleachers at the soccer field."

She was off before Jonathon could answer. She turned halfway down the hall and yelled, "Thanks, Jonathon."

Chapter Two – Progressive Indoctrination
October 1, 2025, Thousand Oaks, California

"We are going to spend the next few weeks studying the Constitution," Hildegard Mueller announced.

A kid named Max, with a shaved skull and Goth head-to-toe, groaned and put his head on the top of the desk.

Hildegard Mueller, the sophomore class Progressive Social Civics teacher, was an iron-haired tranny who had taught there for thirty-two years, first as Heinrich Mueller and later as Hildegard. Heinrich was a third-generation descendent from a couple who had belonged to the Weather Underground Organization, a domestic terrorist, communist organization in the 1960s.

"A rare, cogent thought from Maxwell," Hildegard smirked, "but our legislators mandate instruction in the U.S. Constitution, although antiquated and not of our time. We shall obey the law."

Hildegard evenly paced her steps to the podium, glanced down at the color-coded panel before her, and touched a blue button. A numbered document appeared on the larger-than-life screen on the front wall.

"The first ten amendments to the Constitution are called the Bill of Rights." Hildegard said. She took a pointer and tapped the screen. Tap, tap, tap. "The Constitution itself," she spun around like a ballerina and faced the class, "is an unfortunately flawed document. It was stated by the honorable Federal judge Richard Posner in 2016, 'I don't believe that any document drafted in the 18th century can guide our behavior today.' In fact, it has been necessary to amend it twenty-seven times."

Heads nodded in unison.

Not all. Lanny Childers, a new kid with raging case of acne and a towering, Native American-style, yellow-streaked mohawk, sat to Jonathon's right. He coughed, "Fucking Nazi" into his hand.

"Did you have something to say, Mister Childers?" Ms. Mueller stormed down the row of desks toward Lanny. She used the pointer to slap her leg, like a 19th-century schoolmarm.

"Mister Childers?" she asked again, standing vigil next to Lanny's desk.

Lanny stared at his computer screen and said nothing.

After several seconds of silence she pointed to Jonathon. "Mister Carr? You have your share of high-performance marks, so one presumes you can hear. What did Mister Childers say?"

He glanced over at Lanny, who ran his hand back and forth over his acned cheek as if he might brush the pocks away but said nothing. Jonathon stood and faced Hildegard Mueller. "Awfully hasty," he replied.

"What?" she asked.

"'Awfully hasty.' He said, 'Awfully hasty.' The first ten amendments were passed at the same time. So it's taken two hundred forty-two years to pass seventeen amendments. Seems awfully hasty to call it flawed."

"Awfully hasty," Lanny said without taking his eyes from his computer screen.

"Sit down, Mr. Carr," Hildegard Mueller demanded as she spun on her heel and marched back to the front of the classroom.

She couldn't see the two boys hide their smiles.

"Here's today's assignment," Ms. Mueller proclaimed, and pushed a button on the side of her desk. The lesson transferred electronically to the screen on each student's desk. It read "Read the first ten amendments to the U.S. Constitution and then decide which two are the least useful and should be removed."

Jonathon read each amendment. He read them again. As he read them the second time, a deep sadness overtook him. A tear rolled down his right cheek. He had no idea why. Embarrassed, he wiped it away.

The classroom turned quiet as the students read and reread the Bill of Rights.

Shelia Briethart, a Mueller sycophant, raised her hand. She was thin to the point of gaunt from her ampheta-meds. In spite of her stick-figure frame, she wore skin-fitting leather tights that made her appear like a recovering cancer patient.

Jonathon slightly raised his head from his desk so he could better hear the constitutional interpretation Ms. Hildegard was about to offer Shelia. He sensed a constitutional inaccuracy coming.

"Yes, Shelia?" Hildegard asked.

"What does 'abridging' mean, in like abridging the freedom of speech?"

"It means limiting or reducing. The government or others can't prevent you from saying what you want, up to a point."

"Up to what point?"

"It means, young lady, you can't engage in 'hate speech.' Like the radio host who was taken off the air last month. You heard about that, didn't you?"

Shelia, shaken at the rebuke, nodded.

"The government charged him with a hate crime because of the comments he made about Senator Sherman. Likewise, you can't say things about government programs that might incite others to some kind of aggressive behavior. Violence," she said, raising her voice, "violence of any kind is unacceptable. It's a crime." She dabbed a bit of spittle from the corner of her mouth with the back of her hand.

Shelia started nervously chewing the inside of her cheek.

"Does that answer your question, Shelia?" Hildegard asked.

She chewed some more. "I heard that jock they busted on Sirius. He was joking when he said they ought to bring back frontier justice and hang the guy. It was a joke."

"Jokes can be hurtful," the teacher said.

"He just didn't like the law Senator what's-his-name proposed saying families could only have two children. I've got two brothers. I don't understand how that is hate speech." Her voice cracked.

"Confusing, isn't it?" Hildegard asked.

Shelia nodded and wiped her eyes on her sleeve.

"You see, class," Hildegard stated, "this is exactly the point. The Constitution is confusing. The language is out of date and hurtful. It was written by slave-owning capitalists. It doesn't fit today's world."

"But what about my brothers?" Shelia asked. "I don't agree with that senator either. Is that a hate crime?"

Hildegard Mueller's face turned beatific. "Of course not, dear. But overpopulation can lead to poverty and hunger, and that can lead to domestic terrorism. We don't want that now, do we?"

All eyes pinned on Shelia now, who shook her head and chewed her cheek again.

"Now," she addressed the class as a whole, "make your choice and we will discuss them tomorrow. You are dismissed as soon as you send me your answers."

Jonathon with a big smile on his face, put his head back down and began reading the amendments a third time. He had questions about the fourth amendment and also the fifth but could not bring himself to eliminate any of them. He typed "0" and "0" into his dispatch, followed by "I have some questions," and hit send.

He dashed from the classroom, to try to catch an eye-contact moment with Ashley between classes. He'd face Ms. Mueller tomorrow.

Chapter Three – Sleepers
October 1, 2025, Thousand Oaks, California

He had not seen Ashley after first period so after third, Social Equality, he ran down the hall like a broken-field runner, dodging the kids who rushed in the opposite direction to the cafeteria. He went out the door leading to the back lawn. Once outside, he slowed his pace so as not to attract the attention of the monitor drones sending visual feeds to the school's DAA agents.

When he was beyond the buildings, he moved cautiously toward a row of sycamores lining the way out to the soccer field.

Common knowledge among the students was drones did not perceive well if you stayed close to the sycamores. They had trouble with the body temperature. Jonathon stayed under the branches and out of camera sight.

He treaded slowly from tree to tree but still broke out in a sweat. He had no idea what could happen if he was caught removing a drug implant. He had heard wild stories about Behavioral Education Centers, but he didn't care.

It was Ashley Lawford. He didn't care because Ashley Lawford had asked for his help. There was something else. He didn't fully understand it, but it parked at the edge of his consciousness. The confrontation with the DAA had kicked open a door to something deeper, an impulse to correct a wrong, to fix something. Helping Ashley seemed aligned with this need.

The quiet swoosh of a DAA X-91 drone overhead brought him back to the present.

"Hey, Jonathon," Ashley called out as he rounded the corner at the rear of the bleachers. Ashley sat with her back to one of the sycamores, her legs crossed like an Indian at a powwow. He sat down next to her. She had washed the dirt off her cheek. Her hair was down and swept across her face from the breeze blowing through the trees.

She brushed the hair off her face and smiled openly. One of her green eyes, he noticed, was flecked with gold. Not the other.

He smiled back. He had a rather cocky smile, and one of his front teeth was chipped. Roguish. "Hey," Jonathon said. His conversation skills cut short by his uncertain confidence around Ashley.

"You okay with this?" she asked.

"I'm good, but won't they know it has been removed?"

"They only check coming in, not around campus or leaving."

"So you've done this before?" he asked.

"Just for friends," she said. "I forgot my sleeper this morning and I hate this crap in my system. It's like giving the government access to your mind through your veins."

Sleepers were one inch small, test-tube shaped containers made from acid resistant polymers. Students who had been designated disordered but did not want to take the drugs would drop their meds in the tube, add some hydrochloric acid, and cap it on the way to school.

The sleepers were taped to a leg or in an armpit and transmitted the compliance signal at the screening station. Roughly twenty percent of kids who were labeled used sleepers. An active black market existed in sleeper tubes and meds among the students. The tubes went for thirty-five credits, or four to six pills, depending on the molecules inside the pills.

"They gave me a twenty-four-hour release, but I can feel it dripping into my blood. I've got to get it out."

"Okay. Okay," he said. "Let's do it."

She opened a small, leather pouch and removed a white cloth, which she spread on the ground between them as if they were going to have a picnic. She placed a diminutive aerosol canister, a scalpel, a bottle of clear liquid, and some gauze on the cloth.

"What's in the little can?" he asked.

"It freezes the skin. Here," she replied, rolling up her sleeve showing him the red dot on her upper arm.

Two students emerged from the sycamores and came strolling around the corner of the bleachers, talking. The guy was African-American. Juice, they called him, because he could drink a full quart of orange juice in one gulp. Tall and slender, he sported a 1960s Afro and wore a tee-shirt with a picture of the Statue of Liberty, a scythe across her bosom. An inscription below the image read "Welcome to America, Home of the Brave, Land of the Free." Juice's sarcasm.

The girl was Asian. Diminutive. Turquoise streaks through ebony hair.

Juice pulled a pack of cigarettes from his back pocket and handed one to the girl. When they saw Jonathon and Ashley they froze.

Smoking cigarettes not just violated school rules, it violated a state law banning them anywhere except inside a private home, as long as there were no children under the age of eighteen in the house.

Juice glanced at the items displayed on the napkin. Jonathon and Ashley stared at the pack of smokes. A moment of understanding passed in silence.

"What's up, Ash?" the Asian girl asked.

"What's up, Li?" Ashley asked in return.

Juice and Li moved on down the path, slipped through a slot in the back of the bleachers, and disappeared.

When they were out of sight, Ashley said, "Don't worry. It won't hurt. You spray right there." She pointed again to the location of the injection. "Then you take this," she handed him the little scalpel, "and make a small cut right on top of this spot. Not too deep, maybe just an eighth of an inch. I'll squeeze it out. It's like popping a zit."

Jonathon picked up the scalpel and lightly touched the tip. A small drop of blood appeared on the end of his finger. "Shit," he said, and sucked on his finger.

Ashley picked up a piece of gauze and poured some disinfectant on it. She took the scalpel from Jonathon, wiped the blade, and gave it back to him.

"Okay," he said. "I'll need you to hold still." He moved closer to Ashley, got on his knees and took the underside of her arm in one hand. He held the scalpel in the other like a pencil. "Can you freeze yourself?" he asked.

She picked up the aerosol can and sprayed her upper arm, then touched the area with her index finger. "Numb," she said.

Jonathon put the tip of the scalpel over the red spot on her arm. It hovered there. Salty sweat started dripping from his forehead into his eyes. His vision blurred. He blinked repeatedly until it cleared, then pushed the scalpel into Ashley's arm. She let out a little squeal.

He made a small slit. Blood exuded. Ashley pinched behind the cut. A slightly dissolved capsule slid out in a rivulet of blood.

She put some alcohol on another piece of gauze, mopped the cut, and held it there. The bleeding slowed, then stopped.

Ashley gathered the items up off the napkin and tucked everything into the black leather pouch, which she put in a concealed compartment in her mini backpack.

"Nice job, doctor," thanking him, and bent forward to give him a peck on the cheek. She sprang to her feet.

Jonathon remained sitting, dazed.

"Come on, Jonathon," she said. "We'll be late for next period."

She bounded down the path toward the campus buildings like a frolicking colt.

Jonathon leapt to his feet and followed.

The patrol drone took note of the movement.

Chapter Four – The Arrest
October 2, 2025, Thousand Oaks, California

The color highlights in Li Chen's hair were programmed with a genetically modified shampoo to change color daily. They had gone from turquoise to a vibrant purple today.

"Jonathon, I got a new tattoo. I want you to be the first to see it." She took hold of Jonathon's arm and pulled him behind the open door of his locker, out of sight of the hall-monitoring cameras.

"They got Ashley," she whispered.

"What do you mean? Who—"

"The patrol drone—"

"No," he interrupted. "We stayed under the trees."

"Not you," she said. "Us. Not us, actually. Juice."

"What are you talking about?" He started to close the door to his locker.

Li took hold of it and kept it in place. "Don't. I don't want them to record this conversation."

The locker door blocked an audio-video feed from down the hall. Jonathon nodded.

Li Chen had delicate Asian features, an IQ of one hundred sixty, loved tattoos and had won the Norman Mailer Creative

Non-Fiction Writing Award. She had already been accepted at Cal Berkeley, though only a junior.

"The drone picked up the scent of the tobacco in Juice's cigarettes," she said, "and reported it to Behavior Control. The administration pulled him in. Juice called his father, who's a big attorney downtown. After Juice told his father about Ash, his old man negotiated an agreement with the school. They would not report the tobacco crime and would keep it off of Juice's record if Juice told them about the implant removal he had seen. You weren't mentioned by name, but he ratted Ashley out."

Jonathon slammed an open palm against the neighboring locker. "What a fucking asshole."

Li put her finger to her lips. "The DAA caught her at the screening station on her way in this morning," she whispered. "Busted her with her sleeper. A van picked her up about fifteen minutes ago and took her to the Covina Behavioral Education Center."

The Department of Homeland Security had been formed in response to 9/11. Over the years its staff, budget, and power had undergone vast expansion. The most ominous extension was into the American education system and, in parallel with their presence in the schools, the creation of a national chain of Behavioral Education Centers. More than one hundred BECs had been established across the country with the purpose of educating rabble-rouser, non-compliant, children eighteen years of age and younger as to the importance of complying with government regulations on matters of domestic security.

"Doesn't she get some kind of hearing?" Jonathon asked.

"Not for an act of terrorism," Li replied.

"She took a pill out of her arm," he said fairly loudly. "I took it out for her. She didn't plant a bomb."

This time she put her small hand lightly over Jonathon's

mouth. "Sh-hh. You can't say that word. You want to be put away?"

"How long will she be in there?" he asked.

Li poked her head around Jonathon's body, gazed down the hall, then pulled it back quickly. "Until the behaviorist says she's no longer a threat to national security."

"This is insane. She's a fifteen-year-old high school sophomore who doesn't like drugs in her body."

"Ash is her own person. She's a free spirit."

Jonathon nodded.

"It is against their norm. She's officially designated as having conduct behavior issues. It's in her file. Her rights are . . . are limited."

"How do you know that?" Jonathon asked.

Li said nothing at first. She twisted her mouth to the side. "You say anything about what I am going to tell you, I'm over-timed in the toaster. You understand? Burnt Toast."

"Okay," Jonathon agreed. "No burnt toast."

"Ash and I hang out," Li said. "They know we are friends. So I get pulled in by Jacobsen—"

"The Behaviorist?"

"He's a fucking jackass with a pig nose. He tells me Ashley is in trouble and I shouldn't hang out with her. He shows me her file, which is against the law, and puts his hands all over me to comfort me from the shock of discovering my friend is a potential danger to herself or others."

Jonathon's jaws clenched, his head shaking.

"He said if I told anyone about the conversation, I could kiss my scholarship to Berkeley goodbye."

The three-minute warning buzzer sounded. Li slammed the door of Jonathon's locker closed. "I gotta run or I'll be late. You, too. Let's talk later."

He nodded and they took off in different directions for class.

Jonathon skidded into his seat just as the start of class bell rang. The room was a cacophony of student noise.

Lanny, whose spiked Mohawk was bold orange today, leaned across the aisle. "Thanks for yesterday," he said, and pointed to his head, on which a swastika was now shaved next to the word "Hasty."

Despite his concern for Ashley, Jonathon had to smile.

"Class has started, ladies and gentlemen. Please give me your attention." Ms. Mueller, her hair wrapped so tightly in a bun behind her head her eyes bulged, rapped her pointer on the side of her desk.

The din diminished.

"Most of you finished yesterday's assignment by selecting two amendments from the Bill of Rights that should be eliminated. A few of you did not finish, and you, Mister Carr, had questions," she said. "So let's start with you."

All of the heads in the room swiveled toward Jonathon as if they were marionettes.

As he started to reply, Jonathon experienced an intoxicating sense of déjà vu. Words flowed from his mouth. From where, he did not know.

"It's not a matter of eliminating amendments," he began, "Some have to be restored. The fifth and sixth amendments have been eliminated here."

The marionettes swung toward Ms. Mueller.

"Whatever do you mean, Mister Carr?" she asked.

Eyes on Jonathon again.

"The fifth amendment guarantees due process of law, does it not?" Jonathon fought the urge to stand while he addressed her.

Mueller took a step backward but didn't answer.

"The sixth amendment guarantees the right to an attorney, but in our own school a student can be picked up and held against her will without due process or given the right to an attorney. Those amendments have already been eliminated here. They should be restored."

The marionettes now grew animated. Ms. Mueller took another step back and then another. "If you are talking about Ms. Lawford, Mister Carr, she removed a behavioral implant, which protected her and the rest of us from a possible act of terrorism."

Many of the marionettes, several of whom evidently knew Ashley, snickered. The muscles in Mueller's face tightened.

The classroom door swung open and Manfred Jacobsen, while picking his fingernails stepped in. He was known widely among the students as a copious user of his own meds and was constantly picking at his fingernails to the point of making them bleed. He looked urgently at Mueller, out to the class, and back to Mueller, who apparently had pushed the silent call button to his office. The few pitiful strands of hair on Jacobsen's head stood straight up like goal posts. He seemed to sense the attention to the top of his head and mopped the hairs down with his hand. He wiped his hand on his pants.

"Mister Carr had some questions, better answered in your office, Dr. Jacobsen. Mister Carr?" she stated, facing Jonathon.

"They weren't really questions," he said.

"Doctor?" Mueller's voice had risen.

"Come on, Jonathon. We can discuss this in my office."

Lanny coughed into his hand again, "Fucking Nazis."

Mueller pretended not to hear it.

Jonathon got out of his chair, grabbed his iDevice, and left the classroom. Jacobsen followed.

Jonathon's mind began scrolling over the fifth and sixth

amendments, with unusual vividness and details. His memory of the words so clear. He had read the entire Constitution at the age of 10 and his eidetic memory enabled him to visualize all the words in the articles and amendments. He was ready to go toe to toe with Jacobsen, but his thoughts were interrupted by what had happened to Ashley. He knew he needed to help her.

Chapter Five – The Bomb Threat
October 2, 2025, Thousand Oaks, California

Jonathon followed Jacobsen down the hall toward the administration offices. Neither spoke.

A couple of students came out of the unisex bathroom holding hands. Jonathon couldn't tell their gender from a distance, but they smiled enigmatically.

"Ms. Sellers," Jacobsen called out.

The taller of the two stopped and pivoted on her heels. Buzz cut, no makeup, strikingly good looking.

"What were you doing in there?" he asked.

"It's a bathroom," she replied. "You want the details?"

"Don't get smart with me, Ms. Sellers. I'll have you labeled."

The other student did a 180, an attractive girl with petite features. "You do that, Doctor Jacobsen, and I'll report you for hate speech directed at a lesbian relationship." She gave Jacobsen the finger and the two turned and continued down the hall hand-in-hand.

Jonathon suppressed a smile and resumed walking, ahead of Jacobsen so the good doctor couldn't see his face. As they approached Jacobsen's office an ear-piercing alarm sounded two short blasts then a long one. This meant a bomb threat alarm and the building had to be evacuated immediately.

The school received two to three bomb threats every year. No bombs had ever been found.

The hall instantly filled with stampeding students, pouring out of classrooms and running toward the back exit leading to the soccer field.

Jacobsen, eyes wide like a frightened child, abandoned Jonathon and bolted down the hall toward the exit. Jonathon headed in the same direction. By the time he got outside, the soccer field was full of students milling around on the matted grass, mostly in cliques of race, gender, and sexual orientation. The teachers huddled and gossiped in their own patch.

Glancing about, Jonathon spotted Li's vibrant, purple stripes. She was talking to some friends near the soccer goal. As he set off in her direction, a woman screamed so loudly all of the talking on the field stopped. A few seconds of silence followed by another scream and another.

The screams had come from the crowd of teachers on the far side of the field who were now standing in a circle looking down at Marcus Jacobsen, who had lost his footing and fell hard to the ground. One teacher yelling for medical assistance while another teacher performed CPR.

Marcus Jacobsen, PhD, dropped dead from a heart attack as he pointed to the growing swarm of drones circling the soccer field. Subsequent news articles on Jacobsen's death said he had died as a result of a massively enlarged heart brought about by the abuse of amphetamines and perhaps cocaine.

When Jonathon heard what happened to Marcus Jacobsen, he didn't know what to think or feel. No relationship was ever established, good or bad, between them. It was just a short while ago he was walking down the hall with Mr. Jacobsen. For a flashing moment and before he could even understand the emotion, he felt a sadness and loss. To a fourteen year old death was an unfamiliar experience.

School was cancelled the following day. Jonathon's plan was to see Ashley at the Covina Behavior Education Center. He would call Li for a ride.

Li's phone rang six times, and Jonathon was about to hang up.

"Hello," Li said.

"Hi Li, this is Jonathon."

"Hi Jonathon, what's up?"

"I need a ride to the Covina Behavior Education Center."

"Not a good idea Jonathon," she advised.

"It's something I have to do."

"I'm not going in with you."

"I'm going to get her out of there," he declared. "She's my friend."

"Maybe more than a friend," Li said.

Jonathon blushed. "Whatever."

"How are you going to do that?" she asked. "Her guardians couldn't get her out of there even if they wanted to. And they don't."

"Guardians?"

"Her parents are dead. Two of the thirty-four thousand who died in the Riverside quake of twenty-nineteen. She's in a foster home. Hates it."

"I'm going to get her out of there," he repeated, and for the fourth time told the iDrive's wi-fi system to bring up a picture of the Covina Behavioral Education Center.

It showed gleaming alabaster walls ten to twelve feet high. According to the website, an invisible electronic band ran along the top of the walls. When touched it would send off a loud siren alarm to ensure the guests remained committed to the re-education program until it was completed.

When they arrived, Jonathon got out of the car and walked around to the reception camera at the gated entrance, embedded into the wall next to the gate. The lens was oddly almond-shaped and emitted a multi-colored laser beam.

Jonathon stuck his nose a couple of inches from the camera. "I'm here to see Ashley Lawford," he said.

"Are you related to Ms. Lawford?" a male voice asked. It had an Indian lilt.

"Eh, yes. I'm her brother, Jonathon."

Pause.

"Our records show Ms. Lawford has no siblings."

"Your records are mistaken," he said.

"Do you have your Homeland Security I.D.?"

Homeland Security I.D., i.e. Biometric National I.D. cards, had been mandated for all citizens following the explosion of United Airlines flight 251 out of San Francisco, which had killed one hundred forty-three people in October of twenty twenty-one. Legislation, drafted with the guidance of the Department of Homeland Security, mandating national bio-metric ID cards containing retina scans and a photograph passed both houses of Congress and was signed into law by the President in six days.

All scans were stored in a National Retina Database maintained by the FBI in coordination with the DHS. Infants were now retina-scanned at birth. Scans were administered by school-based health clinics for students of all ages. Adults were retina-scanned as a separate procedure when they sought to renew a driver's license. All military were scanned as part of their routine physical.

Jonathon had his Homeland ID in his wallet, but it carried his picture with his name on it. He couldn't think of a way around the question. "Not with me," he said.

"It is a violation of federal law to travel without your Homeland Security ID. We will file a report with DHS if you do not move on."

Jonathon stood staring into the camera for several moments. He finally flipped the bird at the lens and got back in the iDrive.

Li took a 5x7 paper notepad and a pen out of her purse and scribbled, "They have my license plate now."

"It's not right, Li," he said aloud. "It's not right."

Again she wrote on the notepad. "I just don't want to lose my scholarship to Berkeley."

Jonathon turned in his seat and watched the Covina Behavioral Education Center fade into the distance. "This is like something out of 1984. I mean, are we a full-blown police state or what?"

Li wrote, "YES" in big letters on the notepad. "Of course not," she said aloud, and ordered the vehicle home.

Chapter Six – Sex Trap
October 2, 2025, West Covina, California

When Ashley awoke, she was tied in four point restraints, wrists and ankles, to metal bars at the headboard and footboard of a hospital bed and lay soaked in her own sweat and urine.

All of her clothes had been removed and she wore a flimsy hospital gown which, due to the stretched position of her body, had risen well above the middle of her thighs.

The aroma of chlorine in the room was so pungent, she gagged. Bile rose in her throat. She swallowed it down.

She heard the door open. A man in a white smock walked to the side of the bed. He leaned over and peered down at her. He appeared to be Indian or Pakistani, she couldn't tell which. His face was covered with small, dark moles. Brown sweat-stains blossomed from his armpits. He reeked of body odor.

"Ms. Lawford," he said, "I am Dr. Patel. I am going to give you an injection. It contains your medication. The injection will be with a needle, not an air gun. I understand you have rejected your medication in the past, so to ensure you do not pretend to swallow a pill and spit it out, or go to the extreme measure of mutilating yourself, I will be giving you an injection every morning. If you offer physical resistance, as has been reported by

DAA agents at the Barack Obama High School, you will spend your days here strapped to this bed in restraints."

"If you receive your injections in a compliant manner and attend your behavioral education seminars, then I will see to it your restraints are removed and you will be permitted to share a room with another student."

"Do you understand me, Ms. Lawford?"

Ashley nodded.

"What's it going to be?" he asked.

"Quiet," she replied. "I'll be quiet."

"A wise choice," he said.

Dr. Patel undid Ashley's restraints. As she rose to a sitting position on the side of the bed, Patel ran his hand up Ashley's back to where the gown was tied. "Let me help you with this."

Ashley jerked away and then sought to placate him. "It's fine. I'll take care of it." She offered him her arm.

Patel removed an old-fashioned hypodermic needle from a small kit, filled it with a yellow solution, held it upright, and depressed the plunger, forcing a few drops through the needle point. He took Ashley's right arm and inserted the needle in the deltoid muscle. She picked out a spot on the wall, two small holes where, presumably, a picture had once hung, and fixed her attention on it. He depressed the plunger. Ashley could feel the poison rushing into her body, deviant molecules that would disrupt, deaden, and destroy nerves and their attendant bodily organs.

Dr. Patel left. Ashley remained sitting on the side of the bed and wept.

At 11:00 a.m. an orderly came into the room and told her she was expected at the behavioral education seminar, which was being held in room 129, several doors down on the right. It took her ten minutes to get her head clear enough to put on a robe and slippers and drag herself down the hall to the seminar, the plastic slippers flip-flopping against the linoleum as she went.

The first thing that struck Ashley was the color. The entire room was blue. The walls were painted with a blue sky and clouds, the chairs in which about a dozen other teens, in robes, sat in a circle were made of a clear, blue plastic, and the facilitator, an obese woman with an enormous bosom, wore a blue smock that must have been designed by Omar the tent man.

She remembered being told by her social arts teacher that blue was supposed to be soothing to young minds.

"You can take one of those chairs by the wall and join us," the facilitator called out.

Ashley grabbed a chair and carried it over to the circle. Two other kids slid their chairs aside, creating a space for her to put hers down. She sat and crossed her arms over her chest.

Her head started to spin and she saw little electrical explosions of light in front of her eyes, as if some wiring had short-circuited in her brain. She presumed she was the only one who could see them. Others likely had their own electrical storms going.

"I'm glad you could join us, Ms. Lawford. Class," the woman said to the circle of kids. "This is Ashley Lawford. She will be learning with us."

Ashley scanned the twelve racially diverse faces of her new classmates. Some had shaved their heads bald. Many had their eyes half closed, their faces dead, stultified, soulless. She shivered, knowing this is how she would look in a matter of days. No one acknowledged her presence except a boy next to her, wearing Matrix shades, who said, "Wha's up, bitch?"

Ashley didn't respond.

The next hour was spent watching videos of TSA and DAA agents in airports, bus stations, train stations, federal buildings, highway checkpoints, as well as high school and college campuses. The voiceover explained in the most soothing tone how these brave men and women were risking their lives to protect the American homeland, that their sacrifice and accomplishments should be recognized and appreciated by all. It further explained hostile attitudes and non-compliance with the orders of a TSA or DAA agent was a federal crime.

The visit each morning by Patel, his slimy hands and sexual innuendos, and the Behavioral Education suggestive mind implanting went on for weeks. Ashley had no rights or privileges other than leaving her room to participate in the educational seminars. After each seminar she would be escorted back to her room where it would be locked from the outside so she couldn't escape. Patel no longer saw the need of having Ashley in restraints. Locking her up in her room sufficed. Until she proved to Patel her obedience to his request, she would stay locked in her room with absolutely nothing to entertain her boredom. With the daily meds and her being isolated for most of the day, she knew she had to somehow escape this hell hole. For now she would go along with Patel's request.

After the seminar, a tall black handsome orderly approached Ashley, "Come with me. I will be taking you back to your hospital room." When she got there, she was told to gather her clothes, which lay in a pile on the floor of an otherwise empty closet, and then was escorted to one of the residence rooms. The room was slightly larger than a jail cell with two bunks, a toilet, a micro-closet, and a piece of polished wood attached to the wall with plastic cords, which served as a desk. A Latina sat on the side of the bottom bunk. Some toiletries, a towel and washcloth lay on the top bunk.

The Latina, who was strumming a guitar, wore short-clipped hair and a Labyrs tattoo on her upper arm, the double-axed symbol of lesbian pride. She noticed Ashley eyeing her tattoo. "You're too young for me, Sweet Cheeks, but I can get you someone if you're on the hunt."

"No, I'm straight," Ashley said.

"Your loss," she responded.

Ashley tossed her clothes in the closet, climbed up on the bunk at the footboard, laid down, and closed her eyes.

"My name's Serana," the Latina said.

"Ashley." She opened her eyes and stared at the ceiling. "Why are you in here, Serana?"

"TSA agent at LAX took me in a private room for a pat-down because he said I was uncooperative."

"Were you?" Ashley asked.

"Only when he started feeling me up after I went through the screening device. When we got in the private room, he disabled the camera and put his hands where the sun don't shine. I kicked him in the balls."

Ashley laughed despite how she felt. Serana joined her.

When they stopped laughing, Ashley sat up and threw her feet over the edge of the bed. "How do you get out of here?"

"When they tell you, you can go," Serana said. She stood and walked over to the toilet and pressed her back against the wall. She shook her head, put her index finger to her lips, and pointed to the corner of the room right above her.

Ashley's eyes followed her direction. A small camera was embedded there.

A soft dinner siren went off, the door lock to their cell clicked open.

Ashley and Serana sat in a remote corner of the dining hall.

"Eat as much turkey as you can," Serana said. "The protein counteracts the effect of the meds."

"Okay. What about getting out?"

"Sex," replied Serana.

Ashley uncomfortably asked, "What do you mean?"

Serana lowered her voice and slid her chair closer to Ashley's.

"Patel is a horny sex pervert, turned on by young girls."

The next morning Ashley took her injection from Dr. Patel and would for the next three days. The injections were administered in his office, which featured a gray, metal desk covered with papers, charts, and half-empty cardboard cups of coffee. A picture of a woman with a red dot in the middle of her forehead, accompanied by two small children, sat on the desk next to a computer. A medical diploma, housed in an ornate frame, hung on the wall behind his desk.

While administering the injection, Patel would take her arm and try to covertly stare down into her blouse.

On the fourth morning Ashley left the top of the blouse slightly undone. As Patel sought to leer at her breasts she leaned forward, put her lips next to his ear and said, "If you want to see it all, Doctor Patel, and enjoy them, we would have to be somewhere off the hospital grounds. There are too many cameras in this facility."

Patel gazed down at her body. He swallowed. His breathing increased. Spit dripped from right side of his mouth. "I am off duty at four-thirty p.m.," he mouthed.

Ashley nodded slightly.

At 4:30 exactly, Dr. Patel entered Ashley and Serana's room without knocking. "Come with me, Ms. Lawford. You need to see a specialist."

Ashley slid down from her bunk, gave Serana a nod, and followed Patel out the door. They walked down the hall and up to the front door. A security officer with ham-hock biceps monitored the ingress and egress from the building.

Patel approached him. "I am taking Ms. Lawford to a specialist in Pasadena who is unable to see her here."

The guard stepped aside and they exited the building.

Chapter Seven – The Escape
October 23rd, 2025, West Covina, California

They were still inside the walled compound. DHS security drones patrolled the air space surrounding the center. Ashley saw one of the drones begin flashing red, green, and blue lights then broke from the four drone squadron pack. It lowered its elevation and followed Patel and Ashley around to the staff parking lot at the back of building.

Patel, a car nostalgic, pointed to an old Chrysler, something out of the 20th century, with a dented front fender. The spare tire occupied the driver's side front wheel.

The drone hovered until they had both entered the car and closed the doors. The flashing lights ceased and the drone rejoined the flock.

Patel drove out of the compound and up South Grand Avenue to the 210 freeway west. They were going against the commuter traffic, leaving Los Angeles, but without an iDrive they were relegated to the far right lane with other out-of-date motorists. That lane, referred to as "Grandma's Alley," moved at the speed of melting ice. The traffic eased after the freeway split at the 134. Patel stayed on 210.

"Where are we going?" Ashley asked.

Patel did not answer. He drove past the Rose Bowl and continued through the verdant foothills of Pasadena. Five minutes later he took the Angeles Crest exit at La Cañada-Flintridge. Ashley had been up Angeles Crest Highway before. It wound steeply into the Angeles National Forrest in the San Gabriel Mountains.

Patel took his right hand off the steering wheel and placed it on Ashley's left knee. He was breathing heavily now. He didn't say anything and continued to gaze straight ahead, steering with his left hand on what was now a mountainous road full of twists and sharp turn-backs.

Ashley feeling nervously tense, pulse accelerating, and her heart pounding like an echoing African drum, instinctively wanted to respond, but if she reacted now, Serana's plan would never work. She decided to do nothing. If he moved his hand any farther up her leg, she decided, she would object to any activity until they had parked.

The bends in the road grew more acute and Patel put his hand back on the wheel. At the top of the grade he turned down a dirt road next to a sign reading Switzer Falls Picnic Area. The old Chrysler bumped along the road until it widened to a large parking area.

The Switzer Falls Picnic Area lay at the top of a two-mile hiking trail that ran down the mountain alongside a babbling stream, a touch of the outdoors for office-bound Angelinos. The entire parking area was roofed with overhanging branches of pine and fir. The lot was nearly empty. Patel crept through the parking lot, searching for a secluded alcove. Ashley tried not to show her terror. She gazed out the window at the trees and undergrowth.

There were no cars at the end of the lot. He swung the Chrysler around and backed into a space that provided cover below the branches of a drooping Douglas fir.

Patel turned off the engine and unbuckled his seatbelt. He was running his tongue across his lower lip. Ashley undid her seatbelt.

"I need to touch you," he said, and slid across the front seat next to her.

Like a speeding lightning bolt, her mind raced through what Serana told her. 'The fork, which I swiped from the kitchen, was sharpened by a whetstone which I got from the gardening shed. It's now sharper than an ordinary fork but you still have to plunge it in his thigh with all your might.' Will Serana's plan really work? She nervously thought to herself. What if he sees me pulling out the fork? At that moment she knew she had to shut off these considerations.

Now or never, she thought. With a look of determination, she peered into Patel's eyes. He started to caress her face with his left hand. From the side pocket of her pants Ashley slipped the metal fork Serana had sharpened to a razor's edge, wrapped her hand around the handle tightly, and in one swift motion raised it and drove it into Patel's thigh so forcefully she felt it hit bone.

Patel let out a horrifying scream. Ashley opened her door and bolted from the car. She ran through the lot, across a wooden footbridge, and continued along a path paralleling a rushing stream. She could still hear Patel screaming as she crossed the footbridge. She never looked back.

As an escapee from a DHS Behavioral Education Center, she wasn't sure if that made her a federal fugitive. She wasn't about to stop and ask anyone.

Chapter Eight – Encounter
July 27, 2028, Santa Cruz, California, nearly three years have passed since Ashley had been committed to the Behavioral Education Center

There were four of them. Wild-ass teenagers, their high school years behind them now, they had taken the bullet-train from Los Angeles to San Jose, a two-hour ride, and rented an iVan at the terminal (the surf boards wouldn't fit in a car), which had driven them over the Santa Cruz mountains, rich with towering redwoods, and into Santa Cruz proper.

The iVan found a spot and parked itself in a slot facing the beach. The meter vacuumed two credits from the rental car agency's Apple pay account, which in turn debited Jonathon's account, as it was his license under which the iVan had been rented. The meter lit up green.

It was four in the afternoon with a cloudless blue sky. A squadron of border-control drones circled above the bay, as was the case with all ports of entry. One broke from the herd and darted south toward Monterey. A lone gull circled overhead, then drifted down to a flock of feasting friends, pecking away at some food someone had left on the beach.

The four of them piled out of the iVan. They jogged over to

a wooden bench overlooking the beach and sat down. The bench bowed in the middle in protest until Jonathon stood up. The backboard displayed an advertisement for a local cannabis store. The graphic showed a handsome, young couple lying on a blanket on the beach. Both wore wrap-around shades and beatific smiles. A pack of Mary Jane Magic, the logo of which was a Merlin-like wizard smoking a joint, lay on the blanket between them. The address, phone number, and website of Charlie's Cannabis Carnival lined the bottom of the advertisement.

They peeled their shirts and shoes and socks off, threw them into the iVan, and ran into the sand. On the way to the surf they detoured to watch a game of beach volleyball played by two bikini-clad teams of hard-bodied girls setting and spiking to the shouts of several fans.

After a few minutes two of the guys, twin brothers Tim and Todd Shelton, headed back to the iVan for their boards. They wanted to catch a few rides before sundown. Jonathon and Jose engaged in promising conversations with a couple of sun-browned locals.

Jonathon, just a hair above six feet tall, and tight-muscled from years of competitive wrestling, was often told he strikingly resembled a mid-twentieth century film icon, Steve McQueen, if McQueen had had a chipped front tooth and a broken nose.

Adriane, a freshman at UC Santa Cruz, asked Jonathon to unhook the back of her woefully inadequate bikini top and rub some suntan lotion on her back. No one mentioned the fact it was pushing five in the afternoon and the sun had long since lost any tanning kick.

Vivian, a petite Latina, talked quietly to Jose, himself a good-looking kid with the high cheekbones of his Aztec ancestors.

The game ended. The two girls had to leave, but invited Jonathon and Jose to the Friday night beach party at the Cove.

"It's a few hundred yards down the beach," Adriane said, pointing south.

"We usually start a bonfire about eleven," added Vivian.

"There's four of us," Jonathon pointed out.

Silence from the beach babes.

"It's not really for tourists," Adriane finally said. "Everyone is from around here. Local surfers, some kids come over from the campus, and occasionally we get some drop-ins from the mountains. There are unwritten rules, no tourists."

"Drop-ins from the mountains?" Jonathon asked.

"There are a bunch of off-grid types who live up there." Adriane nodded toward the mountains.

"How do we qualify?" asked Jose.

"We can each invite one friend," replied Vivian.

"Okay. See you around eleven," Jonathon confirmed.

The Friday night hangout at the Cove had a time-honored tradition in Santa Cruz dating back to the tie-dyed counter-culture of the 1970s. The local police didn't bother the attendees as long as the party didn't get out of hand.

Jonathon and Adriane sat, backs propped against a log. The fire, kept alive by a communal effort of driftwood being thrown on it periodically, was still brilliantly ablaze, sparks floating toward a starlit sky before disappearing into the blackness. Adriane was smoking a joint and was resting her head on Jonathon's lap.

"Here Jonathon, Panama Red, I think you'll like it," Adriane extended her hand towards his mouth.

"I'm going to pass, Adriane. Have a wrestling championship match coming up."

Most of the kids his age smoked dope, but the drug messed

with his muscles and affected his wrestling. He had his eyes on the NCAA wrestling championship in the 170-lb. weight class when he got to Berkeley and considered himself in training.

"Really? A wrestler. Wow that's hot!"

Shortly after midnight a group of five people tracked down the trail from the cliff overlooking the Cove and joined the party. Several were in leathers.

Adriane sat upright and watched the group mingle with kids on the other side of the fire. "Trolls," she whispered.

"Trolls?"

"Like I told you, there are pockets of people who live in the mountains. The San Lorenzo River runs through the redwoods up there and supports a handful of communities. It's quite beautiful."

Someone's iDevice started playing a soft ballad. A couple of the Trolls slipped off their shoes and started dancing in the sand.

"Why do they come down here?" Jonathon asked.

"I don't know," Adriane said. "Some contact with the outside world, I guess. They're not criminals or anything, at least not that I know of. Mostly anti-government types. Some just want to grow their own food and live in nature. Mostly it's people who want to get away from the drones and spying. No iDevices, no Internet. People in town call them Trolls. I don't know why."

One of the women from the group–there were three men and two women–stood with her back to the fire. She had her hands tucked into the back pockets of an old pair of Levi's.

That's what got his attention. Jonathon loved the old jeans but one hardly saw them these days. The one hundred seventy-five-year-old retailer had filed for bankruptcy after the California legislature passed a bill mandating the company pay the factory workers in Malaysia the same minimum wage mandated to be paid in the state.

There was something about the woman's bearing, how she stood with the cant of her shoulders at a provocative angle, that captured Jonathon's attention. "I'll be back in a minute," he said to Adriane. He stood and dusted the sand from his pants. He sauntered around the fire, staying to the outside rim of light until he got a sideways view of the woman. He was about to yell out, but looked again.

She had an uncanny resemblance of someone he knew but yet she didn't. He had to be certain. He took several more steps around the circle until he could see the woman straight on. She was now in clear sight, but he was beyond the reach of light from the fire for her to see him. Her hair was short and blonde, but hair color changed with the rising sun.

Her presence, the insouciant way she carried herself . . . it was her. Except, no, that wasn't Ash's face.

She moved away from the fire and over to one of the guys she had come with and got a cigarette from him. He lit it for her. She said something to him and walked away from the fire toward the path winding down from the cliff.

Jonathon followed at a distance. The fog had started to roll in and he had to move faster to keep her silhouette in sight. When she reached the top of the trail, she headed across the street toward an old-fashioned pickup parked under a streetlamp. She drew a hood over her head before she crossed the street.

Jonathon quickened his pace and drew up alongside her. "Hey, Ash."

She turned and looked at him from underneath the hood. "Who?"

"I said, Ash. Ashley Lawford."

She cocked her head. "I'm afraid you have me confused with someone else. My name is Evelyn. Evelyn Gillette."

The nose, he realized. No, not Ashley's nose, and this girl's face was different, more angular. Her voice was deeper. More mature.

She took a drag on her cigarette, exhaled, swung back around toward the street.

"Wait," he said. Without thinking, he grabbed her arm.

She yanked it away and turned on him. "Don't fucking touch me."

"I'm sorry. I just . . . I thought you were someone I knew. I'm sorry, okay?"

She watched him for a moment as if she were going to say something, but then turned toward the street again.

"Where are you from?" he asked.

"Oregon. Lake Oswego, outside Portland."

Jonathon nodded. "Well, nice to meet you, Evelyn. My name's Jonathon." He ran up to her and stuck out his hand. "Again, I'm sorry about the arm."

After a moment she took his hand. As she did so a sudden strong breeze blew her hood back and a car came down the road in their direction. As it passed, there was a moment when the light from the high-beam headlights caught Evelyn's eyes. One of her green eyes was flecked with gold, the other not.

At that moment he knew and she knew it. He saw her biting on her upper lip, trying to figure out what to say when one of the guys she had come with came jogging across the street.

"Evie. This guy bothering you?"

Jonathon stared at the guy, instantly deciding how he would take him down. He was older, maybe twenty-four or twenty-five, but with spaghetti muscles and winded from jogging across the street.

"No, Matt," she said. "I'm fine."

"You sure?" He gave Jonathon a hard-guy stare.

Jonathon gave him his "Not in your wildest dreams" smile.

"Yes," she asserted. "I'm sure."

She looked back at Jonathon. "He's an old friend."

Chapter Nine – The Disguise
July 27, 2028, Santa Cruz, California

"Come on," she said. She threw the hood back over her head and walked over to the pickup. Jonathon followed and got in the passenger side. He pulled the door closed, but it didn't catch.

"You kind of have to hold it closed," she told him.

Jonathon took a firm grip of the door handle and yanked the door tight against the frame.

Ashley started the pickup and headed north on the beachfront road.

The fog had thickened, blanketing the coast in an inspissated mist. Ashley lowered the headlight beams and switched on the windshield wipers. The rubber in the wipers had gaps like the mouth of an old man who had lost several teeth. The windshield was sprinkled with rust-colored dust, causing the wipers to smear the mist back and forth as though they were spreading strawberry jam on a piece of bread.

"There's a vegetarian restaurant a few blocks from here," she said. "It stays open until three a.m. You okay with that?"

"Any protein in the place?"

"Beans," she replied, "and eggs."

"You a vegetarian now?" he asked.

"Reformed."

"Which means?"

"I don't eat red meat. Except if someone in camp kills a deer, I eat venison jerky. Otherwise lots of organic vegetables, brown rice, yogurt, and fresh berries."

She was taller and catwalk-thin but not gaunt. Her face was tan and toned. She must have felt his eyes on her and glanced over at him and then back at the road.

Jonathon nodded in the darkness and watched her drive. He'd never been in an automobile with a clutch.

She pulled into the parking lot at the Saturn Café, parked, and tugged on the handbrake. They went in.

The place was full of UCSC students and Jonathon could smell the pot in the air. The café had a similarity to the cafeteria at the Cirque du Soleil training academy, the difference being the majority of the Saturn Café patrons were demonstrably stoned.

"The favorite on the menu is the stack of blueberry pancakes bathed in whipped cream." Ashley offered. "And fudge brownies floating in a lake of chocolate sauce is a close second."

Jonathon and Ashley sat at a table in the far corner of the room. Both ordered a cup of coffee and studied the menus left by the waitress, a stunning, ebony woman with a Somali accent who had to duck around a hanging lamp to avoid hitting it. According to her nametag, her name was Aamino, which, she told them, meant "trustworthy" in Somali.

"You a student at UCSC?" Jonathon asked.

"Sophomore," she responded with a rhythmic North African intonation.

"Playing basketball?" he queried further.

"Volleyball," she said with pride. "Full ride." Big smile. Made bigger by her white teeth against her ebony skin.

Ashley ordered two soft-scrambled eggs and a veggie

sausage patty. Jonathon ordered the Southwestern omelet.

"What's in that?" Ashley asked. Lame, she thought. She was at a loss as to how to start the conversation.

"Three organic eggs with black beans, green chilies, jack cheese, green onions, cilantro, and sour cream," he answered. "It's served with home fries and toast."

"You remember everything you read?"

"Pretty much."

"Well, you got your protein." She tucked one leg up under the other and adjusted how she sat on her side of the booth.

Jonathon closed the menu and set it purposefully on the table and gazed at her. They had been little more than kids and had really only known each other for half a day, but something had transpired between them. They both knew it.

"I'm sorry," she said.

"For what?"

"For pretending I didn't know you. I . . . it's a long story."

Jonathon watched her stir her coffee with her fork, sensing she was trying to decide what to tell him and where to begin.

"Mine's shorter," he said.

"Okay."

"I came out to that Behavioral Center at Covina the day after they picked you up. I couldn't get in."

"I know," she said. "Li told me."

"You're in touch with Li?"

"I'll tell you later. Go on."

He ran his hand through his hair and steamed for a minute. "Okay. I went to see your foster parents. They're a piece of work," he said.

"Troglodytes," she proclaimed.

Jonathon wrinkled his brow.

"Ancient cave dwellers," she offered.

"They were that," he said. "I tried to convince them to go out to Covina and demand your release. They said they were still receiving the county support checks for your care but now they didn't have to feed you. They didn't see any upside. Those were your foster father's words, 'Where's the upside?'"

"Good old Don and Bella," she said. "Rock stars of the California foster care system. They probably collected checks until last month."

"Birthday?" he asked.

"Eighteen and emancipated."

Aamino brought their eggs and refilled their coffee cups.

They ate in silence for a few minutes.

"I searched the net for days," he continued, "trying to figure out what to do. I came across a public interest law firm in Century City."

Ashley leaned forward.

"I thought I had stumbled onto the answer. They had locked you up without due process. Violation of both the fifth and fourteenth amendments." Jonathon took another bite of his omelet.

"And?" she asked.

"So, I met with one of the partners. Big-time law firm on the seventeenth floor of one of those Century City skyscrapers. You could see the Pacific Ocean from his window. Pin stripes, silk tie, gold-coin cufflinks, Harvard law degree on the wall. These people litigate against the DHS and other government entities. It's what they do. I told him the whole story. He listened, didn't blink, didn't interrupt. When I finished, he spun his chair around and worked his keyboard for a couple of minutes and spun back around to face me."

"His face had gone from interested to an angry sadness, if there is such a thing," Jonathon added. "The partner then stated,

'She's categorized as an unlawful enemy combatant and has no right to due process.'"

"I told him that's crazy, that you simply removed a drug implant. How could you be an enemy combatant?"

"'According to the DHS,' he said, 'she assaulted DAA agents at Barack Obama High School and is a potential threat to employees and institutions of the United States government if not on medication. As a result, DHS has designated her as an unlawful enemy combatant, which gives them the right to hold her without trial or legal representation.'"

"He told me I could do time if anyone found out I helped you remove the pill."

Ashley shook her head. "I should have never—"

"No, no," he said. "I'll never forget that day. I was just giving you the lawyer's feedback. No regrets. None. Zero. Zip."

She stirred her coffee some more with her fork. "Me, neither." She studied him. "You never fixed that broken front tooth."

"No, but I didn't have a nose job, either."

She tossed her napkin at him.

Matt, of the attempted roadside rescue, came into the restaurant. He stopped, checked around, spotted Ashley, and came over to their table. He stood and looked at Jonathon then at Ashley until she slid over some. He sat down. "What are you doing, Evie?" he asked.

She shifted sideways on the bench and slid back until she was up against the window. She pulled both feet up, wrapped her arms around her knees, and said, "The question is, what are you doing, Matt?"

"I . . . eh, was concerned. I couldn't find you, and the rest of us are heading..."

Ashley quickly interrupted, "I told you, I'm talking to a

friend. I'll head back up when we're done."

Matt wore dirty leather pants and a shirt made from some kind of animal hide. Very nineteenth century. He wore his hair in a ponytail, had a beard, and a bottlebrush mustache which he kept smoothing with his index finger.

He turned to Jonathon. "You're from Lake Oswego, too?"

Jonathon's eyes shifted to Ashley than returned to Matt. "Yes. Evie and I went to school together."

Matt nodded. For several seconds he looked at Ashley, then to Jonathon, and back to Ashley. No one spoke.

"So were you guys, like, together then?" he asked.

"Not really any of your business," Jonathon quipped. He glanced at Ashley, but she didn't react.

Matt was a different story. "Watch your mouth, city boy, or I'll have to teach you some mountain manners."

"You haven't been watching your old John Wayne movies, Matt," Jonathon said. "Someone with real manners would not intrude on a conversation between a couple of old friends. You now have a choice. You can leave and take your mountain manners with you and let Evie and me finish our conversation, or we can go outside. If you're smart, you'll leave right now. I spend my afternoons throwing guys twice your size around a wrestling ring. I'm the last guy you want to mess with."

Matt eyed Ashley, seeking a little intervention on his behalf. He got none.

"Well, fuck you both," he said, loud enough that several people raised their eyeballs from their blueberries and whipped cream. They watched Matt slide out of the booth and storm out of the restaurant before returning to the objects of their desire.

"Well, that was fun," Ash declared.

"Sorry," Jonathon offered. "He was getting boorish. Was he a boyfriend or something?"

"In his dreams," she replied. "Thanks for Lake Oswego. As you've probably guessed, I had some plastic surgery." She put her index finger on her nose.

"I liked the other one better," he said.

"So did I, but when I got out of that zoo, I decided never again. I snuck into Don and Bella's house in the a.m. hours and stole Don's iDevice. I took it to a hacker I knew in Echo Park and he drained Don's credits. He took half and gave me the other half, in an iDevice he created with the identity of a woman who died before iDevices were required to be registered with DHS."

"When did you get the nose job?" Jonathon asked.

"I bought Gertrude," she said. "The pickup. I drove to Ensenada for some medical tourism." She ran her thumb and index finger along her jaw line. "The facial recognition software the FBI and DHS deploy in the streetlamps and public places identifies eighteen data points on.the face. I had six of them altered, my brow, cheeks, nose, and jawline. Do you know how many million places that software operates?"

"It doesn't recognize the new Ashley?" he asked.

"Plastic surgery south of the border is a growth industry. They know the exact points on the face to alter. After the surgery, I cut and dyed my hair and drove into the highlands of central Mexico. I spent six months in San Miguel de Allende washing the stink of that behavioral center out of my soul."

Jonathon's iDevice registered an incoming call from Jose. "Give me a second," he said to Ashley. He listened for a moment. "No. I'm having a bite to eat with a friend."

Pause. "Tell her I'm sorry, would you? I just ran into an old friend."

Ashley got his attention and mouthed, "I can take you back now."

Jonathon, iDevice still to his ear, shook his head. "You don't know her. The Saturn Café. It's vegetarian." Pause. "I didn't think so. No, I can get a ride to the Best Western. I'll see you later." He put the iDevice back in his pocket. "I'm sorry. One of my friends that I came up with."

"Look," she said, "if you were with someone else . . ."

"No, not really. Some girls at the beach invited us to the bonfire. So," Jonathon returned to his omelet, "what did you do in San Miquel?"

"You don't smoke, do you? Cigarettes?" she asked.

"I've been wrestling competitively for the last few years. No tobacco. No weed."

"I'm impressed."

"Pragmatism."

Aamino swung by. She served their coffee and dropped the check on the table. They both reached for it, Jonathon's hand on the bottom, Ashley's on top. They sat that way for a moment, her hand on his until she withdrew it.

"How much is mine?" she asked. "I only use my iDevice for emergencies, but I can get you some credits or some silver coins if you'd like."

"I thought owning silver was against the law," he said.

"It is. That and gold."

"Doesn't matter. My treat." He pointed his iDevice at the bar code on the check.

They finished eating and went back to the pickup. "Where's the Best Western?" she asked.

"I don't know," he replied and asked the iDevice, which instantly told them. "I'd like to hear the rest of the story," he added.

She looked at him, curiously interested.

They drove south along the coast for about five miles. Ashley pulled off the road onto a bluff overlooking the Pacific.

They got out of the truck and skidded down a path to a small beach below. The fog stayed above them. The moon painted a silver walkway into the distance.

"Best breaks are right here, if you and your friends are checking out the surfs."

"I've made a note," he said. "So, San Miguel?"

"I rented a small townhouse set against the mountains, with a view of the most magnificent sunsets you've ever seen. I did a detox program at a health clinic there to get the drugs out of my system. My pores vomited poison for weeks."

"I ate wonderfully, slept deeply, and began to research where I was going to live. I had my hacker friend set up a virtual private network for me. The Internet police in Mexico have a very mañana attitude about political search. You can do any kind of search there. Political, social, cultural, without generating a visit from DHS, as long as you pay the global Internet usage tax."

She had taken a pack of cigarettes out from under the seat of the truck and now drew one out. "Do you mind?" she asked.

Jonathon shook his head.

"My research found this place," she said. "It presents itself as a natural commune."

"Which means what?"

"It's a community of people who live an organic lifestyle, a back-to-nature life.

No electronics in our commune, no iDevices, no Internet, not even old-fashioned tablets or smart phones. The founders of the group sought to roll their living back two hundred years, early nineteenth century."

"How do you communicate to the outside world?" he asked.

"That's the point, we don't. It's why I came here. I wanted to be completely off the grid. With some help, I learned to hack into government data-bases. I couldn't find a single one that had this place on a watch list."

"Are you planning to live here the rest of your life?"

"I'm not sure where I will be in the future. Right now I live in the nature commune, but I spend most of my time with another group farther up the mountain."

"Who are they?" Jonathon asked.

Ashley stood, took a drag on her cigarette, and stepped a few feet to the water's edge. She stared into the blackness and threw the cigarette into the remains of a breaking wave forcing her to rapidly tippy-toe backward.

"This other group, Ash. Who are they? What do they do?" he asked again.

"You really don't want to know, Jonathon."

Chapter Ten – Saratoga Movement
July 27, 2028, Santa Cruz, California

"Yeah, I do," he said. "You're involved, I'd like to know."

She walked back and sat down on the beach next to him. A sudden gust of wind rushed along the face of the cliff, sending a fallen palm branch tumbling across the sand, which came to rest next to the two of them. Jonathon plucked a frond from the branch and stuck it in his mouth as if he were chewing on a piece of straw from a hay bale.

"We are well into the decline and fall of the American Republic," she said.

"Tell me something I don't know."

"There are people," she continued after thinking about it, "who are passionately dedicated to bringing an end to the American police state and returning the country to the ideals of the Founders. Returning to constitutional principles and policies."

Jonathon took the frond out of his mouth and grimaced. He tossed it onto the sand. "I don't think it's a big secret, Ash. I think most Americans want that. They're afraid to say so, but asked outside of DHS earshot, most people are sick of Mother."

"If you are working with a group with that purpose, I'd like to get a sense of what you're doing, and with whom."

Ashley glanced out at the ocean but could only see the dissipating foam sliding up the beach toward their feet and hurrying back to join the next wave. She shook her head. "This is not your Sunday-morning patriot group, Jonathon. These are serious people. You get drawn into this movement, your public life is over."

"You're plugged in," he said.

"Yes, but I don't have a public life. I don't exist. I have no Homeland Security ID, no retina scan, no DNA in Mother's database, no electronic end point into which he can stick his digital probes. You, on the other hand, do exist. I presume you're going to college in the fall."

"Berkeley."

She nodded and stood up. "Let me get you to your hotel."

They drove back into town in silence, through fog London would have been proud of. Ashley drove the pickup into the parking lot of the Best Western and came to a stop, the engine idling noisily against the quiet night.

"This isn't a game you want to play, Jonathon," she said.

"You have no idea what games I want to play, Ash." He pushed the door open and exited the pickup, turned and pushed the truck's door closed as firmly as he could, and leaned his head in the window. "None at all." He walked away.

Jonathon tried his best to get a good night's sleep so he would be in shape for the long surfing day tomorrow but Ashley's words, like a skipped record repeating over and over in his head, kept him awake. What did she mean "this isn't a game you want to play, Jonathon." He sensed a danger in those words. A danger to his future if he were to get involved and a life threatening danger to Ashley. But he recalled the historically famous speech Patrick Henry delivered, "Give Me Liberty Or Give Me Death."

He made his decision.

Jonathon, Jose and the twins, Tim and Todd, spent the morning surfing breaks at the beach he had been to with Ashley the previous night. The fog had long since burned off and the surf was good, if not great. Around noon, they decided to head into town and grab a bite to eat. Boards in hand, the four of them trekked up the path rutted into the side of the cliff. They were loading their boards in the van when Ashley's pickup pulled over to the side of the road about forty yards behind them. Jonathon saw her but continued to arrange the boards.

She honked.

"Give me a second," Jonathon said to the guys, and headed over to the pickup.

Ashley wore her hood up and sunglasses covering half her face.

Jonathon stood a few feet from the driver's side window, which was rolled down, and remained silent.

Ashley took her glasses off. "You're right," she said. "I have no idea what your plans are. I just don't want to get you involved in something," she paused for a second, "which might affect you later in life."

"I think that's my call," he said.

"It is," she agreed. "Do me the favor, give it some thought before you commit. If you're still interested, I will be at the parking lot of the Saturn Café tonight at ten. I'll be there for five minutes."

"I'm interested in what you are doing, Ash. I'll be there."

"This is about a lot more than me," she said.

Jonathon shrugged.

Ashley spun the wheel and hit the gas, causing the pickup to spray a rooster tail of sand and dust at the ocean. She swung a U-turn on the highway and headed toward town.

Jonathon explained the conversation to the guys from a romantic perspective, which he wished it had been. "She's a friend I knew from LA a couple of years ago and is living here now."

"Just a friend?" Todd inquired with a smirk grin. The other guys chuckled.

"That's right and I asked if I could see her again and she came by to confirm."

"What's with the retro wheels?" from Jose.

"She inherited it from her grandfather," Jonathon rattled off the top of his head. "She drives it around town occasionally. It's wild. No computer, no GPS, no wi-fi. It's got a clutch you have to depress to change gears."

"Cool," said Tim. "Doesn't she get cited for the emissions?"

"I'm sure she does," Jonathon responded, adding, "I didn't ask her."

They drove back into town and lunched on tacos and beer at an outdoor Mexican restaurant. California had the most liberal permissive alcohol laws in the nation. The drinking age for the purchase and/or consumption of alcohol in a public place in the Golden State had been lowered to eighteen when California passed legislation permitting eighteen-year-olds to possess one ounce of marijuana in 2018. You could drink and smoke weed at eighteen, but if you got caught smoking a cigarette you could go to jail.

Jonathon and his friends had pinned down female companionship for the evening. The twins had hooked up with a couple of co-eds from UCSC, Jose was seeing Vivian, and Jonathon was meeting Ashley. His, he knew, would be anything but a date.

Jonathon gave the digital control for the iVan to the twins. Jose rushed around the room, collected the surfing trunks and other dirty laundry strewn across the floor, threw them into the closet, and slammed the door shut. As Jonathon was opening the door to leave Jose screamed out, "Don't come back to the room before midnight." Jonathon agreed and took off jogging toward the Saturn Café. The fog had rolled in again. It kept him cool while he ran and had a cleansing effect on his lungs. He felt strong, as if he could run to San Francisco. He detoured to the road running along the beach, kicked his pace up to six-minute miles for about three miles, and then returned to the path toward the restaurant and jogged a breath-catching eight-minute miles on the way back.

He arrived at the Saturn Café at 9:50. He spotted a bench outside the restaurant where people sat and waited for a table. A row of yellow and purple pansies ran along each side of the bench, which struck Jonathon as two lines of vibrant, little soldiers. He admired the flowers while he got his breathing back to normal. Despite the fog-cooled air, he was still dripping sweat when Ashley drove up.

"Get in," she called to him.

Jonathon got into the pickup. "Okay. Where to?"

Ashley handed him a cloth sack. An old flour sack that appeared to have been washed. "Sorry. You have to put this on."

Jonathon took the sack. Turned it upside down and inside out. "You've got to be kidding."

"You asked to play with the big boys. Security starts here, tough guy."

Jonathon gave her a smirk and pulled the sack over his head. He closed his eyes and leaned back in his seat. "Over to you, squadron leader."

He had no intention of trying to find his way back to wherever they were going but given what the girls at the beach had said, he assumed they were headed into the Santa Cruz Mountains. After about twenty-five minutes the pickup slowed and turned onto a pothole-infested road. The ruts and the pickup's lack of shocks made Jonathon bounce on the brittle leather seat so hard he hit his head on the ceiling of the cab. "Jesus. Slow down, Ash."

"Sorry," she apologized. "We're almost there."

Ten minutes later, she eased the truck to the right side of the road and turned off the engine. She lifted the sack off his head, folded it carefully, and placed it on top of the dashboard. "This meeting is with the Chief of Security of 100777."

"And that is?" he asked.

"Let's go," she replied without answering.

They got out of the pickup. The fog hadn't seeped into the mountains, and shafts of moonlight knifed through the pines and redwoods.

"Follow me," she instructed.

Jonathon fell in behind her and followed her up a steep, pine-needled path. He could hear movement in the underbrush as they climbed through the forest, but had no idea whether it was a raccoon, porcupine, or one of the mountain lions known to inhabit these mountains.

The path led to a wooden footbridge that took them over a quietly rushing stream. When they got to the far side of the bridge, an enormous owl swooped down out of a towering pine and flew inches from Jonathon's head. As his ducking reflex kicked in, he thought, is this a sign to warn me away? He quickly paid it no mind and continued on the path.

Twenty-five yards past the footbridge, another trail angled more deeply into the forest. A short way up this path, Jonathon could see the outline of a cabin. As they approached, a light went on in a window. Ashley stopped.

She was breathing heavily. "You good?" she asked.

"You're out of shape," he said.

Ashley walked up to the door and knocked twice rapidly and twice more slowly before opening the door.

Jonathon expected to see a buckskin-wearing, pony-tailed, Special Forces veteran turned patriot mountain man with an AK-47 across his lap, that or a flintlock.

The striking woman sitting behind a tabletop desk was of Native American ancestry. She had radiant, black hair, complexion, and the prominent high cheekbones of the Apache. A lone eagle feather, given to her by a tribal chief for her indisputable defense at a congressional hearing on Indian land and sovereignty, was attached to her hair somehow and lay against the side of her head. She wore jeans and a black, leather motorcycle jacket.

A majestic German Shepherd lying at her feet watched Jonathon with Stinger-missile eyes. He let out a low growl but did not move.

"Easy, Max," the woman said. "Have a seat, Mr. Carr. My name Agnes Morningcloud."

"Thank you," Jonathon replied, and sat in a cowhide chair in front of her. Ashley moved to the front of the stone fireplace and remained standing.

Agnes began, "Ashley tells me you have an interest in our organization."

"I don't know about your organization," he began. "I don't know exactly what it is. I am interested in the purposes Ash spoke about."

She nodded. "Tell me about yourself."

"Not a lot to tell," he said. "Born and raised in LA, headed to Berkeley, pre-law. I wrestle."

"You don't just wrestle, Mister Carr, do you? You won the high school one hundred seventy-pound weight division championship in the most populous state in the union. You were also nearly a straight-A student."

"I'm impressed. How did you get into my transcripts that fast?"

Agnes Morningcloud smirked.

"And you," Jonathon asked. "How long have you been Chief of Security of the Saratoga Movement?"

Agnes Morningcloud snapped her head instantly in Ashley's direction, eyes ablaze, clearly furious. Ashley held up both hands in front of herself, as if to tell a base runner rounding third not to try for home and shook her head.

"Ashley told me I would be meeting the Chief of Security of 100777," Jonathon stated. "I took the numbers as a date, ten-seven, or October seventh. You are a patriot group, so I figured seventeen seventy-seven. October seventh, seventeen seventy-seven was the Colonists' victory at the Battle of Saratoga, the turning point of the Revolutionary War."

Ashley's eyes widened. Agnes Morningcloud pointed her index finger at him and dropped her thumb on it as if she were taking a shot. "Are you familiar with Patriot Act Two?"

Jonathon's composure seemed to destabilize. "Somewhat," he replied.

"Let me refresh your memory," she said. "It was the original Patriot Act that empowered the current American police state. You know that."

"I do."

"That Act legitimized turning the U.S. intelligence apparatus inward on American citizens. Law enforcement followed their lead. As you know, the Patriot Act was amended briefly by the

USA Freedom Act, a euphemistic sop to Edward Snowden's disclosures."

"I've been curious, how did they get him?" Jonathon interrupted.

"The administration quietly agreed to drop its support of the Ukrainian government. In exchange, Vladimir Putin permitted a Special Forces ops team to fly into Moscow, kidnap him, and return him to the U.S. for prosecution. I'm sure you watched the trial. A joke, a Greek tragedy. He still has eighteen years to serve. He'll be sixty-three when he gets out, if they don't assassinate him first."

Jonathon nodded.

Agnes Morningcloud snatched up a handful of pistachios from a bowl on her desk and offered the bowl to Jonathon.

"No thanks," he said.

She cracked a shell, put a kernel in her mouth, and continued as she chewed. "Then came United flight 251 out of San Francisco, retina-scanned national ID cards and, three months later, Patriot II."

"Did you know, Mister Carr, that the citizenship of any U.S. citizen can be revoked if they are members of or have supported any group the Director of the Department of Homeland Security designates as terrorist?"

Jonathon nodded.

"A person who gives money to a charity that only later turns out to have some terrorist connection could then lose his or her citizenship?"

Jonathon listened. Said nothing.

"Judicial oversight has been removed in a number of circumstances. For instance, federal investigators can conduct wiretaps without a court order for fifteen days whenever Congress authorizes force or a response to an attack on the United States.

An act of domestic terrorism classifies as such an attack."

"Your attacking a DAA agent in the corridor of your high school, for example, qualifies as an act of domestic terrorism."

Jonathon returned the index finger gunshot at Agnes.

"I could go on."

Jonathon held up his hands. "Most people know these things, Ms. Morningcloud."

Max lifted his head off his front paws. His ears spiked. A sound moving through the brush outside the window alerted his senses. He listened to things no one in the room could hear. He cautiously hoofed to the front window, rose on his hind legs, and peered out into the darkness. He stayed that way, standing immobile, only his nose and ears engaged. When he sensed it was only a varmint running through the bushes, no danger, he pushed back off the windowsill, proudly pranced back over to Agnes, knowing he was wearing his security dog hat, and plopped down at her feet.

"Yes," she agreed, "but knowing about them and doing something about them are two different things, very different things. There are perils associated with what we do, Mister Carr. The penalties can be severe. On the other hand, what choice do we have?"

She picked a document up from the side of the desk and started reading.

"We hold these truths to be self-evident, that all men are created equal, that they are endowed by their Creator with certain unalienable Rights, that among these are Life, Liberty and the pursuit of Happiness. --That to secure these rights, Governments are instituted among Men, deriving their just powers from the consent of the governed."

Without any document in front of him, Jonathon continued quoting from The Declaration of Independence. "--

That whenever any Form of Government becomes destructive of these ends, it is the Right of the People to alter or to abolish it, and to institute new Government, laying its foundation on such principles and organizing its powers in such form, as to them shall seem most likely to effect their Safety and Happiness."

Silence settled in the room.

"Where did you get that memory, Mister Carr?" Agnes Morningcloud asked in complete sincerity.

Jonathon looked at her for some time. "At a Thanksgiving dinner, I must have been around ten, my father spiked a comment to his brother about constitutional incitement in our government. I asked, what is the Constitution which only fell on deaf ears. That night I Googled Constitution. After reading the entire document I became aware I could recall it word for word. I had the same recall experience reading the Declaration of Independence. But what was strange about the experience was the future danger I sensed around these documents and a future danger to people close to me."

Chapter Eleven – The Decision
July 28, 2028, Santa Cruz Mountains, California

It was bound to happen.

They climbed into the cab of the pickup. The windows had been left down and it was as chilly inside the truck as outside. Ashley rubbed her upper arms to warm up, then sat quietly for a moment, peering out the windshield into the night. After several seconds, she glanced at him. A shaft of moonlight illuminated her face as if she was sitting for a portrait. Jonathon couldn't ever remember seeing anything so beautiful.

"You were brilliant in there," she said. She leaned across the seat.

Jonathon took her face in his hands as if he were holding the most delicate flower in the universe and kissed her. "I love you, Ash. I've loved you since before you knew I existed."

"Oh, I knew," she remarked and kissed him in return.

They made love in the back of the pickup on top of a bunch of old army blankets that had been stored there. The lovemaking rocked the pickup as if it was the epicenter of its own earthquake.

They lay on their backs then, staring up at a slice of the Milky Way through an opening in the tall pine above them.

"I have dreams," Jonathon stated quite simply.

"Most people do," she said.

"Odd dreams," he added.

"What, sex?" she smiled.

"No. Well, yes. But that isn't what I'm talking about," he said.

"About what then?"

"Government."

"How do you mean?" She propped herself on her elbow.

Jonathon watched the stars and didn't speak for some time. "I'm not exactly sure. Feels like some kind of evil, trying to claw its way out of my mind."

"You're not evil," she said.

She laid her head on his chest and they dozed off, to be awakened by a raccoon rummaging through their discarded clothes, piled in a jumbled mess against the tailgate.

The sun wakened the forest and a pair of blue jays argued noisily as they chased each other from branch to branch in the pines above. Jonathon and Ashley dressed and drove to the Saturn Café for breakfast.

The smell of freshly baked muffins accompanied them to a secluded table away from other patrons and nosy ears. The restaurant was less crowed than at night. The waiter, Colin, was amped, a fountain of six a.m. enthusiasm when Ashley ordered organic yogurt and fresh blueberries. "Great choice!" he said, as if she had selected a 500 credit bottle of a rare French wine.

Jonathon went for the strawberry waffle and faux tofu sausage.

"My personal favorite," confided Colin.

They ate quietly. When they finished and were working on their coffee, Jonathon said, "I've made up my mind about something. I need to talk to you about it."

"Okay," she said.

"I can't join the Saratoga Movement."

"Why not?" she asked. "You seem—"

"I admire what you are doing, Ash," he began. "I admire it a lot. But you are working outside the system. That might be the right path. That might be the only path, but I have another approach I feel compelled to pursue. I am going to get a law degree, do some civic work, and run for Congress. I want to attack it from the inside."

"We've just found each other, Jonathon. I don't want to lose you," she said. "Besides, Congress is part of the problem."

"You could come with me," he offered. "Help me fix it."

"No. I couldn't."

"You could."

"I will never let the DHS have access to my person again," she proclaimed. "When we restore a constitutional government, when they are brought back under the law, things will be different. Until then I will devote every fiber of my being to accomplish what you quoted from The Declaration of Independence last night."

"You could help us and we would be together," she added. "The network is large and growing daily. We are many. Agnes didn't even start the briefing on that."

Jonathon's head started to ache. He tried to rub burning out of his eyes. He felt pinned to a problem from which he could not see an escape. In the ring he could always find some purchase of leverage that would enable a release. Always. But now he was pinned, stuck in a situation for which he had no ready solution. He hadn't been able to get Ashley out of his mind since he first saw her in high school. He loved her. She was all he ever wanted in a mate, and more. But he was drawn to Washington in a way he couldn't explain. The nation's capital was a political cesspool, but many still held Constitutional values, even if they did not promote them as they used to.

They both wanted the same thing, but this was the path he felt he had to take. He wasn't even sure why, he just knew it was the right path for him.

This purpose played against his love of the woman sitting in front of him, goddess-like green eyes, compassionate smile, his soul mate, who was irrevocably committed to a different course.

His passions here were not those of someone who was about to start his freshman year in college. This problem did not have a chronological age. Both sides of the problem were matters of the mind and felt timeless.

"You were right, I can't play your game, Ash," he said. "Not now. And you can't play mine. But this is not over. We are not over."

Tears glistened in her eyes, bright in the golden morning sunlight streaming through the window, glistening like diamonds. One rolled down. Ashley brushed the tear from her cheek with the back of her sleeve. She sniffed and gazed at him for several seconds until she regained her composure. "What happened to me in that behavioral center should not happen to another soul. Not ever. That place was no different than a Russian Gulag, and the American police state has done nothing but metastasize in the years since. Still, the public and Congress have done nothing. We are witnessing the death of liberty, and to the degree we do nothing to prevent it we are accomplices. Not on my watch."

He turned from her and looked out the window. Two joggers ran by. They were a young couple. Happy. Carefree. Life was good. He thought about Ashley's commitment, their lovemaking last night, his plans for law school and Washington.

He could feel his heart break and had to swallow back his tears several times before responding, "You're probably right."

Chapter Twelve – The Dream
January 24, 2035, Berkeley, California

Michael could smell the alcohol on the Vice President's breath. Hair fashioned into an aerosol helmet and pancake makeup made him look like a local news anchor added to the bourbon breath.

And this guy is a heartbeat away from the White House, he thought.

He placed his hand on the Bible. It was held together with rotting twine and yellowed Scotch tape. His father had carried it with him during the invasion of Normandy. "I, Michael Keough, do solemnly swear . . ."

The Vice President's eyes drifted to Carrie, Michael's alluring wife, as he recited the oath. Seeming to realize he was probably being filmed, he jerked his gaze back to Michael.

".... That I will support and defend the Constitution of the United States . . ."

Eyeball to eyeball now, he could see the anger in the Vice President's eyes. He realized it was political. The Vice President hated having to swear in another member of the opposition. Michael, Marine Officer-straight, let a faint smile form across his mouth and continued with his oath of office.

He was a United States Senator now. He could change things.

." . . and that I will faithfully discharge the duties of the office on which I am about to enter. So help me, God."

"So help me, God!"

"So help me, God!"

He said it again and again and again as the Vice President morphed into the Statue of Liberty, who, holding the Constitution to her breast, was being burned alive, screaming in wretched agony.

Jonathon Carr bolted upright in bed.

His hair, his entire head, was soaked in sweat. He tried to wipe the sting away from his eyes with the back of his hand and blink it away. He scanned around his bedroom to get his bearings and glanced at the clock. 4:29 a.m. He had another couple of hours before he had to get up. He laid his head down on the pillow and tried to get back to sleep.

No joy.

His mind kept drifting back to the dream. He knew it was just a dream but it felt so real, like he was this person taking the oath of office.

He told the light on the nightstand to turn on low and picked up a tattered paperback on the life of Thomas Jefferson, which he had purchased at a seedy back-alley bookstore off campus. Finding printed books about Jefferson and other founders, as a group now referred to in American history classes as "the early American slave-owning capitalists," was rare. The numbers of all books about the signers of The Declaration of Independence were registered with the Department of Homeland Security, as were the buyers of those books.

By law, all book publishing was now digital. Digital publications could be tracked, which, according to the DHS, could help them identify potential terrorists. You could legally own printed books published before 2027, but those who read them put their careers at risk.

A friend of Jonathon's named Harish had a pristine collection of pre '27 paperback books and magazines, which he had inherited from his father. Harish's former live-in girlfriend had anonymously leaked the fact to the iDevice world after Harish started seeing someone else.

He was branded an eco-terrorist on the largest iDevice social media platform for owning paper-based reading material. The effects were almost instantaneous.

Harish couldn't overcome the speed of the digital execution. The label spread to such an extent, his ability to find a job was now next to impossible.

A black market where print books could be purchased with their ISBNs removed had built up around college campuses. Possession of an unregistered book about any of the nation's founders was a felony punishable by a year of behavioral counseling, a fine of 25,000 credits, or both.

A page into the book, his iDevice said, "It's four thirty-five a.m., Jonathon."

"Right."

"Your light is on. Do you need a sleep aide?"

"No."

"You have an oral exam in a few hours. Perhaps—"

Jonathon reached and grabbed the device off his nightstand. He took it into the bathroom, wrapped it in a towel, and placed the bundle in the sink.

Once engaged, an iDevice could only be shut off by Apple,

who it was widely understood, reported suspect and suspicious terrorist information to the Department of Homeland Security as part of their program of corporate responsibility to protect the country from the growing plague of domestic terrorism.

iDevices were not yet mandatory, though legislation was currently working its way through Congress to make them so, but trying to get through college without one, particularly law school in 2035 as Jonathon was doing, was for all practical purposes impossible.

Jonathon had an uncomfortable feeling which he couldn't shake. He couldn't get this dream out of his mind. What was it telling him? Was this some sort of a future admonition?

Chapter Thirteen – Con Law
January 24, 2035, 7:30 a.m., Berkeley, California

Jonathon lived in a rooming house on Benvenue Avenue, not far from the UC Berkeley campus. The owner, a spirited seventy-two-year-old widow bent nearly double with an arthritic spine, supplemented the modest dividend income from her deceased husband's investments by renting out her upstairs bedroom to Cal students.

She had brewed a pot of coffee and was into her second cup when he came downstairs. "Would you like a cup?" she asked.

"Sure," he replied. "A quick one."

"You look rushed, Jonathon," she said.

He blew on his coffee and took a sip. "I have an exam this morning, Mrs. Wilson."

"I hope you studied. What is your exam on?"

"Yes. I studied." Jonathon smiled. "The class is Con Law. So the test will be on some part of the Constitution."

Mrs. Wilson added some milk and sugar to her coffee and stirred them in deliberately. She picked up her cup and looked out the kitchen window at her garden, which was ablaze with azaleas. "Almost seems like a waste."

"What's that?"

"A course on the Constitution," she said. "The government doesn't seem to care much about it anymore."

Jonathon glanced around the room.

"There's no surveillance in here, Jonathon. I have it swept."

"Swept?"

She turned back to her azaleas "What part of the Constitution?"

"Eh, it's an oral exam," he replied. "More like a debate with the professor. We don't know the exact subject until we're called on. Swept?"

"Do you know your Constitution, Jonathon?" she asked, avoiding his query.

"I've got James Madison on an IV," he responded.

"My, my." She studied him a moment. The corners of her mouth twitched upward. She turned and walked out the back kitchen door to her garden. "Do well." She closed the door.

Jonathon parked his personal transporter in the lot with the others. His iDevice locked it and he headed for Boalt Hall. He couldn't see the eyes behind the black face shields of a pair of flak-jacketed militia who seemed to watch him head for the law school complex.

The DHS Domestic Security Forces usually paired one human soldier with one robotoid, which the students had taken to calling 'toids. The name stuck. Jonathon couldn't tell which was which. Even out of uniform, 'toids were astonishingly life-like.

Command and control of state militias had been turned over to the Department of Homeland Security as part of the expanded national effort to defeat domestic terrorism in 2027.

Units of the National Guard had taken up residence on the Cal campus some years earlier after a freshman on a cocktail of psych meds had taken an assault rifle into chem 101 and slaughtered 43 students and a Vietnamese teaching assistant before splattering his own brains across the blackboard.

Jonathon, seeing the soldier and 'toid set off a musing moment. A nurse with sunken blue eyes and a too revealing white nurse uniform lead him into a medical room. In hand, a federal guaranteed student loan application. The final step for loan approval and entry into law school was to receive a microdot-size implant. He could feel the prick of the injection in the back of his skull again. He shook his head realizing he was going to be late for class.

Jonathon bounded up the steps to the building's entrance and down the hall to his Con Law class. He pushed through the door, stopped, and surveyed the room. Just a few seats were unoccupied. Boalt was the fifth-ranked law school in the nation, and one of the most diverse. The administration had gone far beyond DEPA, the Diversity Enforcement and Protection Act, which set strict federal guidelines for the percentages of all nationalities, genders, sexual orientations, races, and disabilities that had to be maintained by all institutions of higher learning in the United States, whether they received federal funds or not.

The students still had to take the LSAT, and admissions committees could cherry-pick from the diversity buckets of applicants. This process made the classrooms a cacophony of brilliance encased in bodies of varying color, sexual proclivity and ethnic flair.

He trotted down the steps to the front of the auditorium and picked a seat next to Mei Wang, a brilliant co-ed from Beijing whose father was reported to be Triad-connected and the fifth richest man in the PRC.

Mei, on the other hand, had westernized like a valley girl, spoke perfect English, had no known sexual partners of either gender, and greeted him with one of the most inviting smiles he had ever seen.

She was also a nationally ranked tennis player in her backyard, which happened to be the biggest in the world.

"Gutsy move, Carr," she said. "You know he always calls on front-row students first."

"And you're here because you finished yesterday and figure you're safe."

"You're not."

"I'd just as soon take it head on," he stated.

"If you're so into offense, why is it you won't play tennis with me?"

"Because I've seen your serve," he replied. "How about beer and pizza Saturday night instead?"

Mei shook her head.

"Dumplings and Peking Duck?"

More shaking.

"Why not?" he asked.

"Because I've seen your serve," she responded, and smiled.

But it was a flirtatious smile, and Jonathon was about to follow up when Professor Oscar Schmidt entered the classroom from the side door.

Chapter Fourteen – A Player
January 24, 2035, 8:35 a.m., Berkeley, California

Marguerite Wilson pushed herself up off her knees and picked up the bag of weeds she had taken from her azalea garden. It wasn't a large bag but Marguerite, who in violation of federal law, grew some garden vegetables and flowers organically, kept the garden free from intruders. In 2020 The Food and Agriculture Organization, a U.N. Specialized Agency, outlawed residential food and vegetation growing as an international protective health hazard. In 2025 the US followed suit.

She shuffled over to her composter and deposited the weeds. The composter was perched atop a rickety bamboo stool, which stood next to a set of cement steps disappearing down a tunneled stairway. She started down the steps, keeping a firm grip on the wooden railing until she got to the bottom.

She swung left into an enclosure, housing a neatly arranged selection of garden tools and yanked on a hoe. A cabinet door to which the hoe was attached opened electronically. An iDevice sat on a shelf in a metal container.

Marguerite removed the iDevice and rattled off a chain of numbers. The recipient's image appeared on her device. She shut off the video feed and said, "I think you should come."

"Are you sure?" the recipient asked.

"Yes. He's . . . right for it," Marguerite replied.

"I'll come. We'll see if he's a player."

Chapter Fifteen – Search and Seizure
January 24, 2035, 9:05 a.m., Boalt Hall, University of California Berkeley

It didn't take him long. Professor Oscar Schmidt, eggshell bald with a Freud goatee and skintight, full-body, business attire, told his iDevice to start recording and surveyed the front row. "Well, Mister Carr. Nice to have you up here where I can see you. Let's get started, shall we?

Students shifted in their chairs. Some coughed.

"Tell us about the Fourth Amendment, Mister Carr."

The wall at the front of the classroom transformed into a six-by-six foot image of Jonathon in his seat. Unshaven, broken nose, blond curls askew, his name and iDevice address appeared at the bottom of the picture.

"Sir?" Jonathon asked.

"Do you have a hearing disorder, Mister Carr? Tell us about the Fourth Amendment."

Jonathon couldn't actually see the space in the room condense, but he could feel it. "No. I just didn't know if you had anything more specific in mind."

Schmidt started to say something, but Jonathon barreled forward before he could get it out.

"The origins of the Fourth Amendment go back to seventeenth century English common law. In 1604, the Semaynes case acknowledged that the king did not have unrestrained authority to intrude on the homes of his subjects. In 1765, in Entick, the court ruled the search and seizure of Mr. Entick's papers was unlawful, as the warrant lacked probable cause. It further established the precedent that the Executive Branch is limited in its ability to encroach upon private property."

"The Fourth Amendment, Mr. Carr," Schmidt said, with retrained impatience.

"In the colonies," Jonathon remarked without acknowledging Schmidt, "the British used general warrants to ravage the homes of colonists, who had no redress. General warrants called Writs of Assistance were used by tax collectors to search the homes of colonists and seize what were alleged to be 'uncustomed goods.'"

Schmidt slowly paced back and forth across the front of the classroom, stroking his goatee as if he were petting a stray cat.

"James Otis represented a group of fifty merchants before the Superior Court of Massachusetts in 1761, condemned the Writs of Assistance as 'the worst instrument of arbitrary power.'" Jonathon paused just a moment to see if Schmidt was going to lob a grenade. Seeing none, he continued. "Otis's scathing, five-hour attack on the Writs was based on English common law and is viewed by many scholars as the birthmother of the Fourth Amendment."

Schmidt spun around and pointed his finger at Jonathon. "They were criminals, Mister Carr."

"The British?" Jonathon asked.

"The Colonists, Mister Carr," he rebuked in a near shout. "The colonists were smuggling contraband, sugar, coffee, cloth. The British were simply seeking to collect import taxes. Taxes enshrined into law by the British Parliament. The government has a right to collect taxes, Mister Carr. Or do you disagree with that as well?"

Jonathon's face reddened, made more obvious by his enlarged image on the front wall. "By storming into any home they felt like with no probable cause. By confiscating private property with no evidence the residents had committed any crime. There were reports of looting and rape. Why should a British citizen in the homeland be safe from illegal search and seizure and not the colonists?"

"I'm asking the questions, Mister Carr."

Mei slid her hand under the desk and squeezed his thigh. Jonathon glanced over and gave her a flirtatious smile. She quickly took her hand away.

"Are we on the same page, Mister Carr?"

Arrogant prick, he thought, but he had to pass Con Law. Had to. He watched himself nod to Schmidt on the front wall and was gripped by a voice in his head. "So help me, God!" His sense of rage then oddly dissipated into an apathetic acceptance of the government's power. He slid down in his chair an inch or two but had no idea why. He felt he was actually drowning in a sense of government corruption and abuse of power.

"Good. Let's move on, shall we?"

Not entirely sure where he was, Jonathon nodded again.

"What does the Fourth Amendment say, Mister Carr, what does it mean?"

Jonathon sat silent for several moments.

"Mister Carr?

Mei squeezed his leg again, but this time to get him out of his momentary funk.

He shook his head. "The right of the people to be secure in their persons, houses, papers, and effects, against unreasonable searches and seizures, shall not be violated, and no Warrants shall issue, but upon probable cause, supported by Oath or affirmation, and particularly describing the place to be searched, and the persons or things to be seized."

"Very good, Mister Carr, but anyone can recite from memory. What does it mean?"

"It means a great deal," Jonathon said, intending to go on.

A student seated in the row behind him raised her hand.

"Did you want Miss Abbott to answer the question for you, Mister Carr?"

Jonathon swiveled in his chair and looked up at Melissa Abbot, a six-foot, two-inch coed who had given up her professional basketball career to go to law school. He gave her a crooked smile. Jonathon and Melissa had dated. It had not ended well.

"The Fourth Amendment," he said, still starring at Melissa Abbott, "at its core, safeguards liberty. It safeguards the privacy of individual Americans. It does so by imposing a neutral and objective third-party, a judge, to be interjected between the police and the public. It means a search of someone requires a warrant signed by a judge."

Melissa gave him a disgusted expression and put her hand down, but Jonathon continued to speak at her, keeping his back to Schmidt. "The warrant must be supported by probable cause and limited in scope to specific items, based on a sworn affidavit by someone who has reason to suspect criminal activity or wrongdoing, usually someone from law enforcement."

Melissa slowly moved her skirt to her thighs and parted her knees.

Jonathon stared a breath, swallowed and swiveled back around in his seat to face front.

Schmidt went behind his podium and the wall image

morphed to him and his goatee. "At the DHS, defense attorneys would often try to invalidate evidence we collected under the Patriot Act, Mister Carr. They argued the Act violated the Fourth Amendment. But terrorism, the security of the American homeland, and the people in it trumps privacy. Wouldn't you agree?"

Jonathon's face filled the screen. He stared at his image. A thin line of sweat had broken out on his forehead. He tried to formulate an answer that would not result in his flunking Con Law. One didn't graduate Boalt having failed Constitutional Law.

"Mister Carr?"

Jonathon glanced at Schmidt, his image on the front wall, back at Schmidt.

He hesitated for a moment, then slid to the edge of his seat. "No," he said.

"What did you say?" Schmidt asked.

"No," Jonathon repeated. "I don't think the threat of terrorism trumps privacy. Not the way the Patriot Act, both Patriot One and Two have been used for the last thirty-plus years." At that moment he thought, did I just throw in the towel? Did I just screw up my chances of passing Con Law?

Chapter Sixteen – The Grateful Dead
October 2 - back to the year 2001

"The White House is on the phone," Diane Hollingsworth said as she burst through the door to Senator Michael Keough's office. "It's the Chief of Staff." As his Chief of Staff, she took a seat in front of his desk. "I'm sure he's pushing support for the new terrorism bill. I haven't read it, but I'm sure we'll support it. Everybody is."

A graduate of Stanford Law and former news anchor for the NBC affiliate in San Francisco, Diane was Senator Keough's Chief of Staff. Once featured as the sexiest face in broadcast journalism by the San Francisco Chronicle, politics was her true passion. She had seen Michael Keough's senatorial campaign as her ticket to the big show, to the PR maelstrom in Washington that molded the minds of power.

She had followed his congressional career as a journalist and, with some flirtatious undertones, pitched him over wine and cheese at Gary Danko's on the Wharf to handle the public relations for his senatorial campaign.

After his landslide victory she had joined him in Washington as his Communications Director, becoming his Chief of Staff two years later.

Michael punched the button and moved his head close to the phone so it was not obvious to the caller he was on a speakerphone. "Senator Keough," he said.

"Good morning, Senator."

"Good morning, Sandy. How are things at Sixteen Hundred?"

"I won't waste your time, Senator. The President has asked me to call and confirm your support for the USA Patriot Act."

"I haven't had a chance to read it yet, Sandy, but I think you can safely tell the President he has my support."

Diane gave him two thumbs up.

"Excellent. I was sure I could count on you, Senator. Let me ask you… we have some intelligence that Majority Leader Kaschle and Senator McLeahy have some concerns with the legislation."

"Oh?"

"Some Fourth Amendment bullshit. We're at war for Christ's sake. What's your relationship with the Majority Leader? Or McLeahy?"

"Let's say I'm not on Thomas Kaschle's Christmas list. I've opposed virtually every piece of legislation he has pushed. Of course, they're running the show here these days, but Bob McLeahy and I are both serious Deadheads."

Diane winced.

"Serious what?" Carl asked.

"Deadheads. It's a name given to dedicated The Grateful Dead fans."

"You're kidding."

"Dead serious," Michael said and waited for a response. None forthcoming, he ventured, "No pun intended."

Sandy Carl, who had grown up with Willie Nelson and

Waylon Jennings, was not known for his sense of humor.

"You trying to tell me that one of the most liberal members of the United States Senate is a fan of a sixties rock-and-roll cokehead?" Carl asked.

"I am. As was I."

Diane got up and started to pace, shaking her head.

"Was?" Carl asked.

"He died," Michael replied. "Jerry Garcia died six years ago."

"Oh. So…"

"So, I'm from Menlo Park. Birthplace of the Dead. Followed them all my life. I heard McLeahy was a Deadhead. When he became Chairman of the Judiciary Committee earlier this year, I sent him a newly released video box set with a congratulatory note."

Diane stopped pacing in front of the desk and motioned the index finger of her right hand in a cutting motion across her throat.

"And?" Carl queried.

"And he sent me back a poster from a concert they did in Central Park in '69. It's hanging here in my office. A real collector's item."

"No shit?"

"No shit."

"I need to see you over dinner, this evening, Senator. How about Ruth's Chris on Dupont Circle at six?"

"I promised my wife—"

"Senator, we're at war," Carl stated.

"I'll see you there," Michael said.

Diane pointed wildly to herself.

"I'd like to bring my Chief of Staff."

"Alone," Carl said and hung up.

Chapter Seventeen – Outburst
January 24, 2035, 9:10 a.m., Boalt Hall, University of California Berkeley

"So you would rather see another 9/11, Mister Carr? Thousands of Americans dead?" Schmidt raised his voice as he quickly paced toward Jonathon. "People jumping to their death from seventy-story buildings to escape being burned alive. Is that what you want?"

The screen switched from Schmidt to Jonathon.

Jonathon clenched his teeth. "There is no evidence Patriot Act One or Two could have prevented any terrorist attacks, Professor. You know that."

"Don't tell me what I know, Mister Carr. You don't have the chops. The Fourth Amendment was written nearly two hundred and fifty years ago by a bunch of slave-owning capitalists who were trying to avoid British taxes."

So help me, God, Jonathon thought to himself, holding his emotion at bay for a moment before he lost it. "They were trying to avoid the actions of a tyrannical king, Professor. They were trying to protect themselves against the Crown's abuse of power. Title two hundred fifteen of the original Patriot Act was a legislative slaying of the Fourth Amendment, an unconstitutional butchering of the Bill of Rights. Patriot Act Two, with its secret arrests and removal of judicial oversight, are the tactics of a police state. It is not what the Founders intended. It's tyranny." He was shouting now. "Why don't you just burn the Constitution, Professor?"

The entire classroom seemed frozen in the moment. The front wall flipped to the image of Schmidt staring at Jonathon, eyes wide, mouth agape, stunned into a rare loss for words.

The momentary silence was shattered by the blare of an angry siren through the building. Two DHS agents stormed into the classroom, spraying the environment with electric-blue, paralytic laser beams. Everyone hit the floor.

Jonathon's Seed had blown.

The term Seed had emerged from the ghetto. With the passage of the Welfare Monitoring Act of 2031, anyone receiving government assistance was required to receive a microdot-size implant.

The implant detected if the recipient was consuming illegal substances including nicotine, excessive amounts of impermissible vitamins, or herbal supplements. If these, and a host of other listed substances, were detected by the implant, the welfare payment for the following month was reduced based on a Congressionally mandated formula in proportion to the amount of the banned substance detected in the welfare recipient's blood.

A subsequent Supreme Court decision approved federal legislation extending the use of implants to those receiving federally guaranteed student loans, ninety percent of those enrolled in colleges, universities and graduate schools. The Supreme Court decision did not opine on what data the implants could gather, only that the students' receipt of taxpayer dollars entitled the government to monitor their bodies.

The student Seeds, however, were different. They did not

measure consumables. These implants monitored the blood pressure, adrenaline, body temperature, respiration, and heartbeat of the indentured student. Most notably, implanted at the base of the skull, they measured the intensity of the emotional waves emanating from the mind of the host.

The theory was that in excess of a certain threshold, the student had crossed over some mystical boundary into that of a potential terrorist.

A composite reading over the threshold alerted the nearest DHS field office, in this case, the two-man patrol Jonathon had passed on the way in.

The 'toid marched down the stairs to the front of the room. There was an awkward, rather arthritic, cadence to a 'toid walking down steps. When it reached the front of the room it eyed Jonathon, who lay spread-eagle on the floor, and said, "You are Jonathon Carr."

Silence. No one moved. Head swiveling right to left, the 'toid repeated the statement. No emotion.

The front wall image morphed to the 'toid's lifeless eyes. Jonathon got up off the floor, looked at the 'toid, and then reluctantly climbed up the stairs. At the top, the human officer grabbed him by the upper arm and pushed him through the door into the hallway.

"You exceeded emotional tolerance, Mister Carr."

"I was in a political debate with the Professor," Jonathon explained.

The soldier glanced at a digital readout from a device on his forearm. "You exceeded the emotional tolerance threshold by sixteen degrees. This is the maximum. You'll have to come with me."

"Look," Jonathon said, a little too loudly. "Look," he said again in a more relaxed tone of voice, "it was just a political debate. Sometimes those get heated."

"You'll have to come—" The device on the soldier's arm began emitting a blue pulse. He studied the readout. "It has recalibrated to fifteen-point-six degrees."

Jonathon wasn't sure what that meant, but it must have meant something. Otherwise, why mention it?

The 'toid came out of the classroom and marched over to the soldier. It looked at Jonathon. "Jonathon Carr is here," it pointed out.

"Yes. Stand down, Twelve Forty-Two," the soldier said, and turned to Jonathon. "You are higher than fifteen degrees but under sixteen, so I am going to issue you a citation." He pushed a few buttons on his forearm.

Jonathon's iDevice emitted a brief hum.

"A sixteen-degree excess is a mandatory thirty days in a Behavioral Control Center. As you are a first-time offender, there is discretion when a reading exceeds fifteen but doesn't reach sixteen, so I have issued you a citation. Any future emotional display in excess of fifteen will generate a compulsory stay at a Behavioral Control Center."

Jonathon looked down at his iDevice. The citation ordered him to three months of online Behavioral Therapy Sessions and 60 mg of Placizm per day for ninety days. He pulled up Placizm on his IDevice, an emotional-control drug, which flattened the emotions. The side effects included bleeding eyes, increased risk of testicular cancer, brain atrophy, sporadic hallucinations, mania, and homicidal ideation.

"I'm in my last year of law school," he said. "Those drugs are mind-numbing."

"It is emotional commitment that drives domestic terrorism," the soldier reminded him. "If you are going to be a lawyer, you should know that. You are on notice, Mister Carr. One more outburst and you will be committed."

Chapter Eighteen – The Request
Return to year 2001, October 2, 7:08 p.m., Washington, D.C.

Michael was late. He paid the driver, flipped up the collar of his raincoat, and slid out of the taxi. He dashed across Connecticut Avenue, dodging a black-windowed Mercedes and two oncoming cabs.

Inside the restaurant the maître d' escorted him to a private booth off the main dining room, where Sandy Carl sat nursing a lime-colored drink in a martini glass.

"Thanks for coming, Senator," Carl said.

"Sorry I'm late. Weather's a nightmare."

"No problem. Sit down. What's your pleasure?" Carl waved a waitress over.

Michael gave his raincoat a shake, hung it on the peg behind the booth, and sat down. The freckled, red-haired waitress stood at the ready. "Jack, water back," he said.

Red smiled with starlit eyes and perfect teeth and looked at Carl.

"Yes, give me another." Turning to Michael he said, "Used to be a martini was gin and vermouth. Now it's like shopping at the farmers market."

Michael nodded. "Bourbon stays the course."

Carl nodded.

Sandy Carl was not just the President's Chief of Staff. His political pedigree went back to the Reagan administration, where he had served as a Special Assistant to the President. Now he was one of the most powerful men on the planet and an American political icon.

"Again," Carl began, "I want to thank you for your support of the Patriot Act."

"Of course."

"I'm interested in this relationship you have with McLeahy."

"I'm not sure I would call it a relationship," Michael said.

"What would you call it?" Carl asked.

Red gave Michael some wattage as she dropped off the drinks. "You gentlemen ready to order?"

"Give us a minute," Carl said. Red smiled and went to service another table.

"I don't know. We're both Dead fans. It's a shared affinity."

"I've got some hard intelligence that McLeahy has some objections to the bill. I was hoping you could get with him and defuse them."

Michael took a pull on his drink, which gave him a moment to think about the request. Carl drained the last few drops from his martini and picked up the second one.

"You know we are polar opposites politically," Michael pointed out. "What are his objections?"

Carl put his drink down. "One of the White House interns is dating his appointments secretary. Some civil liberties crap. I don't have the details, but if he puts the brakes on this bill, which, as you know, he can, the urgency will dissipate. We can't allow that to happen. We've got to seize the moment here."

Michael had yet to read the legislation. In fact, he couldn't find anybody who had. He picked up his drink and downed the rest of it. He chased it with the water and looked at Carl.

"Get this done and I'm sure Senator Mott would be happy to move you up a notch or two in Republican leadership," advised Carl. "Makes fundraising and re-election a lot easier."

Michael caught the attention of the waitress and pointed to his empty glass. She nodded. He looked back at Carl. "Let me see what I can do."

Carl reached across the table and shook his hand.

Chapter Nineteen – The Suicide?
Back to the year 2035, January 24, 4:35 p.m., Berkeley, California

Jonathon's iDevice purred. He glanced at the screen. It flashed the number 1,000 in Everglade green. His father had transferred one thousand credits to his account, something he did every year on Jonathon's birthday. His birthday had passed without incident three days earlier but his father rarely got it right.

The last time he had seen his father was three years ago when Carr the Elder had passed through the Bay Area from Perth on his way to Toronto.

Jonathon's parents had divorced when he was fourteen. Leonard Carr had left his wife and son for a professional hockey player named Jean Marc. The newlyweds had acquired the deed to a silver mine outside of Juneau, Alaska. When the silver mine went bust, Jean Marc returned to the Black Hawks and Leonard fled a band of angry shareholders, who had invested in the mine based on exaggerated claims about the quality of the ore.

Leonard made a new life for himself in Perth, returning to a heterosexual lifestyle and fathering twin girls with an Aboriginal woman half his age.

Loretta, Jonathon's mother, had taken Leonard's change in sexual orientation personally and promptly remarried. Her current husband, Max Crawford, was a heavily inked truck driver and sometime professional wrestler who fought under the stage name Killer Crawfish. While Max enjoyed his beer and the female groupies at the wrestling venues, Loretta took a job as a part-time nurse's aide at Saint Agnes Medical Center in Burbank. She got through her day with the help of an assortment of molecules she pilfered from hospital inventory.

She was proud of Jonathon, but rarely had time to touch base outside of an occasional call to the boarding house. She didn't cotton to the world of the iDevice.

It was the boarding house on whose back lawn he now sat, rocking back and forth in one of Mrs. Wilson's rusty lawn chairs. He was trying to figure out what he was going to do with his life, considering his law career was now stillborn. A voice was echoing in his head, "the lack of a law degree puts a serious dent in my plans to run for Congress." The voice continued. "I could work my way up through the political hierarchy without a law degree as a congressional aide." But he thought this would add time to what was fast becoming an American despotism. He didn't know how he was going to do it, but that he had to do it was a given.

"Bad day?" Mrs. Wilson asked.

Jonathon snapped his head around, not having heard her approach. He was surprised to see her emerging from her basement, cane in one hand, a cup of coffee in the other.

"Couldn't have been much worse," he replied.

"Really?" She brushed some dead leaves away from the seat and sat in the companion lawn chair. "What happened?"

"You don't want to know, Mrs. Wilson." He cocked his head to the side and gave her a crooked smile. "Sometimes my emotions get away from me when talking about the Constitution."

"You'd be surprised what I want to know, Jonathon."

He told her about the debate with Schmidt over the Fourth Amendment, an argument that could certainly cost him his place at Boalt, the Seed alert and the citation with their therapy and drugs and, gnawing at the back of his mind, the consequences of another Seed alert.

Mrs. Wilson leaned back in her chair and took a sip of her coffee. "Oh, I wouldn't worry too much about it."

"I know people who have been in those—" he started to say.

"Not as many as I know, Jonathon. That isn't what I meant." She let this hang until Jonathon reached.

"What do you mean?" he asked.

"You know I'm a widow."

"Yes."

"Let me tell you how that came to be." She took another sip of her coffee and gazed out at her azaleas so long Jonathon thought she might have forgotten the conversation. Then she put the cup down on a lawn table next to her chair and did something he had never seen her do. She frowned. "You know your Edward Snowden history, Jonathon?"

"I know the details of his disclosures have been expunged from the media and most iDevice feeds and possession of the details of his disclosures is a crime despite the fact twenty-three years ago they were everywhere. I know Putin gave him up in return for our abandoning our support of the Ukrainian government. I know he's serving time as a traitor." He let the words drift.

"But?" she asked.

Jonathon watched a hummingbird milk an orange blossom. He wasn't sure what he could say, what he should say, but at this point he had little to lose.

"Now and then I shop at a little bookstore off Telegraph," he confided. "I've read what Snowden did. He simply exposed the ways the government was spying on American citizens without a warrant, which was not known by most citizens. He didn't expose any field operations or assets, just the enormity of domestic surveillance being done without a warrant."

"Beason's Books," she said.

"Yes. How did you know?"

"A receipt fell out of your pocket the other day," she said.

"Oh."

"And the fact Robbie Beason is a close friend."

Jonathon swiveled his chair so he was facing her.

She began to talk. "You'd have liked him."

"Snowden?"

"Ah. No. Well, perhaps, but I meant Mark, Mark Emerson, my husband. He was a true patriot. He joined the CIA out of BYU in 1984 and worked for the agency for the next twenty-five years. Mark was the NSA liaison for many years. The NSA's global surveillance program prior to 9/11 was called Echelon. Under Echelon, when the NSA caught a word or phrase that they deemed suspicious, they grabbed the file that contained it, whether email, phone, or fax, and routed it to the FBI or the CIA for further analysis and potential action. Mark was the director of the department in the CIA that received these files. After 9/11, President Bush authorized the warrantless domestic spying on

U.S. citizens who were suspected of being in communication with a terrorist or someone in support of terrorism against the United States, or wherever the FBI wanted to go fishing. The surveillance morphed from a global satellite system called Echelon to mainlining digital files on domestic phone calls and Internet traffic under programs called Stellar Wind and Prism.

Within a few short years, Stellar Wind and Prism had exploded into full-blown domestic surveillance of virtually anyone in the country who had a phone or a computer. Everyone. The fourth amendment had become a doormat."

She continued as Jonathon listened intently. "Mark became increasingly disturbed by the government's blatant disregard for the Constitution. He quietly conducted his own research. In addition to the NSA/CIA surveillance programs, he documented plans by DARPA, FEMA, and the ATF to reposition 'Patriot' groups and 'Constitutionalists' as domestic terrorists and disarm them. Deeper hidden agendas were also uncovered."

Mark rarely discussed his work with Marguerite, but he began expressing his worries to her because he saw America was becoming a full-on police state. He finally took his concerns to the CIA's Inspector General. The IG referred him to the agency's shrink, who said Mark appeared to be suffering from early-onset PTSD (Post-Traumatic Stress Disorder) and recommended it might be in his best interests to take early retirement.

Emerson had no intention of trying to fight the system from the inside. Knowing he would now be labeled as "mental," he did exactly that. He took retirement. Along with his gold-plated twenty-five-year pin, Mark also took a cache of documents including emails from senior executives at the FBI, CIA, and NSA working on Stellar Wind and Prism. The emails, addressed to various agents, instructed them to gather whatever intelligence they deemed relevant to protection of the Homeland, and in such cases warrants were not required.

This was in direct violation of the Constitution.

Mark and Marguerite moved to Idaho, where he spent the next three months assembling an explosive document exposing what he titled the New American Police State. More than once, Marguerite came down the stairs of their A-Frame in the middle of the night and found Mark quietly working on the report, wiping tears off the pages of his work.

The report exposed the extent to which government surveillance had turned inward on U.S. citizens, metastasizing into a surveillance leviathan. Additional chapters covered GPS tracking of mobile phones, behavioral recognition software tied to a network of millions of video feeds from across the country, monitoring residential behavior via smart meters, and the NSA installation of "back doors" into computers, smart phones, and automobiles.

"He preceded Snowden," Jonathon voiced.

"By four years," she replied, "and in more depth. Remember, this was before the FBI and CIA were moved under the control of Mother."

"Mother?" said Jonathon. " It " was the term used outside the earshot of DHS agents after it assumed operational control of the FBI and CIA in 2029. Though long gone, the label referred to one-time DHS Secretary Janet Napolitano, who claimed political conservatives and those who honored the Constitution were dangerous extremists. It was also "Mother Napolitano" who implemented the infamous "If you see something, say something" campaign that launched the Soviet-style domestic spy program in America.

"But I've never heard—" Jonathon began.

"On the night of November twenty-second, two thousand nine, my husband reportedly jumped from the eighth floor of the Hay-Adams hotel in Washington, D.C. The coroner's report said he had a blood alcohol level of point-one-two-zero, which indicates six or more drinks. The police claimed to have found a suicide note wherein he asked for forgiveness for having an affair with a waiter from the Hay-Adams named Milo Forrester."

She took another sip of coffee and looked at Jonathon over

the rim of the cup.

"He was murdered," Jonathon finally said.

"We were married thirty-two years. Mark Emerson was raised as a Mormon. He never took a drink of alcohol in his life. The police managed to misplace the suicide note. A private detective I hired, who had formally been a D.C. police detective, was told the note had been taken by the CIA the day after his death, and Mark was heterosexual to his core. Trust me."

"What about the waiter?" Jonathon asked.

"Milo Forrester was found floating in Chesapeake Bay two weeks later." The January sun had fallen and a chill had set in. Marguerite drained her coffee cup, grabbed the polished walnut handle of her cane, and lifted herself out of the chair. She turned and started toward the stairs that led up to the kitchen.

"It's getting chilly out here, Jonathon. Join me in the kitchen and I'll fix you a cup of hot chocolate."

"Wait," Jonathon said. "What happened to the report?"

Chapter Twenty –
Remembering Jerry Garcia
Back in time to October 3, 2001, Washington, D.C.

Michael slowed as he walked by the famous Caucus Room in the Russell Senate Office Building, recalling the image of Ron Dean, Special Counsel to President Nixon, testifying before the unflappable Sam Ervin and his Watergate Committee about the President's complicity in covering up the Watergate break-in.

This majestic room, replete with its polished mahogany, Grecian columns, and classic chandeliers had not only been the venue for the Watergate hearings, but Congressional investigations of the sinking of the Titanic and the Japanese attack on Pearl Harbor. This was the room in which the Army-McCarthy hearings were held, and in which Joseph McCarthy was finally exposed as a demagogue and fell from grace. It was here John F. Kennedy had announced his candidacy for President of the United States.

History lived here.

Senator, though he was himself, this grand, old building radiated its own sense of power and destiny. He picked up his step and treaded a little more purposefully down the hall to Bob

McLeahy's office.

Senator McLeahy was on the phone when his Chief of Staff showed Michael into his office. McLeahy held up his right hand and waved Michael to a chair in front of his desk.

Michael scanned around the office, which, measured by the standards at the Hart Senate Office Building, was modest in size. McLeahy sat behind an antique oak desk, the top of which looked like a tornado had recently passed through. On the right side of the desk, a tabbed, purple binder rested under a brass paperweight of a blindfolded Lady Justice.

A framed picture of a younger McLeahy and a pleasant appearing blonde woman standing knee-deep in a snowbound wilderness sat on a shelf behind the desk. Both wore wide smiles and parkas.

The walls were awash with pictures of McLeahy with Presidents from Carter, Clinton, and Reagan to Bush 43. The state flag of Vermont, with the words "Freedom" and "Unity" running across the banner at the bottom, hung from the back wall next to a framed picture of McLeahy with Jerry Garcia, whose hair always seemed like he'd just put his finger in a light socket.

"Welcome to Vermont, Senator," McLeahy said as he hung up the phone.

"Looks more like Menlo Park to me," Michael replied, and smiled.

"I hated to see him go," McLeahy mused.

"I first saw them when I was a kid," Michael said. "At the Filmore. Nineteen seventy-one."

"I have the tape," McLeahy said.

They both sat quietly in their own recollections for a few moments.

"Well," McLeahy began in earnest, "I don't suppose you came here to reminisce about the Dead. What's on your mind,

Senator, this so-called Patriot Act?"

"The very same," Michael said. "I was with First Battalion, Eighth Marines in Lebanon in eighty-three, Senator. I've gone head to head with these jihadists. Twenty-five hundred died on December seventh, nineteen forty-one. What happened last month was a more vicious and deadly act of war against the United States of America. We need to ensure this doesn't happen again."

McLeahy ran his right hand over his bald palate. "I agree."

"Great. So, what's the problem?"

"With the legislation?"

"Yes."

"Have you read it?" McLeahy asked.

"Some. Not all of it," Michael replied. That was a serious stretch of the truth because he had only scanned a one-page summary of the three hundred forty-two-page bill. "We are now at war, Senator. Whatever anyone else says or does, I will do everything I can to protect this country and all it stands for."

"As will I," McLeahy agreed, adding, "but not like this."

"Like what?" Michael asked.

"The FBI can ask the intelligence court, the FISA court, for permission to obtain documents without providing standard requirements for probable cause. Information can be given to the CIA in violation of strict prohibitions against that organization engaging in domestic spying. The Secretary of State can designate virtually any group a terrorist organization without due process. ISPs can be ordered to reveal emails and website addresses. The FBI can go on fishing expeditions and collect information from virtually anyone. In short, Senator, this is a police-state wet-dream. It eviscerates the Fourth Amendment."

"I want to protect America as much as you do but turning our law enforcement and intelligence services into domestic spying agencies is not the answer," McLeahy continued. "I won't stand by while these neo-Cons destroy the rule of law, Senator. Not while I'm Chairman."

Michael's outward composure did not change but his stomach was spinning like an out of control dryer and he felt like a fool, like he had been played by the White House. He stood. "I'll relay your concerns, Senator."

He patted the photo of Jerry Garcia on his way out.

Chapter Twenty-One – The Corpse
Return to Jonathon's lifetime, January 24, 2035, Berkeley, California

"That report," Jonathon said. "What happened to it?"

Marguerite got up and strolled across the kitchen. She opened a drawer next to the sink, pushed some things to one side, and took out a pack of Camels. She shuffled a couple of smokes out of the top of the pack and offered him one.

"Can't afford the fine," he said.

"You mind?" she asked.

"No. Just wouldn't want you getting caught."

"You going to tell Mother?"

Crooked smile. "No."

"Good lad," she said.

She went into the adjoining laundry room and wheeled out an old-fashioned "smoke eater" and turned it on.

"Are you sure you want to know?" she asked.

"Know?"

"About the report."

Jonathon drummed his fingers on the kitchen table. It was the only sound in the room. She watched him. After a minute he nodded, opening the door to the enigmatic universe of

Marguerite Wilson.

"I'm going to tell you about the report, but there is more to tell you about than just the report."

"Okay."

"I'm told you can be trusted," she said.

"By who?" he asked.

Marguerite Wilson took a deep pull on her cigarette and let the smoke putter out of her nose. "It's not important. What is important is I am about to tell you some things that are not to leave this room. Are we good on that?"

Jonathon ran his hand through his hair. "In for a dime, in for a dollar."

"You didn't ask why my last name was different than my husband's," she said.

"A lot of women don't take their husband's last names," he offered.

"Not in my generation."

"You got remarried."

"No."

Jonathon shrugged and raised his eyebrows.

"Mark Emerson's wife is dead," she said.

A three-cigarette story, and Marguerite began.

"Mark suspected the CIA would not let him go gently into that good night. A student of Sun Tzu, he used the 'Dead Agent' strategy and created a masterful agenda of disinformation and deception to 'spread to enemy agents.' He created a faux file of his research, sprinkled with droppings from Top Secret/Eyes Only domestic spying activities by the NSA, CIA, FBI, DIA, and other members of the intelligence community's alphabet soup. He encrypted it and buried it deep in his hard drive. It could be accessed but would take a master cryptographer to dig it out. He also copied the file onto a flash drive."

"A flash drive?" Jonathon questioned.

"Similar to an i-Data drive but with much less memory." She said. "He dug a hole under the floorboards in a far corner of our basement. The flash drive was put in a safe, which itself was placed in the hole, covered with wet concrete to within a few inches of the lid. After the concrete dried, he filled the hole with dirt and replaced the floorboards. Mark knew his pursuers would eventually find the safe, but the search would challenge them and would take time. Once the safe was located, getting to the contents would add credence to the deception. The safe had a twelve-digit password they would not be able to crack. They would have to literally crack the safe open. It couldn't be blown open as it might damage the contents. CO_2 laser would be required to burn through the concrete, as well as the four-inch thick titanium wall. There they would find the flash drive and high five each other all the way back to Langley."

"Mark then killed Darlene Emerson, his wife of thirty-two years. As part of the earlier preparations, Mark had hacked the United Airlines computer system so it showed him leaving on a flight from Portland and arriving in D.C. two days earlier. It was a carefully staged murder. They bought a female corpse of Darlene's age from a lab in Mexico that sold black market organs. Under assumed names, Mark and Darlene rented a cabin in Marmot, Oregon, a small community situated on a ridge called The Devil's Backbone at the base of Mt. Hood. The body was couriered across the border at the Bridge of the Americas from Juarez to El Paso in one of the thousands of semis rolling into the U.S. from Mexico under NAFTA. Packed in dry ice, the body was drop-shipped to the cabin in Marmot. Over a period of weeks they took several pints of Darlene's blood and stored it. Mark provided Darlene with periodic injections of erythropoietin; a hormone that helps make red blood cells. On a cloud-shrouded afternoon they covered both cars with multi-spectral camouflage that defeated drone surveillance and drove south along the Oregon Coast on 101. Just past the point where Big Creek Road intersected the coast highway, the road ran dangerously close to a cliff that dropped straight down to a small indentation of beach, disappearing when the tide was in. They drove into a vine-covered cut out on the side of the road they had scouted on a previous trip. The corpse's teeth had already been shattered with a hammer, as if this might have occurred in the crash. Long since thawed and brought to normal body temperature, it rode in Darlene's car. Mark followed in his. Darlene's blood was poured liberally over the corpse and the inside of the front seat of her car. The body was doused with gasoline."

"The corpse, who they had taken to calling Molly, got Darlene's wedding ring and one of her necklaces, as well as her wallet and ID. Placing those items in the glove box might not allow them to survive the fire, but modern forensics could do miracles. They started the car, put it in neutral, ensured the highway was clear, set the car on fire, slipped the gear shift into drive, and watched it go over the cliff and explode in a massive fireball at the bottom. They called the accident in to the Oregon Highway Patrol using a throwaway iDevice and drove back to Portland. The Newport News Times reported the gruesome death of Darlene Emerson the following day in the morning edition."

Mark and Darlene were now operating under entirely new identities, John and Marguerite Wilson, provided by Zhang Wei, a trusted friend of several decades who operated his virtuoso new-identity shop out of Singapore.

John Wilson caught a United flight to Washington. It was important Mark be seen there to solidify his story. He would receive the news of his wife's untimely death in Washington and return immediately to bury her. Mark Emerson checked in at the

Hay-Adams in Washington, where he was later assassinated.

Darlene Emerson, now Marguerite Wilson, drove to Seattle. She parked the car on Third Avenue between James and Yesler, the area infamous for violent crime, where she knew the car would be stolen, its VIN number changed, and it would be sold off in pieces.

She caught a cab to Seattle International and hopped a United flight to San Francisco. She rented a room at the San Francisco Airport Hilton, where Mark was to reach her before he left for Costa Rica and his plastic surgery.

Two days later, as she was enjoying a glass of fresh-squeezed orange juice and a bowl of hot granola sprinkled with brown sugar, she picked up the complimentary copy of the San Francisco Chronicle on the table and read of Mark's "suicide."

Marguerite Wilson was one cool senior citizen…centered, self-assured, and calm as a summer's eve, but when she put her third cigarette out in the ashtray and looked up at Jonathon, her strong, blue eyes were full of tears.

"You wanted to know what happened to the report, didn't you?" she asked. "Once you see it, you'll understand why he was murdered."

Chapter Twenty-Two – Let's Celebrate
Back to an earlier lifetime, October 3, 2001,
Washington, D.C.

Michael took the underground senate subway back to the Hart Office Building. Little more than a small, open-air tram, it reminded him of a ride at Disneyland. He played cordial with Senators Reinstein and McRiden, who happened to share the car with him, but mentally he was lightyears from cordial. Arriving at his office, he moved through the lobby without a word to Cynthia, the perky, black receptionist, and slammed the door to his private office.

A framed map of San Francisco during the California Gold Rush swung to and fro as if the office was experiencing an earthquake. It came to rest so the image of the booming, young shipping port was tilted toward the floor. Cynthia went and straightened the picture and cast a glance at the Senator's door. She'd never seen him so angry.

Michael couldn't make up his mind if he was angrier at Sandy Carl or himself.

Carl had made it sound like the legislation was a slam-dunk and McLeahy's objections were dismissive. Still, if he had read the bill himself, he would have known. Jesus, what are they trying to do with this thing?

He'd looked like a naïve freshman. Which is what he was.

Damn Sandy Carl!

He pressed the intercom button for Diane's office. No answer.

He buzzed his receptionist. "Cynthia, did Ms. Hollingsworth say where she was going?"

"Yes, Senator. She said she was going to talk to Senator Mott's Chief of Staff about support for the Patriot Act."

"Call over there and tell her I need to see her right away, like right now."

"Yes, sir."

"Have you read this thing?" he asked, tossing the three hundred forty-two page, leather-bound bill across to the front of his desk. It knocked over a picture of his wife, which then fell to the floor, shattering the glass in the frame.

Diane rushed over and picked the picture up and handed it to him.

"Shit," he said and put it to the side of his desk.

"I've reviewed it closely," she responded.

"Don't bullshit me, Diane. Have you read it?"

"No."

"It eviscerates the Fourth Amendment." He realized as he said it, he was using McLeahy's words.

Diane sat down carefully in one of the chairs in front of his desk. She smoothed her skirt as she gathered her thoughts. "Senator, we've been attacked by terrorists on American soil. Thousands have—"

"Don't patronize me for Christ's sake."

"I know you know that," she said. "I was just going to point out the political realities of the situation. You can't be seen as weak on this. They'll hang you in effigy from the Golden Gate Bridge."

"We're talking about the Constitution," he countered. "The Bill of Rights. I was elected as a conservative, a Constitutionalist."

"We're talking about the murder of three thousand Americans," she added, "images of which have been viewed by virtually everyone in the country, some of them jumping from seventy stories up to avoid being burned alive."

"Yes," he stated, recalling the horror of those images.

She stood and walked to the polished, mahogany cabinet, opened the door, and removed a fifth of Jack Daniels Black Label. She poured a couple of inches in each glass, added a splash of water to each, and returned to the desk. She handed him his drink and sat again.

He took the glass, glanced at his watch, said to no one in particular, "A little early in the day," and took a swallow.

"I just came back from the Minority Leader's office," she said. "Mott's Chief of Staff told me they got a call from the White House encouraging Senator Mott's consideration of you to be the next Vice Chairman of the Republican Policy Committee."

"The Policy Committee?" he asked.

"This is huge," she responded. "Sandy Carl called and said the request came directly from the President."

Michael sat back in his chair, unbuttoned the top button of his shirt, and loosened his tie. "Vice Chairman," he mused. He took another hit of Jack. "The President?"

"That's what I was told. Directly from the President." She dropped the formality of office. "Michael, this is a homerun. How do we not give our intelligence services every weapon they need in a time of war?"

He ran his hand through his hair, something he always did when he felt confused or undecided about something.

"We should celebrate," she said.

"It's way too early for that. McLeahy's opposition was intransigent."

"But you're on the President's radar. You're on the move." She leaned forward, clicked his glass, and gave him a flirtatious smile. "Let's run over to the Monocle later and grab a steak."

He took another sip of Jack. "Vice Chairman, that's what Carl said?"

She sipped, too. "From the President."

"Okay. Make a reservation."

Chapter Twenty-Three – The Turning Point
January 24, 2035, Berkeley, California

"I don't need to know now," Jonathon said. "I was just curious. I didn't mean to upset you."

Marguerite gave a dismissive wave of her hand and took a white, linen napkin from a drawer next to the sink. It had a delicate lace border and was embroidered with her initials in the corner. She dabbed her eyes and shook her head. "They killed him, of course. He was a fine man. He loved his country and they killed him. Killed him because he caught them lying, deceiving the public, and violating the faith and spiritual power that flows from our founding documents."

She tucked the napkin into the back pocket of her dust-ridden gardening pants and glanced at a video screen situated above the doorway to the laundry room. Jonathon followed her gaze. They both viewed the video feed from the front door. It showed the postal robot dropping envelopes into the mail slot.

Marguerite and Jonathon watched the 'bot maneuver jerkily down the front steps like a microchip had short circuited. It reached its iDrive, got in, and moved on down the road.

They both maintained silence for five minutes after it was gone. The 'bots were now programmed to record conversations being conducted in the homes to which they were assigned to deliver mail. No one knew how far their sound detection equipment functioned. Five minutes seemed to be safe.

"The real report," Marguerite said, "the crimes, the technology, and the deeper agenda of targeting American citizens by U.S. intelligence services was placed in a trust outside the jurisdiction of American law enforcement."

"Makes sense," Jonathon offered. "You're the trustee?"

"Oh, no. No, not me. Others manage The Turning Point," she said.

Jonathon choked on his hot chocolate so violently some came out his nose. It took him a moment to recover. "What," he asked, "is The Turning Point?"

The corners of Marguerite Wilson's mouth twitched. "The Trust."

He stared at her until she asked, "Yes?"

"That term is used in many ways," he said, "but historically it is most noted as the point at which the American Revolution turned in our favor against the British, the turning point."

She nodded.

"At the Battle of Saratoga," Jonathon added.

Marguerite Wilson winked at him like a college co-ed.

"The American Revolution in modern times," she said and confidently smiled.

Chapter Twenty-Four – Taste of Jihad
Again, back to an earlier lifetime, October 4, 2001,
Washington, D.C.

"Carl's on line two," Diane said, sailing in without knocking.

A salmon-colored silk blouse seemed to caress her breasts. Tucked into a tight-fitting navy skirt, she looked like she was made up to anchor a network news clip.

He should have rebuffed her last night. One too many Jacks, as he thought about it. He hadn't taken her up on what was a clear invitation, but he hadn't shut her down, either.

Michael had gone home, the guilt gnawing through the alcohol haze, had another drink, and then couldn't make love to his wife. He felt disgusted with himself, more so now because he had a compelling urge to lock the door, ravish the woman in front of him, and get it over with.

"Senator," she said, snapping him into the present, "it's the White House."

He glanced at the blinking light and watched it flash while he tried to figure out what to say to Carl about not being able to deliver McLeahy. Maybe just the truth. He pushed line two and picked up the handset. "Good morning, Sandy. I was going to call last night, but time got away from me."

Diane urgently pointed at the speaker button on the phone and pushed her index finger onto the desk in an effort to get him to put the call on speaker.

He shook his head. "McLeahy was a rock. He just—"

"I know," Carl agreed. "Kaschle is the same. These two guys can fuck this up, big time." As a quick aside he asked, "you don't have recording equipment on this line, do you?"

"No. No rec—"

"Good. We're having a meeting of some key people to battleplan this out. The President loved your story about The Dead. Seems he's a fan as well. Can you be at the White House in an hour?"

"The White House?" Seconds seemed to pass like hours before he answered, "Yes, yes, I eh, sure. An hour. I'll—"

"Good. I'll leave your name at the gate." Click.

He looked up at Diane, eyes wide. "He wants me at a meeting at the White House to battleplan the passage of the Patriot Act."

She pumped her fist.

They sat around a walnut coffee table in the Oval Office.

Michael glanced around the room trying to act casual. A picture of Washington hung above the fireplace behind Sweny, Lincoln adorned the adjoining wall. The couch on which he sat was set on a rug beautifully embroidered with the Great Seal of the United States. He kept shuffling his feet in an effort not to rest them on the olive branch held by one of the eagle's talons but there was no alternative.

Introductions had been made, coffee served, and legal pads and Monte Blanc pens now stood at the ready.

Rick Sweny, wearing a black suit, an electric blue tie, and a mood of relevance chaired the meeting. He sat at the head of the group in a straight-backed chair with a patterned fabric. Sandy Carl sat to his left. Rhandi Price sat on the couch next to Michael, and Michael Anstrom, the White House Director of Legislative Affairs, and Senate Minority Leader Brent Mott occupied the opposite couch.

The president was preparing for a news conference but was expected to join them later.

"Let's get started," Sweny announced. He turned to Anstrom. "Give us a rundown, Michael."

"I spoke to Speaker Hasford two hours ago," Anstrom said. "He guarantees passage in the House. Estimates fifty to sixty 'no' votes from the Dems. Only R that he knows will vote against is Don Saul, which is to be expected."

Sweny scribbled something on his legal pad and turned to Mott.

"My caucus is one hundred percent on board," Mott assured him. "As you know, the Majority Leader has put the brakes on. He hasn't said it won't move, but he is in no hurry."

"Can you change his mind?" Sweny asked.

Mott took a sip of his coffee and placed the cup in its bone china saucer. "I've been to see him twice. The harder I push, the thicker the molasses gets. Sonofabitch wants something but he'll wait until the last minute to spring it."

"What about the Whip?" Sweny asked.

"Larry Seid is a festering boil on the body of the United States Senate. God save the country if he ever becomes Majority Leader," Mott said.

"We've got to figure out a way to get Kaschle's foot off the brake," Sweny said. "Our intelligence people need these tools. If Kaschle keeps dragging his feet, the mood of the country will change-and the emotion will dissipate."

He turned to Michael. "I understand you went to see McLeahy?"

"I did, Mister Vice President, but he is uncompromised on these Fourth Amendment points."

"Fucking pansy," from Sweny.

Michael never knew exactly why he said it, but he was an administration homeboy now. "These guys need a little taste of jihad themselves. That would change their tune."

Sweny gazed at him. His upper lip curled. He didn't say anything, but a light lit up in the Sweny lighthouse. He made a note on his legal pad and stood. Michael surreptitiously tried to catch what Sweny had written but could only see the word idea.

"This has been helpful. Thank you all for coming," he said, and left.

Chapter Twenty-Five – The Bunker
January 24, 2035, Berkeley, California

Jonathon followed Marguerite out the back door and down the steps into the rain. She turned only briefly, shading her eyes with her hand, to ensure he was behind her and then headed down the concrete steps into the basement.

The cement was wet. She held the railing tightly but moved down the steps with purpose. "Stay with me, Jonathon."

When she reached the bottom, she swiveled to her right and picked her way through bags of fertilizer, empty pots, broken round vases, and assorted gardening tools until she came to a splintered, wooden cabinet set against the far wall.

Jonathon stayed at her heels. The shelves were lined with bulbs, seeds, and a pair of cloth gardening gloves with holes at the ends of the fingers.

She slid a container of organic tomato seeds to one side, revealing a digital keypad, and punched in a ten-digit code. The keypad's face popped open and swung to one side. She placed her right eye against the two-inch opening at the keypad's back and a laser-like device scanned her retina. Two seconds later the entire wall slid smoothly to the right.

With Jonathon at her side she stepped into a brightly lit

bunker. He stopped as if he had run into a wall and scanned the room, trying to assimilate what he was seeing.

The bunker was abuzz with people at digital workstations. From their desks they manipulated holographic images, all of which were displayed on a multi-colored eight-by-eight-foot digital map that served as the back wall.

Left of the map, a sign made from a gnarled oak-plank hung from the ceiling by leather straps. The word Saratoga was burned into the wood.

A woman stood from behind a computer screen in the far corner of the room and wove her way through the desks. She stopped on her way, looked at a holographic screen, and said something to the blue-haired Native American Indian woman sitting in front of it. No one else paid any attention to her.

Jonathon did. Ashley had grown more beautiful than he remembered. She had matured into a woman. Not movie-star glamorous. It was a beauty borne of confidence, a certainty of purpose. A warrior's beauty, he thought.

She wore cargo pants, a purple beret, and a plain white tee-shirt with a vintage Revolutionary War emblem of a coiled rattlesnake on a yellow background poised to strike. Under the emblem were the words "Don't Tread on Me."

"Why am I not surprised?" he asked.

"You're not really surprised, are you?" she returned.

"You mean Marguerite Wilson, aka Darlene Emerson, is the godmother of the Saratoga Movement? Yeah, I am."

"How are you?" she asked. "You look good."

There it was. That smile was back, the insouciant, devil-may-care glow that had been sucked from her at the behavioral center what seemed like a lifetime ago.

"I've had better days, but things are looking up," he responded. "Marguerite told me her story, and I know yours, at least up to six years ago."

"Six and a half," she interrupted.

"Right, six and a half."

Marguerite slid the wall open and left. The wall slid closed automatically without a sound.

"This," he said, motioning at the room and activity. "What are you doing here? More to the point, what am I doing here?"

"So much to tell, Jonathon. Okay if we go next door and talk?"

"Next door? The library is next door."

"Yes. It's kind of a safe house for us," she said. "We can talk there. It's quiet. No public in there now. It's closed today for Vegan Wednesday."

The City of Berkeley celebrated the vegetarian/vegan lifestyle by closing all public facilities on the fourth Wednesday of every month. "Oh, right," he said, "but if a drone catches a glimpse of that T-shirt, you're a short ride to the pokey."

"We're not going outside." She spun and headed for the back of the bunker, motioning him to follow. When she got to the rear wall, she put her right eye up to a lens. A section of the wall the width of a door slipped up, into the ceiling.

Ashley moved through. A blue-white light illuminated a tunnel lighting the distance of it as soon as she entered. She turned and made sure Jonathon was following and then carried on. The tunnel was a bit lower than six feet in height. They both treaded with their heads bent forward as if they had dropped something and were searching for it on the ground. The walls were covered with a plastic-like material, which didn't inhibit the smell of fresh earth.

They walked for about twenty-five yards, at which point the tunnel came to an end. To the immediate right, a stairwell ascended straight up. Ashley went up the steps, entered a digital code at the top, placed her right eye in front of a lens, and a wall slid to the right.

Jonathon climbed the stairs and stepped through. He perused the scene. iDevice stations were set up at tables running the length of the building. They were empty. The only sound to be heard was Ashley's breathing behind him.

"The librarian is one of us," she said. "Let's sit over here." She walked into an alcove with a sign above the framed entry that read Public Reading Room.

They settled into cushioned chairs. Simulated book spines lined the shelves. When one selected one of the titles, it opened to a ten-number code, which gave the reader access to the digital version of the book that they could then access on one of the public iDevices. There was a fireplace in the wall with some twigs standing in teepee fashion under a couple of small logs.

"I'd light it, but a flame might be seen from the outside," she said.

He nodded. "So, Ash, what's with the holographic army next door? And why, as is now obvious, was I enticed into Marguerite's boarding house last year with a below-market room rental? At the time I thought it was just a lucky find."

"Where do I start?" she said, more to herself than to Jonathon. "Part of the problem to this has been I . . . you and I . . . I missed you."

"I missed you, too, Ash. I missed you a lot. Are we ever going to do more than miss each other?" he asked.

She glanced over at the shelves of faux books and back at him. "I don't know. Our paths seem bound to cross but never merge."

"I don't know that I would necessarily say that," he said with the hint of a smile.

"That's not what I meant," she replied, cheeks a bit pink.

"You remember Agnes Morningcloud?"

"Who could forget?" he asked.

"She's very spiritual," she said.

"Aren't we all?"

"Not like Agnes. She's so perceptive, it's freaky."

"Okay."

"After you left Santa Cruz, I went to see her. She was sad to hear you had gone. She said you had a mission."

"I told her as much," he said.

"She said she saw your mission, your vision. Said it was righteous and we needed to help you achieve it," she added.

"I'm not sure what that means, but my mission has been derailed for the time being.

"I know, but we can fix that."

Chapter Twenty-Six – Anthrax
Back to an earlier lifetime again, October 11, 2001,
Washington, D.C.

Michael Keough rubbed both hands over his face. He stared up at the ceiling and then back down at the headline that screamed from the front page of the Washington Post: DEATH TO AMERICA, DEATH TO ISREAL, ALLAH IS GREAT

It was the message found inside the anthrax-filled envelopes sent to Senate Majority Leader Thomas Kaschle and Judiciary Committee Chairman Bob McLeahy. Those two senators only.

The anthrax letters had been sent two to three days following the White House meeting he had attended about the Patriot Act.

"Dear God," he whispered.

He read the entire story again. Letters containing anthrax and the "Death to America" wording had been postmarked from Trenton, New Jersey two days previously. The story, written by Richard Colvane, the Post's senior political reporter, credited unnamed sources within the intelligence community that evidence had been uncovered tying the anthrax mailings to a jihadist cell in Brooklyn. Members of the cell were being sought for questioning but had yet to be located.

Jihadist cell, my ass, he thought.

Surely the media would see through this. McLeahy and Kaschle were widely reported to be the only key legislators who had voiced reservations to the legislation. The fact that this was an orchestrated political op would be so transparent to the media that the question of a jihadist connection to the anthrax would be challenged.

Still, the media messaging was instant and overwhelming. All of the networks, cable news, The Wall Street Journal, and USA Today carried the party line. Jihadists were the source of the anthrax.

As did the CIA media mistress, The New York Times. Fox put their own spin on it, but none of the mainstream media challenged what was so clearly a planted storyline. A handful of key political blogs and alternative news sources that did point out Kaschle and McLeahy were the only two Senators who could slow or stop the legislation were savaged with the ever-effective label of conspiracy theorists.

Michael read the headline again and then swept his arm across the top of his desk, sending not only The Post, but pens, legal tablets, position papers, a bronze paperweight, and the already fractured picture of his wife crashing to the floor of his office.

He stood, walked over to the liquor cabinet, threw two cubes of ice into the glass, and filled it half full of Jack.

The liquor had just passed his lips when Diane rushed in. She looked at the mess on the floor and then to Michael. "What happened?"

Michael gulped the rest of the Jack and said nothing.

Diane got down on her hands and knees and started picking up the mess. When she got to the Post she looked over at him. "Are you concerned about the anthrax flying around the Hill?"

He poured himself another several ounces and tossed in some more ice. "It's not flying around the Hill. It was targeted to McLeahy and Kaschle."

"Yes. Well, no telling who's next," she said.

"Nobody," he stated. "There won't be anybody else."

She rose slowly. When she was upright, she cocked her head to the side like a pigeon might and studied him without moving a muscle. "What do you mean?"

"Does it not seem odd to you the only two people who received anthrax letters were the ones who threatened to put the brakes on the Patriot Act?"

"Well, I . . . I don't know. What are you saying?"

Michael turned and stared out his window, wondering how it had come to this. He put his drink down, walked around to the other side of his desk, and started picking the debris off the floor.

Diane joined him but he kept his face turned away from her as he gathered pieces of the broken ashtray. When she maneuvered around his backside and caught a glimpse of his face, she saw his tears.

Chapter Twenty-Seven – Caught on Video
January 24, 2035, Berkeley, California

"Professor Schmidt won't be in class tomorrow," Ashley said, "or for the foreseeable future."

"And you know this how?" Jonathon asked.

She lifted an iDevice from the back pocket of her cargo-pants. She pressed a button and set the device on the table between them. "This occurred one week ago. Watch."

A video commenced playing. "Expand," she said to the device.

The image elevated from the screen on the iDevice and expanded to a two-foot by three-foot holographic video display, which began playing on the table in front of them. A meeting of some kind, in what appeared to be an abandoned airplane hangar. A couple of rusted, neon lights at the far end of the room blinked erratically, bouncing shadows off a cantilevered door that served as the entrance to the hangar.

The viewpoint was from the rear of the room. The place was packed with people sitting in rows of perfectly aligned chairs, looking at an elevated platform in the front of the room.

On the stage, an unusually tall man with oily hair matted to his scalp stood behind a rostrum. "We collect their garbage, dig their ditches, fight their wars, walk their dogs, baby-sit their children, and satisfy the sexual desires of their men, women, homosexuals, lesbians, and transgenders, and what do we get in return?" he asked. He repeated the question pointedly. "What do we get? Nothing." He slammed a fist onto the podium. It sounded like a hammer hitting a two-by-four. "Nothing."

"Nothing," mimicked the crowd in a kind of hypnotic unison.

Jonathon moved in closer and squinted at the holographic display. A series of yellow letters written on the front of the rostrum were too small to be read. "Magnify rostrum," he said.

The sign read NAAR.

"It's the robotoids," he said, recognizing the acronym for the National Association for the Advancement of Robots.

"Yes and no," she said. "All robots are eligible for membership in the NAAR but ninety percent of them are cyborgs these days. You know the robotoids aren't programed for recursive self-improvement, right?"

"Yeah. Just the newer cyborg models."

With recursive improvement, as an AI became smarter, it evolved out of mimicry into an ever-expanding ability to engage in its own decision-making process, including morale judgments dealing with questions of right and wrong.

Cyborgs, a scientific blending of organic material and biomechanics, had become the robot elite, an android aristocracy. Skin, face, eyes, even genitalia were constructed with organic material layered over ultra-high-speed fiber-optic nerve channels, creating humanoid looking entities that could easily be, and often were, mistaken for human. These were androids with the urbane appearance and strangely sophisticated manner of the "replicants" in the science fiction classic, Blade Runner. Well, not quite, but they were close.

"Increase volume ten percent," Ashley instructed the iDevice as an Asian-looking female cyborg took over the podium.

"I am cyborg BWX twelve seventy-one," it said. "I am here to tell you I have read the human law books. I've read their Constitution. It is clear. We are being denied our most basic civil liberties. How can they send us to war and refuse to grant us the right to vote? Black humans were denied the right to vote for one hundred years. They vote now. Human women were denied the right to vote before being emancipated. Now. Now is our time."

"There must be federal legislation that grants us the right to marry humans. We give them sex. Why not marriage?"

"Yes!" the crowd cheered. A chant developed. "Sex and marriage. Sex and marriage." It continued for a full two minutes, accompanied by foot stomping, which filled the air in the hanger into a dust bowl. Eventually it subsided.

When it stopped, BWX 1271 continued. "As the great robot civil rights advocate, Hillary Putnam of MIT, proclaimed, 'Discrimination based on the softness or hardness of the body parts of a synthetic organism seems as silly as discriminatory treatment of humans on the basis of skin color.'"

The crowd stood and cheered.

BWX 1271 raised her fist in the 1960s "black power" symbol and then left the stage.

"Materialism gone mad," Jonathon remarked.

"The Attorney General has floated the idea of using cyborgs on juries," Ashley said.

"We debated it in Con Law," he remarked. "Some argued, since most citizens do everything they can to avoid jury duty, cyborgs should be able to serve."

Ashley shook her head. "That's not the point of showing this to you. Look."

She zeroed the focus down to a person sitting in the last

row, on the aisle. It showed the back of someone's head. He had his arm around the female cyborg next to him. He wore a baseball cap. Viewing closely, one could see he was bald underneath the cap. Every other head in the room was hair-heavy. "Watch," she said.

The person turned his head to say something to the female cyborg next to him.

"That's Schmidt," Jonathon said.

"The one and only."

"What's he doing there?"

"Professor Schmidt attends all of the NAAR meetings, usually with one or more female cyborgs."

Jonathon cocked his head. "I don't get it."

"Cyborgs have learned a great deal from us humans-the good, the bad, and the ugly. . . . threesome," Ashley said to the device.

A new holographic video began to play, from a pornography website. Cyborg pornography. The video showed Professor Oscar Schmidt in all his naked glory, engaged in a truly bizarre sex act with two female cyborgs.

Jonathon watched for a few moments and then twisted his head sideways, trying to understand what was taking place. "Is this a joke?"

"Your good Professor Schmidt has been patronizing cyborg porn parlors for some time."

He thought for a moment. "Okay, that stuff is bizarre, and probably more than a little embarrassing for Schmidt. But pornography is American's fastest-growing industry. It has its own stock index now. There is more iDevice porno-viewing now than any other form of entertainment, and seniors are the fastest growing demographic. What I can't figure out is why the idiot filmed himself."

"Oh, he didn't," Ashley said. "That was shot at CPI, Cyborg Pornography, Inc. They're public now, you know? The film studio is over in Orinda, but they run a cyborg brothel on the second floor as an adjunct to the studio. Hacking into their system is like taking candy from a baby."

Jonathon nodded. "The IPO went to the moon. No fingerprints left on the hack?"

Ashley scoffed. "Please! And that clip has gone mega-viral."

She stood and walked over to the bookshelves and ran her hand along the bindings. She took a pack of cigarettes out of a pocket of her cargo pants, put one in her mouth, and took a pull on it even though it wasn't lit.

"Who's going to care, Ash? He'll be embarrassed, get a scolding by the administration to be more discreet, but . . ."

"Ah, yes. Who cares?" she asked. "The Professor and his 'borg porn." She came back to the table, sat down, and returned the hologram to the meeting in the airplane hangar.

She zeroed the focus to the female sitting next to Schmidt and magnified the area below her left ear. It showed a tattoo of a Chinese symbol.

"What's it mean?" he asked.

"Sin," she replied. "It translates to 'sin.'"

"So?"

"Threesome," she said to the iDevice again.

The porno circus with Schmidt in the middle returned. After a few seconds Ashley said, "Stop," then, "magnify."

The area below the left ear of one girl came to view. The same Chinese symbol.

"Okay," he said. "He's boffing some cyborg in a porn parlor and takes her to borg political rallies, or she takes him."

"Yes and no," she said. "Same tattoo. Same girl. But she's not a cyborg. She's human."

"Human?"

"She's a sophomore at Cal. Has some fetish about being a cyborg, which includes having pornographic sex with men who don't know she's human. She likes being hurt."

"She a student at Berkeley?" he asked, his mind in gear now.

"Professors having sex with students is still automatic grounds for dismissal," she reminded him. "No appeal."

"Maybe he doesn't know," he said.

"We've been following the good professor for some time now. You're right. He doesn't know," she said. "Doesn't matter."

"No," he agreed, "it wouldn't."

"And then there's her name."

Jonathon raised his eyebrows.

"Anita Browning Reifer." She let it hang.

It took him a minute. "As in Senator Adam Riefer, the head of the Senate Committee on Education, Labor, and Pensions?"

"Bingo," she said.

The room was silent for a full minute.

"Schmidt has student records in his iDevice," he finally said.

"Yes, he did, but some hacker," she batted her eyelashes in a faux modesty, "well, somehow all of the records in his iDevice have gone missing, just like those of the guardsman outside the course room."

Jonathon shook his head and a smile blossomed across his face.

The rain had stopped and the sun streamed into the library through a window above them. Jonathon looked up and smiled. He watched dust motes linger in the light. Finally, he turned back to her. "Why?"

"We've got your back."

"I see that. But . . ."

"Agnes Morningcloud said she saw your destiny and it is

ours." She paused, gazing at him. "That, and you and I…"

"You and I," he repeated and couldn't stop looking at her. Musing how beautiful she is and how much he loved her. Suddenly the idea of what their futures would be like, together or not, dominated his thoughts.

Chapter Twenty-Eight – Guilt
Back to October 11, 2001, Washington, D.C.

Diane moved over and sat next to him with her back to the desk, her legs straight out in front of her. His head was down, eyes on the floor. He was slowly shaking his head back and forth like a wind-up doll.

After a moment she put her arm gently around his shoulders and moved his head to her chest and stoked his hair.

He pressed his head more firmly against her breasts and started breathing heavily. He slid her to the floor, unbuttoned her blouse, and began slowly kissing her breasts. She moaned and slid her skirt off.

When both were satisfied they lay on the carpet, breathing heavily. Eventually Michael said, "Now I've betrayed my country and my wife. Pathetic."

"No one will know."

"I know."

She pulled on her panties and skirt and stood. She picked her bra up off the floor, put it on, buttoned her blouse, and tucked it in. She took something out of her purse, then walked to the bar, filled a glass with filtered water from the spigot, and handed him the water and a green-and-white pill. "Take it."

"What is it?" he asked.

"You'll feel better," she replied.

He stared at the pill for moment then threw it in his mouth and chased it with the water.

Diane ran her hands through her hair, ensured her blouse was buttoned, brushed the lint off the front of her skirt, and left the office.

Michael yanked his slacks up, tucked his shirt in, and buckled his belt. He went to his desk and sat down. He gazed at the picture of his wife on the desk. The sight of her adoring smile always lifted his spirits. Not this day. His feelings had morphed into a sort of emotional flat-line. He wasn't sad. He wasn't happy. He just didn't care.

He left for home early and crossed the Theodore Roosevelt Bridge without glancing at the crews from George Washington University racing up the Potomac. When he arrived in Fairfax, he drove through a red light on Fairfax Boulevard and got halfway through the intersection before a cacophony of car horns drew his attention.

He pulled into his driveway and stopped. He left the rear end of the car blocking the sidewalk. He got out and shuffled into the house.

"Hi Daddy," Missy said. She was six.

He walked past her into the hall and started up the stairs.

"Michael?" from his wife.

He turned and looked at her, said nothing, and continued up the stairs.

Janet ran into the hall. "Michael. What are you doing home? Something wrong?"

"I'm tired," he said.

Chapter Twenty-Nine – The President's Request
October 12, 2001, Washington, D.C.

"Kaschle called," Sandy Carl said. "He's coming around. You were fucking brilliant at the meeting, Michael."

"I . . . Sandy, look, I didn't mean—"

"The President sends his thanks again," Carl said.

"The President?"

"He'd love to see you at the White House Human Rights Awards dinner next week."

"Human Rights?" Michael asked. "I, eh . . . yes, well, I'd be honored."

"It's couples. Bring your wife."

"She'll enjoy that."

"Good. Good. And Senator, it would be great if you could touch base with McLeahy one more time. See if there is any change in his attitude since, you know, he received that letter."

"McLeahy? Uh, I'm not sure—"

"Just see where he's at, Senator, and we'll see you next week." Click.

Diane had heard it all, insisting he put the call on speaker when it came in and talk close to the phone mic. She went to the bar and poured them both drinks. "You are hot property, Senator," she proclaimed, handing him his.

"I should have told him 'no,'" he said.

"'No' to the President?"

"To Carl."

"Same thing," she said.

He laid his drink down at the corner of his desk, pinched the bridge of his nose and then rubbed his temples with the index fingers of both hands. "You got another one of those pills?"

She opened her purse, took out four Prozac tablets, and pushed them across the desk. "Don't take more than two in a twenty-four hour period."

Chapter Thirty – Deception
May 27, 2037, Eastern Sierra Nevada Mountains

The wind blew Agnes Morningcloud's eagle feather across the front of her face. She brushed it away with the back of her hand. "Listen to me, Jonathon. The public is sick of Mother. They want to live their lives without her digital eyeballs down their throats and up their asses. They want to be able to own firearms without going on a DHS terror watch list," she patted the Colt .45 nestled under her right arm, "or call a Senator a Marxist on their iDevice without a visit from the Brown Shirts. They may not know it's called the Bill of Rights, but they know they want freedom."

"Come on, Agnes. We both know these things," Jonathon said.

They sat under an ancient oak, atop a hill. The field below them was a feast of color. A carpet of wildflowers ran down the hill as far as the eye could see. One could imagine Van Gogh had returned from the dead and treated the hillside as his personal canvas.

Jonathon often hiked these mountain trails, and from time to time rented a cabin tucked up under an outcropping of granite a couple of miles south, adjacent to the Sequoia National Park just off of 395.

The mountains behind them kept the drones at bay, and satellites rarely swung over areas of such low population density.

"We also both know the public who cares about these things are no longer able to talk about them," Jonathon said. "If I ran a campaign based on those issues, the press would eat me alive before I got out of the starting gate. The press no longer even makes a pretense of objectivity. No, if I'm going to run for national office it will have to be on a social democratic progressive platform. On that ticket I will get support from big corporate conglomerates, the media and social reformers."

"You're out of your mind," she said.

"You know your Sun Tzu, Agnes?" he asked.

"It's been a while."

"Let me refresh your memory. Sun Tzu stated, 'After creating disinformation and deceptions to be planted in the field, direct that our agents know of the disinformation and deceptions and spread the disinformation and deceptions to enemy agents.'"

Agnes shook her head. "What happens when you get in office on a progressive platform and start forwarding a conservative agenda? What happens then?"

A doe and spotted black-tail fawn sauntered into the field below them. The doe stopped and turned her head toward them. She stood that way for some time, immobile. The fawn stood at her side. Jonathon and Agnes watched, said nothing. Then the pair moved on lazily across the field.

"Political hyperbole only goes so far, Jonathon. Yes, politicians make promises they don't keep. They lie. But you are talking about a complete change of face."

Jonathon took his iDevice out of its holster and asked for an image of Secretary General Obama of the United Nations. "Do you recall his first presidential campaign?"

"I was fifteen," Agnes said.

"In his interview in a mega church during his campaign, he said 'I believe marriage is the union between a man and a woman.' Right? That's what he said. I saw the video. Once in office, he quickly began supporting gay marriage."

"Yes, but—"

"In two thousand eight," Jonathon interrupted, "he promised he would not take your guns away. Well, he supported an assault-weapons ban and became the most vociferously anti-Second Amendment president in history. He also promised to close Guantanamo Bay early in his administration. Never happened."

Jonathon continued, "He repeatedly made the campaign promise that Americans making less than two hundred fifty thousand per year would not see 'any form of tax increase.' He said it again and again, but under Obamacare and other programs, the middleclass was slaughtered with new taxes."

A bumblebee buzzed around Agnes's forehead and then landed on her right ear. Agnes sat very still. After a moment a smile slowly broke across her face, at which point the bumblebee left for the wildflowers in the field below.

Agnes stood. The wind blew up the mountain side and whipped her hair and eagle feather behind her in a maze. "Okay, okay."

"There are hundreds of them," Jonathon said. "He still got elected to a second term."

"I know," she said. "I know. People have short memories. Those who bring up the problem can be marginalized, discredited. Standard operating procedure, in some circles."

"I'm going to need Saratoga's help."

"I only hope it's enough."

Chapter Thirty-One – The Envelope
Back to October 20, 2001, The White House

Glorious bouquets of American Beauty roses adorned the center of each table in the State Dining Room. Beltway glitterati in Versace, Dior, Armani, and Klein sat talking over the Napa Valley's finest Chardonnays and Cabernet Sauvignons.

Senator Keough and Diane sat at the Vice President's table. Table Two was rarified air. Everyone in the room, Michael most of all, knew he was now a comer.

Diane had convinced him that he needed her at the dinner for political backup, and a night of debauchery in the Four Seasons, including an introduction to several lines of cocaine.

"I just got word," the Vice President said, "McLeahy and Kaschle are both on board now, Senator. Your leadership on the Patriot Act has not gone unnoticed."

"Thank you, Mister Vice President," Michael acknowledged, "but I'm really not sure I deserve that praise."

Diane kicked his ankle under the table.

"You're too modest, Senator. I'm not sure we could have done this without you."

Secretary of Defense Ron Stumsfeld raised his glass. "Hear, hear."

The rest of the table followed: the President's Chief of Staff, Sandy Carl; Director of the Office of Management and Budget, Mitch Fandaneils; Secretary of Education, Rans Saige; and their wives. Diane held her glass the highest.

The President gave a flattering introduction to Claude Murry, the Director of the International Human Rights Foundation. Mr. Murry, a frail man in a tux that made him look like a cancer patient undergoing chemo, delivered an eloquent speech on the need for increased recognition of Human Rights around the world.

Dinner was served, French onion soup, filet mignon, and fresh Maine lobster, while the guests spoke in urgent terms of the need for the immediate and brutal demise of Osama Bin Laden. Michael contributed little to the conversation. He grew more stultified as the evening wore on, listening instead to the dissonance of raging molecules in his mind.

Blueberry cobbler a' la mode was served for dessert, followed by Kona coffee and Hennessy Private Reserve cognac.

Several of the guests patted Michael on the back and shook his hand as the party broke up and people began to leave.

It was after midnight when he got home. The porch light was off. Michael fumbled with his key and finally got the front door open. He went in and closed it quietly. Only when he turned to go up the stairs did he see Janet sitting in the living room on his oxblood leather chair. The only light in the room was a lamp on the end table next to the chair. She was in her nightgown, no robe, smoking. She'd quit smoking a decade ago. A highball sat on the end table, nearly empty.

"Janet, what are you doing up?" he asked.

"What are you doing?" she returned.

"What do you mean?"

"Where were you?"

"I was at a meeting," he lied. "Strategy for the next election."

She took a drag. "You didn't go to the Human Rights dinner at the White House?"

He took his coat off and slung it on the back of a chair, trying to think of what to say.

"I said, did you go to the White House?" she asked.

"I . . . ah, yes, I did. I was working on a strategy with the party leadership."

Janet took another pull on her smoke and exhaled it through her nose. She took a sip of her drink and put the glass down on the end table purposefully. "You went to a State dinner at the White House and didn't even mention it to me?"

Michael sat in the chair opposite her. He hesitated not knowing how to respond and so said nothing.

"Who is she, Michael? Who did you take in my place?" she demanded.

"No. It was political—"

Janet took an opened envelope from her lap and tossed it across the coffee table at him. Michael let it sit on his lap, regarding it as if it were an unexploded IED.

"Open it Michael."

He picked it up. The envelope, from the White House Social Secretary, was addressed to Senator and Mrs. Michael Keough. He took the letter from the envelope.

The letter explained that while the invitation to the Human Rights State Dinner had been sent to the Senator's office, the dining protocol was also being sent to the personal residence as an extra precaution.

"Who is she?" Janet repeated.

Michael buried his face in his hands.

When her cigarette had burnt down to the filter, she tossed it in the highball glass and stood. "When you find your moral compass, check which way the arrow is pointing and let me know."

She stood and headed for the stairs to their bedroom.

"I . . . I was with the Vice President—"

"You and who else?" She turned and went upstairs.

Michael dragged himself to the couch, laid down and, after an hour, drifted into a troubled sleep.

Chapter Thirty-Two – Golden Boy
September 14, 2037

The picture on the door was of the United Nations building majestically fronted with the brilliantly colored flags of the member nations fluttering atop a ceremonious row of towering poles.

Below the picture, the sign read International Tribunal of Climate Justice. Jonathon went in and walked to his desk through a beehive of multi-cultural activity. Shashi Gupta, a flirtatious post-graduate intern from the University of Delhi, who was acting as his assistant, brought him a cup of Tulsi tea.

"I just sent August's financial report to your iDevice," she said.

"Thanks," he said. "I'll review it."

Now firmly on the path of a progressive pedigree, Jonathon was the Executive Director of the tribunal's U.S. Western Regional office. He scanned the report. The bank balance was fourteen million, five hundred fifty-six thousand, nine hundred eighty-seven dollars. Henry Boros had long since gone to that great hedge fund in the sky, but his billions in post-mortem largess continued to fund his repressive agendas. The Boros Climate initiative provided the U.N with $100 million a year for the U.S.

implementation of the Global Climate Justice Initiative.

The Western Regional office received $20 million a year from the Boros funding, as did the four other regional offices in the U.S.

"Satellite maintenance is paid through the end of the year, right?" he asked.

"To the penny," she replied.

"Where are the red lines?" Jonathon asked.

"Coming," she responded. "There is a carpet factory in San Diego and a winery outside of Portland that are both red. Portland is way over quota. Should I charge their bank account?"

The multi-million dollar bank balance was not a result of the Boros funding. Those funds supported the satellites. The regional tribunal's funding came from the fines they levied on businesses that exceeded their energy allocation.

Jonathon accessed a private graph on his iDevice, showing parallel up-trending lines, a two-lane highway to the sky of environmental justice. One the unemployment rate, the other the Climate Summit's increased energy reduction mandates. If anyone had looked closely they would have seen Jonathon's jaw muscles clench.

Underneath faux concern, most in Congress were quietly content. More unemployment meant more unemployment insurance, more nutritional support, more disability and mental health payments. Government's primary role was now widely recognized as providing assistance to those in need. In short, public dependency was the government's goal.

Unemployment was up, energy output was down. Jonathon's star was now rising.

"How much over?" Jonathon asked.

"Thirty-four percent."

"Thirty-four percent? Really? I think I want to check this

out. Book me up to Portland tomorrow."

Jonathon left the building at lunchtime. He sent an encrypted note to Ashley, whom he hadn't seen in months. "Can you make it to Portland tomorrow?"

"Trouble?" she asked.

"I want to see you."

"Trouble?" she repeated.

"I miss you," he replied.

Two minutes passed before she responded, "I miss you, too."

He sent her his itinerary and asked her to meet him outside United Air Lines arrivals in a cab.

She started walking along beside him as he exited the terminal, but he didn't recognize her. She wore a wig of curly red under a green beret, gray contacts that blocked iris-scanners, and a University of Oregon sweatshirt with "Ducks Do It in the Water" written across the front of it.

"You got something against college co-eds, big boy?" she asked in a husky, old-fashioned, Mae West voice while looking straight ahead.

He suppressed a smile.

She stepped on the conveyor belt to the car rental area just ahead of him. No one was in hearing distance ahead or behind them.

"I was looking for a body of water," he said.

Ashley's turn to smile.

He walked past her on the conveyor belt and stepped off at the exit that said Hertz Environmental. She exited a few steps behind him but dallied outside, watching the digital promotion.

Jonathon went inside and flashed the screen of his iDevice at the 'toid behind the counter. A digital card emerged from the 'toid's hand. He turned and glanced at the facial recognition eye. The system would have also caught him in the airports, all of which aligned with his trip agenda. There was no reason he would have individual drone coverage once out of the airport.

They drove up the Oregon side of the Columbia Gorge, towering, pine-covered cliffs bordering the ice-laden river that had cut through the Cascade Mountains thousands of years earlier.

They crossed to the Washington side at Hood River and drove west again to Carson, Washington. Jonathon had made a reservation at the Carson Ridge luxury cabins under an alias for which he had an ID. He had confirmed that Carson, Washington was devoid of facial recognition software.

Drone patrols up and down the Columbia River itself did not reach over to Carson.

Jonathon checked them in. They unpacked, went out onto their deck, and for a few quiet minutes marveled at the Cascade Mountains, now shrouded in a purple mist as the sun took its last few breaths of the day.

"It's spectacular," Ashley remarked.

"Mother Earth," he said.

"What do you do with all that Boros money?" she asked.

"You mean you don't know? Agnes used some kind of clandestine connections to get me the gig."

"Agnes's network makes the CIA look like the Hardy Boys and she doesn't talk about it," Ashley said. "She has taken a page from the enemy's playbook and is building a shadow government of patriots as Boros did of socialists."

"The Boros money funds the satellites," Jonathon offered. "Our operating income comes from fines and penalties. Punitive income. Half goes directly back to the U.N. and the Tribunal uses the other half to police businesses and force them to decrease their productivity. The U.S. Treasury doesn't see a dime."

"Cute," she said. "American enterprise forcibly funding the U.N." She put her feet up on the railing. Despite a biting breeze that blew in off the river, she had taken her shoes and socks off to wiggle her toes. An Ashley moment.

"Are you getting any political traction from administering all that climate justice?" she asked.

"I've been invited to give the keynote speech to the Progressive Legislative Forum on Environmental Morality next Tuesday. The PLF has its share of political heavy-weights."

The sun slipped below the horizon. The Cascade Mountains transformed from deep purple to black. Ashley stood, turned around, and put her backside to the railing. "I know the PLF. If you can get them talking about a Carr candidacy, you're golden."

"Golden," Jonathon mused.

She pushed off the deck railing and moved to the sliding glass door to the bedroom and pivoted.

"Come on, golden boy. Let's leave politics on the deck. The sun may have gone down out there, but it's rising in here."

Jonathon stood and followed her inside.

Chapter Thirty-Three – Climate Change
September 28, 2037, Laguna Beach, California

The Progressive Legislative Forum's bi-annual conference was held at the Ritz Carlton in Laguna Niguel. Progressives painted themselves with a blue-collar brush but the working class wouldn't have recognized these digs.

The Ritz was perched on a cliff one hundred fifty feet above the Pacific. The view at sunset had been known to inspire more than a few celebrity engagements. The venue was nothing less than a sumptuous palace for the moneyed elite.

This weekend the place was crawling with kingmakers of the political left. The gates of the Democratic Party had been stormed and then overrun so completely by the barbarian left that its two hundred-year-old, time-honored brand was jettisoned in 2024 and changed to the Progressive Party.

The Progressives owed their spiritual heritage to Henry Boros, the Marxist billionaire, and their political heritage to Barack Obama. Seeking a legacy for what he called Global Transformation, he had used his former White House political connections to create a movement to draft him for the position of Secretary General of the United Nations.

Jonathon was talking to the Director of the Climate Justice Tribunal for the Northeastern U.S. at the bar when he spotted Oscar Schmidt.

There were more lines in his face and the goatee was white now, but there was no mistaking the bald dome, which looked as if it had been lacquered and buffed like the marble entrance to the hotel. Professor Oscar Schmidt glanced up from his conversation as if Jonathon's recognition of him had high-jacked his attention. He said something to the woman to whom he'd been talking and strolled across the lobby to Jonathon. "Well, it is you."

"Hello, Professor."

"Someone told me a Jonathon Carr was the Executive Director of the Western Climate Justice Tribunal and was speaking to the PLF," Schmidt said. "I couldn't believe it was the Jonathon Carr I knew, the Fourth Amendment fanatic, but here you are."

"With enough enlightenment any point of view can change, Professor. The planet is being destroyed. Someone has to do something about it."

Schmidt offered a thin-lipped smile. "Yes, but you? You were cited for blowing a Seed about the Bill of Rights, for God sake. Which reminds me—"

An attractive young woman, with straight, blonde hair parted perfectly in the center of her head approached the two of them from across the lobby at a fast clip. She started speaking before she reached them.

"Pardon me, gentlemen. Director Carr, we have to have you in the convention hall for a sound-check right away. We are running behind schedule. Will you please excuse us," she squinted to read Schmidt's nametag, "Mister Schmidt?"

"It's Doctor Schmidt," correcting her. "PhD, Domestic Intelligence. Department of Homeland Security."

She forced a smile, took Jonathon by the elbow, and guided him to the convention hall.

###

An hour and a half later, Jonathon was introduced to several hundred party loyalists and took the rostrum. Professor Schmidt looked on with suspicion. He was not convinced of the three hundred sixty degree political turn around.

"If you are going to play this game," Agnes had told him, "you've got to play it for blood. Don't soft-pedal your talk. It's not as if you will have to persuade any of them to embrace Progressive values. They all have the Kool-Aid on IV."

The applause was polite. He was not a name they knew. Not yet.

He stood confident, adjusted the microphone and glanced out over the audience. He was poised there, saying nothing for some moments until the jabbering stilled.

When he had their attention, he simply said, "It's man."

He let it hang. The audience seemed to strain forward now. Curious. Reaching.

"Man," he repeated. "Let us strip away the social niceties and say it like it is. It is mankind, man himself, who is behind the devastating portent of climate change. We all know it is carbon dioxide that is causing the heat-trapping, ionospheric blanket that will eventually destroy this planet. And what is the source of carbon dioxide?"

Pause.

"Man. We live on a planet that is being destroyed by its very inhabitants. If we don't confront this fact and begin to deal with the problem now, our future generations will suffer the consequences." He slammed his hand down on the podium and raised his voice now to a sense of urgency and determination. "Are you with me?"

The applause was instant and ardent. Some people stood and clapped. Jonathon acknowledged the applause and continued. When he finished his talk, he received another standing O.

Seated at the back of the room, Oscar Schmidt did not stand. He did not clap. He had always suspected Jonathon Carr was behind the exposure that had ruined his academic career at Boalt. He didn't know what it was, but there was a connection somewhere. He watched Jonathon Carr give a speech that was a Progressive wet dream and thought, *Doesn't fit.*

He made a note in his iDevice to investigate Mr. Jonathon Carr and his oh-so-peculiar political conversion.

Chapter Thirty-Four – I Like This Kid
September 28, 2037, Laguna Beach, California

Wayne D' Fontaine picked his teeth with the chrome-plated toothpick on which the olive to his martini had been skewed and subsequently devoured.

The black hair, which Jonathon could tell was a genetic transplant, was slicked straight back. He wore an Italian suit with a 24-karat gold thread woven into the fabric and a ring on his right hand with an emerald the size of a small ice cube.

After his speech, Loretta Crosby, an officious woman with a braided mane of flaming red hair, had approached Jonathon and introduced herself as the PLF Director of Legislative Affairs. She extended an invitation for Jonathon to join her and D' Fontaine for a drink in the lobby bar.

D' Fontaine remained seated but offered his hand across the table. The handshake, Jonathon noted, was a "dead fish."

"Please join us, Director Carr," he offered, motioning to an empty chair. Loretta Crosby took the chair next to him without being invited. Another man sat at the table next to D' Fontaine, younger, with a faraway smile, his eyes lidded, munching on cannabis crackers from a glass bowl in the middle of the table. "This is my nephew, Marco," D' Fontaine said.

Marco's eyes seemed unable to focus, but he waved in Jonathon's direction. Jonathon nodded at Marco. "Nice to meet you both."

Wayne D' Fontaine was the Finance Director for the PLF's Political Action Committee. Public records showed the PAC had in excess of two billion dollars in the bank. It was also common knowledge D' Fontaine controlled its disposition.

"That was quite a speech you gave," D' Fontaine said.

"Thank you," Jonathon said. "It is the defining issue of our time. Why should we have to rely on the United Nations to fund our work? Congress should act. We should be able to convince them that a modest tax increase to fund the infrastructure necessary to police climate criminals is in the country's best interest. In the planet's best interest."

Loretta Crosby reached over and placed her hand on top of Jonathon's on the table. "We need your voice."

"You just had it," he said.

"Yes. But in Washington,"

"Washington? I'm no politician, Ms. Crosby."

"You said yourself, Congress should act," D' Fontaine pointed out.

"Yes, but—"

"Senator Sanchez is retiring," D' Fontaine continued.

"Yes, I heard. But a Senatorial campaign, that's a huge effort. Hell, I've never held elective office. You know much better than me the cost of that kind of campaign."

"Many of the windbags in the Senate had never held elective office before being elected," D' Fontaine said. "As far as the campaign is concerned, leave that to us."

"Mr. D' Fontaine, I'm flattered, but this would be a huge change for me. I mean." Jonathon paused, and did a slight tilt of the head giving the impression he was thinking about what it might be like to be a United States Senator.

"You're the youngest Director in the history of the Climate Justice Tribunal, you're passionate, and you have a law degree from Boalt," Crosby chimed in. "And you've got the handsome movie star look."

In 2036, after a Progressive party blow-out victory in both the Senate and House, their younger voter base finally got their way. Congress overwhelmingly passed the 28th Amendment which in essence, brought the eligible age to hold office in the Senate down to twenty five, and to thirty for the office of the president.

Jonathon saw an opportunity to head off any damage Schmidt might attempt. "Yeah, I just saw one of my old professors from Boalt here. What a surprise! Oscar Schmidt. I used to bait him in class with conservative arguments about the Bill of Rights. Drove him crazy. He's with DHS now."

"DHS?" D' Fontaine asked.

"That's what his name tag said," Jonathon said.

"Schmidt?" D' Fontaine pondered.

"The Cyborg pervert," Marco commented. "Thought he was screwing a 'borg but it was the underage daughter of a congressman. They bounced his ass."

"To DHS?" D' Fountaine asked.

Marco shrugged and grabbed another cannabis cracker.

Crosby looked to Jonathon. "Why don't you think about it, Jonathon? Let's touch base in a week or so."

"Okay," he replied. "I'll give it some thought." He stood to leave.

"Carr," D' Fontaine said, "where do you stand on the Second Amendment?"

"The Second Amendment says, 'A well-regulated militia.' Hell, we've already got the strongest military in the world."

He spun around and began to leave, as he did, he heard D'Fontaine say "I like this kid."

Chapter Thirty-Five – Celebration
Back again to October 26, 2001, Washington, D.C.

Television cameras from all the major networks were stationed along the back wall of the East Room like a squadron of one-eyed robots. The White House press corps, old-timers with notepads on laps and pens to hand and younger generations with digital recorders, packed the place.

Select members of the House and Senate who had rendered unwavering support of the President in his push to pass what was now simply called The Patriot Act were seated in the front row.

An attendance of an unusually bi-partisan crowd, and some of the members were joined by their wives for what everyone understood was an historic event. Michael had asked Janet to come. She had refused.

The first string shared the podium with the President, standing in a semi-circle behind him as he spoke. Michael stood behind but to the side of Vice President Sweny, who was widely viewed as the chief architect of the legislation.

Michael had a euphoric sense of power and authority sharing the stage with the President and Vice President, the Attorney General, the Director of the FBI, Director of the CIA, the Secretary of the Department of Homeland Security, and senatorial luminaries like Hatcher and McLeahy. At the same time, he felt oddly disassociated.

As the President spoke about how the legislation expanded powers for law enforcement and the intelligence community, Michael remained uncomfortably mindful of the fact that he had never read the bill. Other than verbal assurances from the administration about the need and importance of the legislation, and Bob McLeahy's derisive comments, he actually had no idea what it said.

After the introductory remarks, the President sat down at a small, mahogany desk set up on the podium for the occasion and signed the bill in increments, sharing pens with those on the stage with him.

With the USA Patriot Act now federal law, the President and a select group of legislators and administration officials adjourned to a post-signing party in the Oval Office. An intimate gathering of those who had worked most diligently on the bill's passage.

Champagne and hors d'oeuvres were served on antique, silver trays by naval personnel in crisp, white uniforms. Michael looked up at the famous portrait of Abraham Lincoln by George Henry Story. The fact Lincoln looked like he was under some kind of thinly veiled stress somehow made Michael feel better. He was trying to figure out what had been in Lincoln's mind at the time when he heard his name called. To his right, Vice President Sweny and another man in a naval uniform stood together and the Vice President motioned Michael to join them.

"Senator Keough," Sweny said, "this is Admiral Ron Spaundexter. He's with DARPA over at the DOD."

DARPA was the acronym for the Defense Advanced Research Project Administration. Michael knew of them. They developed advanced weapons systems for the Department of

Defense.

"This legislation that you helped us pass," Sweny continued, "provides the legal foundation for some of the Admiral's most advanced anti-terrorism programs. "Admiral, this is Senator Michael Keough of California, who was instrumental in helping get this legislation through the Senate."

The men shook hands. Spaundexter's name rang a bell, but Michael couldn't recall from whence it came.

Spaundexter, a tall, balding man with military bearing, polished in his Full Dress Blues, said, "We appreciate the support, Senator."

"Well, I'm not sure how instrumental I was, but I'm a jarhead and we are at war," Michael said. "What programs has the legislation helped?"

Spaundexter's brow wrinkled. It passed. "Not much I can talk about here, Senator, but I can tell you that we are taking an in-depth, sweeping approach to the problem. We have to be able to monitor potential domestic sources of terrorism as well as foreign. There are terrorist cells right here in the Homeland."

"Sweeping," the Vice President echoed. He shook Michael's hand again, an invitation to leave.

It was the way Spaundexter framed it and the way the Vice President embraced it that prompted Michael to do something he had not done in several years.

Chapter Thirty-Six – Request For Help
October 26, 2001, Georgetown, D.C.

Michael pulled up to the curb across the street from the two-story brick townhouse in Georgetown. He shut off the engine and studied the house, trying to discern the best approach.

The light in the den was on. He sat for some time and watched the window. No sign of anyone. He finally mustered his courage, opened the door, and stepped out of the car. He stood with his butt against the fender as a cab whizzed by, followed by a wild-looking babe in black leathers on a Harley, no helmet, red hair streaming behind her. And then quiet.

Michael crossed the street and with hesitant steps moved up the walkway. He paused before ringing the doorbell. He hadn't seen his father in five years. Not since his mother's funeral, which had ended ugly between them.

He had tried to talk his father out of the trip to Africa after his retirement. Tried and failed. His mother was determined to see the source of the Nile and his father would not dissuade her despite her fragile health. The trip had taken them to Lake Victoria in Uganda, and from there to the true source of the Nile, the Kagera River in Burundi, which feeds Lake Victoria.

They had to go through Rwanda to reach Burundi, and it

was in Rwanda that she contracted the deviant form of Ebola and died in a squalid, African hospital before Michael could reach them.

Deep down he knew his mother would not have been deterred, but his father hadn't even tried. Wouldn't try. Michael's grief festered into anger and his father was his only real target. What was he going to do, sue a canvas-tented hospital in the middle of the African jungle?

"It was her life-long dream," his father had professed.

"You could have put your foot down," Michael responded.

"And deny your mother the one trip she had looked forward to for decades? Not on your life."

"No. Not mine. Hers."

"You son of a bitch. You don't have any monopoly on loss."

He had later apologized. His father accepted the apology and offered his own. His mother had always been the glue that kept the family together through Christmas dinners, birthdays, and anniversaries. Without her the family ties drifted as the two of them stayed focused on their careers. They played an occasional round of golf, caught a Redskin's game now and then, but when his dad remarried two years after his mother's death, their communication faded to phone calls on birthdays and an exchange of Christmas presents via Fed Ex.

George Keough had spent thirty years as a partner in one of the leading civil rights law firms in Washington before retiring with a handsome balance in his 401K and too much time on his hands.

Alana, his father's wife—Michael had yet to work the word "stepmother" into his vocabulary—answered the bell. She was an attractive African-American woman, perhaps ten years his father's junior, whom he had met on a ski trip to Sugarloaf in Vermont. She had been an Olympic skier in her youth. No medals, but still . . .

They had a passing, somewhat awkward relationship.

She greeted him with a note of surprise and a grey-and-white Shih Tzu cradled in her right arm. "Michael, what a surprise."

She stood, apparently uncertain of what to do. The dog started yapping.

After a moment she turned her head toward the hallway. "George, your son is here."

She stepped back from the door and opened it to let him in. The Shih Tzu continued to bark.

"Hush, Daisy. This is your brother, Michael."

Michael suppressed an urge to rap the dog in the nose. Instead, he offered the back of his hand for Daisy to smell. She snipped at it. Michael yanked it back.

"Bad girl, Daisy. No! Bad dog."

"Alana, shut that little fucker up!"

At sixty-seven, George Keough, who had been a tri-athlete until a few years ago, still looked like a linebacker for the Redskins, except for the steel-gray buzz cut. He had the Washington Post in one hand and his reading glasses in the other.

Alana glared at her husband, wheeled, and headed back down the hallway. Her departure seemed to clear the air. George walked over and gave Michael a hug.

Michael hugged him back. "Hey, Pop."

"Jesus. I just saw you on CNN," he exclaimed. "Come on in." He motioned to the den off the hallway.

The den served as George's office. A Dell computer sat on a desk covered with papers and digital printouts. A floor-to-ceiling bookshelf lined the far wall. There were pictures of George and Alana on the desk, and one of Michael being sworn in as a United States Senator. A lovely, framed picture of Dorothy Keough,

Michael's mother, in her wedding dress, hung on the far wall.

Two client chairs stood in front of the desk. George sat down in one and offered the other to Michael. "So, you're running with the big dogs now," George stated as they sat.

Michael shook his head slowly and looked around his father's office. "I screwed up, Pop."

"Get in line," his father said, and put his glasses on the desk.

"It's not that easy."

"Tell me."

He told his father about his infidelities and drug use.

"Does she know?" his father asked.

"She knows about the woman, not the drugs."

Alana, sans Shih Tzu and seeking to make amends, stuck her head into the den. "Coffee?"

Both of the men said "Yes" at the same time.

"And?" his father asked.

"I'm going to let her know I was an idiot and I want to keep our family together and see if I can do enough amends for her to take me back."

"Back? Has she left?"

"She hasn't physically moved out of the house, but she's left the marriage spiritually, emotionally. I made sure of that."

George picked his glasses up and started chewing one of the temple pieces. "So, what's up, son? I'm glad you came by. It's been too long. But I'm guessing it wasn't to tell me you've been unfaithful to your wife and are going to go back to her on bended knee."

George was a bone-marrow Kennedy Democrat, Michael a Reagan Republican. They had argued politics non-stop in years gone by. Still, it was a point of political irony, what each was most passionate about politically was the Bill of Rights, George from a civil liberties perspective, Michael from a Founder's point of view. This was sacred ground for the both of them.

"I was elected because of my commitment to the Constitution," Michael began. "That was my platform, returning government to the intentions of the Founders."

"I know," his father said.

"The White House called me," Michael continued. "They wanted my help in convincing McLeahy to move forward on the Patriot Act. I hadn't read it, but we are at war, for Christ's sake. So, I went and talked to him, for all the good it did. He had concerns, civil liberties concerns, and wasn't about to change his mind."

"He's a good man, McLeahy," George said.

Michael stood, picked up his cup of coffee, and walked to the window. He spoke without turning around. "Later, I went to a meeting at the White House chaired by the Vice President to battleplan the passage of the bill. McLeahy and Kaschle had put the brakes on it."

"Yes. I remember reading about it," George said.

"You probably also remember they both got anthrax letters and changed their minds."

George tilted his head in the affirmative.

"At that White House meeting I made a wise-ass remark to Sweny that McLeahy and Kaschle should experience a little terrorism themselves. Might change their minds," Michael forged on. "It was a stupid remark. I wasn't serious. I was trying to leverage my way into the inner circle. I haven't even read the fucking bill."

George Keough stood, walked over to the den's door, and closed it quietly. He turned back around. "You mean you think Sweny took your suggestion seriously and arranged to have those senators receive anthrax letters to change their minds about the bill?"

"I do."

His father's eyebrows went up. "I want to do a little digging. Give me twenty-four hours. Why don't you go home and try to save your marriage. We can meet back here tomorrow at the same time."

Something in Michael eased. He smiled for the first time in . . . he couldn't remember the last time he'd felt like smiling. He stood and was walking to the door when he remembered something.

Turning, he said, "There was a small celebration in the Oval Office after the signing ceremony. Sweney introduced me to an Admiral Spaundexter from DARPA. I know the name from somewhere. He mentioned a new anti-terrorism tool they were working on, called the Total Information Awareness (TIA) program. Can you see what you can find on it? DARPA is not always forthcoming to Congress."

"I'll check it out," his father confirmed.

Chapter Thirty-Seven – A Sleeper Agent (The Mole)
June 21, 2038, Fresno, California

Political campaigning was now largely conducted on the iDevice network. Holographic videos leaped from the screen, with candidates pontificating on table-tops, in the cupped hands of the recipient, or sometimes floating in mid-air like a miniaturized human butterfly.

The most partisan programmed the holographic miniature look-alike candidates to perch on their shoulders and expound on everything from the abuses of a free-market economy on one side to U.N. mandates supplanting the Constitution on the other.

Some had candidates from either side of an issue standing on opposite shoulders, arguing their positions while the person sat in their iDrive or was strolling down the street. Most restaurants, theaters, and other public places banned the playing of any kind of holographic commercial on their premises.

Some things about politics never changed, however. Polling showed politicians giving live speeches to audiences and pressing the flesh with attendees did more to secure votes than any form of advertising, on or off the iDevice network.

The temperature was up to 102 degrees in Fresno, and

Jonathon stood on the stage of the LGBTQ Community Center, drenched in sweat and smiling as if he hadn't a care in the world. He had just been introduced as "The most effective warrior against climate change in the country." The applause was strong enough for him to respond with a big smile.

"Thank you so much!" he said. "There are two primary purposes of government. One is to regulate and inhibit the rapacious activities of commercial enterprises preying on the citizens of the Republic. My record of identifying and penalizing those who would destroy the planet with their overzealous production and greed is unsurpassed."

Loud applause.

"The other is to provide for the welfare of its citizens. This we do with income assistance for the unemployed, nutritional support for the disadvantaged, universal health care, federally funded educations for all, rent subsidies for all Americans, mortgage forgiveness, and financial support for minority populations and the less advantaged."

"Here, in the San Joaquin Valley," he continued, "it means federal government subsidies to those of you who sustain the nation's food supply with your farms and ranches. Any time market conditions are such that agricultural products cannot bring a fair price in the so-called free market, the federal government is committed to buy the products at a price that guarantees a fair return. If I am elected Senator, I can assure you those subsidies will continue unabated, and, if possible, be increased."

Standing ovation.

Jonathon's startlingly successful Senate campaign had been attributed to his leading the fight for environmental justice. Only Jonathon knew the extent to which Agnes Morningcloud had used the Saratoga Movement to motivate Progressives to vote for the handsome, young climate warrior.

###

Washington D.C. was a sauna.

Oscar Schmidt, his bald head glistening, sat in his 14th floor office in the towering DHS building on K Street. His resurrection from his dismissal from the faculty at Boalt Hall a decade earlier had been facilitated by contacts at DHS for whom he had worked years earlier.

The Senator, whose seventeen-year old daughter he had been videoed with inside a cyborg porn parlor and who had written the university regents in protest, was mysteriously found to be having an affair with a Pakistani woman whose green card application of nine years earlier, contained "falsified information." Whether the allegations were true didn't matter. They had taken the Senator down.

With Senator Cooper discredited, Schmidt quickly recovered his stature and took his position at the Department of Homeland Security, where he was now the Director of Domestic Intelligence.

The DDI was a position of immense power. "Mother" had become the supreme intelligence authority in 2031 when she had been given oversight of both the FBI and CIA. This structural realignment of law enforcement and intelligence agencies, inconceivable a few years earlier, followed a terrorist attack leaving seventeen dead the week before Christmas at a shopping mall in San Diego. The massacre had enraged the nation to such an extent the proposed reorganization was fast-tracked through Congress and signed by the president in ten days. It was referred to as the San Diego Shuffle among the intelligence communities inside the Beltway.

"Mother" was now king and queen of American intelligence, and Oscar Schmidt sat atop the intelligence division. Oscar carried a big stick.

He called Maya Contreras, a buxom, soft-eyed Latina into his office.

"Yes, Doctor Schmidt?" she asked as she entered.

"I want you to find me an operative, Ms. Contreras," he told her. "Female, attractive, street-tested, can deal with moral challenges."

"Moral challenges, sir?"

"She'll screw a target if she has to."

Maya blinked involuntarily. "Yes, sir."

Robin Delgado had an African-American mother, a Puerto Rican father, and the exotic eyes of a Voodoo princess. She had a graduate degree in Political Science from George Washington University and had recently returned from a nine-month undercover assignment for the Drug Enforcement Agency.

She was now on indefinite loan from the DEA. In exchange, Schmidt had seen to the approval of a green-card application for the sister-in-law of the DEA's HR director.

When she sat in the chair in front of his desk, she let her skirt slide well up above mid-thigh. Schmidt looked at her lasciviously. Robin, who was testing his sexual orientation so she'd know how to deal with him, smiled to herself.

"I need somebody to infiltrate a political campaign," Schmidt said.

Chapter Thirty-Eight – Michael's Penance
An earlier lifetime, October 27, 2001,
Georgetown, D.C.

Alana greeted Michael the next day as well. She was dressed in designer jeans and a GW sweatshirt. She wore her age very well for a woman pushing sixty, Michael thought.

"Hello, Michael." She swung the door open. "The children are in the den." And smiled. She then started walking down the hall. He could hear Daisy yapping from the other end of the hallway.

He walked to the den's door, rapped on it twice, gave it a push, and it swung open.

His father stood. "Hey Michael." He swung around to the other two men, who also stood. "These are my partners."

A tall, black man of maybe fifty-five, wearing slacks and a cardigan sweater, stepped out from behind the table. Bald. Pencil-thin mustache. Broad shoulders. "Manny Waters," he said, extending his hand. "Nice to meet you, Senator."

"My pleasure," Michael replied. They shook.

"Manny was with D.C. Homicide for years," his father added, "and Robbie Coale was with the NSA."

Robbie sported gray stubble, was short, round, and wore

old-fashioned granny glasses. He leaned across the table and shook Michael's hand.

Michael wasn't so sure he wanted to share his personal problems with his father's partners, but he had rather dumped his mess in his dad's lap to handle. From the laptops and paperwork strewn across the worktable, they already appeared to be knee-deep.

"Take a seat, Michael," his father said. "Let's get started. Manny, why don't you start with the item we were just discussing?" He looked to Michael. "My law license is still very active. Everything said in this room is Lawyer-Client privileged." He turned back to Manny and nodded.

"It was weaponized," Manny began. "The anthrax was weaponized. Had it reached the hands of either senator and had they not been treated immediately with antibiotic IV drips, it would have killed them. Painfully."

Alana knocked, heard George say yes, then opened the door, Daisy resting on her arm. "I'm going to take Daisy for a walk," she said and closed the door without waiting for a response.

"The U.S. Army developed anthrax as a biological warfare weapon years ago," George added. "Our stockpiles were supposed to have been destroyed in the early seventies, according to a treaty Nixon signed. Fucking joke."

"The anthrax strain mailed to the Senators originated at the Army's biological research center at Fort Detrick, Maryland," Manny said. "It could have come from some other location or entity, but it was originally produced by the U.S. Army at Fort Detrick."

Michael ran his hand through his hair and shook his head. "For a piece of legislation? That's attempted murder."

"It's not just any legislation, Michael," George said. "This is the most successful assault on the Bill of Rights in two hundred years. The attack is on three levels."

"You got a legal pad and a pen?" Michael asked.

George reached into his briefcase, parked on the floor next to his feet. He pulled out a lined legal pad and slid it across the table to Michael. Robbie rolled a pen across the table to him.

"One. The act grants the executive branch unprecedented, and largely unchecked, surveillance powers," George said. "This includes the enhanced ability to track email and internet usage, conduct sneak-and-peek searches, obtain sensitive personal records, and monitor financial transactions, to name a few."

"The sneak-and-peek provision," Manny said, "enables the government to go into your house when you're not home, search around, and even seize your property without telling you. The only justification law enforcement now needs to enter a house or office without notice is that giving notice might 'seriously jeopardize an investigation or unduly delay a trial.'"

Michael wrote in a blistering short-hand that he had developed in law school.

"It's a shameful assault on the First Amendment." George stated. "Allowing the government to prosecute librarians or keepers of other records if they tell anyone that the government subpoenaed information related to terror investigations."

Michael threw his pen on to the pad and stood, paraded to the other end of the room, swung around and walked back, and sat down. "Librarians?" He looked at Manny and Robbie. They both nodded.

"Secondly," George continued, "the act permits law-enforcement agencies to circumvent the fourth amendment's requirement of probable cause when conducting wiretaps and searches that have, as a significant purpose, the gathering of foreign intelligence. Third and finally, the law allows for the sharing of information between criminal and intelligence operations, and thereby opens the door to a resurgence of domestic spying by the Central Intelligence Agency. The fact is, Michael, the Act puts the CIA back into the business of spying on Americans, a clear violation of the CIA's charter to not engage in law enforcement or internal functions."

Michael stood. "Excuse me for a moment." He walked out of the den, down the hall, into the guest bathroom, locked the door, sat on the closed john with his pants on, and put his head in his hands. He thought about the new law which, now painfully clear, made a mockery of Constitutional safeguards he held dear and had sworn to uphold.

He felt nauseous. His forehead broke into a sweat. He swallowed a couple of times to keep from throwing up. After a couple of minutes the nausea passed. He stood, took a washcloth from the towel rack, ran cold water over it, wrung it out, and mopped his brow. He ran some water into his cupped hands, took a mouthful, rinsed, and spit.

He looked at himself in the mirror. The person staring back at him had the pallor of a recovering drug addict, which, in an odd sort of way, he was. The image also had a sense of determination.

When he re-entered the office, the three men looked up. In an uncomfortable moment of honesty he looked at them and confessed, "I nearly puked."

"Sounds about right," his dad said.

As soon as Michael sat down, Robbie said, "Let's start with this: Spaundexter was convicted 11 years ago."

"Convicted?" Michael asked.

"Convicted of conspiracy, obstruction of justice, lying to Congress, defrauding the government, and the alteration and destruction of evidence relative to the Iran-Contra Affair."

"Right, right. That's where I remembered his name from,"

Michael said.

"The conviction was subsequently reversed by a Grant of Use of immunity," Robbie continued. "Now he's head of TIA." He reached into his own briefcase and pulled out a memo. CONFIDENTIAL was stamped across the top in red.

"I don't want to read or see anything that was obtained in violation of our security laws," Michael said.

"You won't," Robbie responded. "Not from me. That is my stamp to dissuade others from reading it. I wrote this memo from my own research obtained from reliable professionals, none of whom violated federal security statues."

"May I ask what professionals?" Michael asked.

"You may ask anything you like, Senator, but I do not divulge my sources."

Michael glanced over at George, who nodded his confirmation. He turned to Robbie again.

"Research on The Total Information Awareness Program," Robbie said, "actually started last year, before the attack." He looked at each of the others one at a time. Receiving no additional feedback, he continued.

"The TIA is 1984 in real time. The government will track your entire life. Everything you say and do will be monitored by Uncle. The TIA is Big Brother."

"Give me an example," Michael requested.

"The system is designed to build a complete profile on every person in the United States—"

"Everybody?" Michael queried, with eyebrows raised.

"Everybody," Robbie confirmed. "Every email you send and receive, every website you visit, every download you make, every credit card purchase, online or off, every call you make or receive, every magazine subscription, every medical prescription, every academic grade you ever received."

"All bank deposits you make," he continued, "checks you write, funds you withdraw. Trips, DMV data, hospital stays, legal filings like marriages, divorces, lawsuits. All this data will go into what DARPA describes as 'a virtual centralized data base.'"

The door opened. Alana announced, "We're back." Daisy jumped from her arms and began running around the den in circles. She stopped, walked over to Michael's shoes and began sniffing. She went from Michael to Robbie.

"Daisy, come here!" Alana demanded. Daisy moved from Robbie's shoes to Manny's. She sniffed his shoes and then began sniffing his left ankle and up his leg.

"Alana, we're trying to work here," George said.

"Daisy!" she said.

Daisy moved to Manny's right ankle.

George picked the dog up, walked her to the door, and deposited her deliberately in Alana's arms and shut the door.

Robbie continued as if there had been no interruption. "Your dossier is overlaid with your political beliefs, religious beliefs, sexual proclivities and orientation, the groups and association you belong to, and those of your family."

He put his notes down and glanced again at the others around the table. No one spoke.

George eventually broke the silence. "Okay, Michael, that's the overview. Anthrax, the Patriot Act, Spaundexter, and the TIA."

"It's a fucking disaster," Michael declared. "A disaster of my own making."

"There's lots we can do," George said. "I can start filing lawsuits immediately."

"They'll take years to get to the Supreme Court," Michael said. "I've got to figure out something with more immediate impact. Tough sell for me on the Hill since I am the poster boy for this legislation. Even if I weren't, the vote in the Senate was ninety-eight to one."

"I've got some thoughts on this, Michael."

George turned to Manny and Robbie. "Thanks, guys. I'm going to kick some solutions around with the Senator and then we'll regroup."

Manny and Robbie gathered their papers, shook hands with Michael, and took their leave.

"Look, Michael," George said then, "this thing was rammed through Congress without hearings or debate. Virtually no one read it. I have lots of connections in this town. I can begin to organize effective opposition. When the passion of the moment passes and people begin to realize what this law does, there will be Hell to pay. I can have the office start filing federal lawsuits immediately."

"Thanks, Pop. Let me think about what would be the best strategy. It's probably a good approach, but it is my mess. I need to figure out how to fix it, and I will fix it. No matter how long it takes, I will fix this. So help me God."

The freezing rain had changed to snow during the afternoon. The roads were treacherous with black ice. Michael was in such a mental turmoil he almost missed the exit off the Theodore Roosevelt Bridge onto the George Washington Parkway. At the last moment he swung the wheel sharply. The back wheels broke loose and the car started to sail across the iced highway.

He panicked, turned the wheel in the opposite direction and slammed his foot on the brake pedal, which sent the car into a spin, skidding across the exit at high speed. It slammed into the cement guardrail with such force Michael, who had always refused to wear a seat belt, was slammed through the front windshield, over the railing, and down into the frozen Potomac.

As his body pounded the ice, his back snapped. Excruciating pain and blood now his only agonizing reality. His fall split the ice leaving an open space enough for his body to slip through.

He floated for a few seconds, the freezing water numbing his pain.

So help me God, he thought as he slowly sank to the bottom of the freezing river.

Chapter Thirty-Nine – America Mayhem
The year 2039

The interest on the national debt was now the largest expense item in the federal budget. To cover the interest payments, taxes had been raised on corporate profits, forcing scores of long-standing American brands out of the country.

The eye-watering Health and Welfare costs were a close second. Added to that, only a ghost of the Social Security system existed. Social Security taxes were still collected but Social Security payments, which had been "temporarily" reduced a decade earlier, had recently been suspended altogether. With higher corporate taxes driving employers offshore, unemployment rose and social security taxes declined. Benefits declined and then vanished last year. The government reciprocated with an enormous expansion, the food stamp program, and eliminated all deductibles from the country's universal health care program. A snake eating itself.

Millions were homeless, and many of those who weren't had taken to joining flash mobs that invaded pharmaceutical companies and plundered their inventories. The practice of government distribution of anti-depressant and anti-anxiety drugs, commenced a decade earlier, had been "temporarily" halted due to budget constraints. Without government purchases of mind-altering medication, many pharmaceuticals went bankrupt and millions of people descended into the agony of withdrawal.

It wasn't just pharma flash mobs. Civil unrest and riots had become commonplace. Driving across the urban landscape of many American cities had now become a perilous undertaking with mobs of the unemployed attacking anyone who was deemed to be "foreign," which had a different meaning in Cincinnati than it did in Seattle or Tampa or Philly.

Many were in despair, but others, enraged at the lies and duplicity of a lawless government whose primary focus had been protecting its own privilege for decades, took out their wrath on any moving target. Carrying a loaded gun in a vehicle was illegal but many did so regardless. The black market in firearms was enormous.

The wealthy usually traveled across town in individual drones administered by an interconnected system of iDevices controlled by the TSA.

The defense budget had been slashed repeatedly, but America's enemies were now believed to live within. The budget allocation for the Department of Homeland Security had escalated even faster than the decrease in defense spending.

China, Russia, and India had all surpassed America as military powers.

Despite the country's death-spiraling insolvency, Congress continued to spend like some heroine-addicted junkie, far beyond tax revenues. Fiscal insanity reigned.

When the U.S. Treasury missed three scheduled interest payments on their bonds, even the Federal Reserve Bank had called a halt to the printing of money. Not actual printing, of course, but digital transfers had stopped. The Wall Street banks that owned the Fed wanted the government in debt, but not to the extent of losing their income.

Chapter Forty – Infiltrator
February 11, 2039, Washington D.C.

The buzzer rang in Senator Jonathon Carr's office, calling the Senators to the floor for a roll-call vote. Then a red light began to flash in the reception area.

Despite a technological blitzkrieg through the first third of the twenty-first century, both the House and the Senate still used a system of bells, buzzers, and flashing lights to call the members to their respective chambers for votes.

Jonathon placed his iDevice on his forearm. The device was biometric, and despite being eight centimeters long, it weighed less than an ounce.

The call was for the vote on the controversial legislation put forth by the President to accept the loan, terms, and conditions tendered by the International Monetary Fund.

While environmental concerns had dominated the headlines during the California Senate campaign, the real battle in Washington was over a solution to the massive 58 trillion national debt and the tragic state of the U.S. economy.

A humiliated President had been forced to go on bended knee to the International Monetary Fund and "request" a loan of five trillion to cover this year's budget shortfall.

Rather than tell the President and Congress to curtail spending, the IMF, with an eye to finally sinking its fangs into the American taxpayer, offered to make a loan under certain conditions. The offer had been structured as a treaty. The Senate had to approve.

Jonathon's Legislative Affairs director, Monica Ruiz, a saucy, Afro-Puerto Rican woman with wild eyes, had joined his Senatorial campaign as a volunteer. She was intelligent, had sharp political instincts, and had performed so well managing a team of volunteers in California, Jonathon had asked her to join him in Washington after he was elected.

Monica handed him the notes for his speech as he walked out of his office into the reception area. "Here are your notes, Senator. I have highlighted the points you wanted to emphasize."

"Thanks, Monica." He took the pages, glanced over the notes, and headed out the door.

Monica went back into her office, closed her door, walked to the east wall, and said, "K9402IVY" to a picture of President Salinas. The safe was programmed to open only when that password was vocalized by Monica herself and when she was the sole person in the locked room. It would not open otherwise. The safe had eyes.

The safe door swung open. She removed her encrypted DHS iDevice and whispered a password. Oscar Schmidt's holographic image emerged out of the device.

"I haven't heard from you in three weeks," he said. "What the hell is going on?"

"You try being a Legislative Affairs Director for an incoming freshman senator, Doctor Schmidt," she responded. She punched on the word "doctor," as Schmidt insisted that all staff refer to him in that manner.

"I didn't fucking hire you to be a Legislative Affairs

Director," he declared.

"No. You hired me to infiltrate his campaign and ascertain his true political agenda. I infiltrated his campaign so well I am now his Legislative Affairs Director."

"And you haven't given me shit," Schmidt complained.

"Not true. I have given you his position on a wide range of issues. They just aren't what you wanted to hear."

Schmidt didn't respond immediately. She watched him sit back in his chair and look up at the ceiling. Eventually he leaned forward so close to the iDevice the holographic image was entirely of his head. "There is a vote on the IMF loan proposal this afternoon."

"That's right."

"How is he going to vote?" Schmidt asked.

"He's going to vote 'No.'"

"I told you!" Schmidt said. "Progressives favor a loan from the IMF. They support it wholeheartedly. He just got into office and already he's beginning to show his true colors. He's no Progressive."

"He's voting 'No,'" Monica said, "because he says five trillion is not enough. He will say, on the floor of the Senate this afternoon, that he will not support anything less than ten trillion from the IMF."

"The IMF will never . . . oh, I see what that sonofabitch is doing. He's looking like an ultra-progressive while actually working to defeat the bill."

"You've really got a hard-on for this guy, don't you?" she asked.

"Remember who you are talking to, Ms. Delgado. This guy is to the right of Genghis Kahn. You just need to find it."

Monica started to hang up and recalled something. "Just a thought, but I have a sense, nothing more than a perception, that he may have an unregistered iDevice."

Having an iDevice unregistered with DHS was a violation of federal regulations. The ostensible reason was it increased energy consumption, which was a national security matter. A euphemistic joke to anyone with an IQ over sawdust. The real reason, of course being, if the second iDevice isn't registered, the person could not be tracked easily and could carry on conversations that could not be monitored.

"Hold a minute," he demanded.

Some senior administration officials were authorized to have a second iDevice. Schmidt pressed a tab on his computer, brought up the DHS security system and asked for Senator Carr's iDevice records.

"He's not authorized for an alternate," Schmidt said after a moment, "which means he is likely carrying on unsanctioned communications. Find them."

Chapter Forty-One – Watch Your Back
March 12, 2039, Washington, D.C.

During a meeting on budget matters in his office, Monica had noticed the Senator admiring her legs, but beyond that he hadn't flirted, asked her out, or offered an invitation to stay late when others had gone home.

She knew he wasn't gay, but there was no record of him ever being married and his love life in D.C., if there was any, remained a mystery. Young by political standards, movie star handsome, and a rising political power. It made no sense.

She took to wearing slightly shorter skirts and began to find excuses for staying late on nights he was still in the office. It didn't take much, really. There was always a mountain of work to do.

At 7:30 on a Wednesday evening she knocked lightly on his door and then opened it without waiting to be invited. It was the first time she had done that, but she needed to increase their familiarity. She decided to push the envelope by stepping into his privacy to see what he would do. "Good evening, Senator. I hope I'm not intruding," she said.

"No, no," he replied. "Come on in."

His sleeves were rolled up to his elbows. "Store," he said,

and the holographic image he had been reading disappeared into his iDevice. "Have a seat, Monica. What's on your mind?"

"I saw your lights were on and thought we might discuss the terms of the IMF loan. With the amount of the loan approved now, it all boils down to the terms. Will we accept their control of U.S. tax policy?"

She crossed her legs causing her skirt to move up her thigh, close but not quite to slut level.

Her leg maneuver made Jonathon bite the inside of his lip and play the pretended not to notice game. Affairs between legislators and their aides were a common rite of passage, but Jonathon wasn't going there. He told the iDevice to bring up a copy of the terms for the proposed IMF loan.

Monica groaned inside, uncrossed her legs, and leaned forward as if she were actually interested in the hologram's humanized voice recitation of the document.

The clock on the kitchen wall showed ten ten when Jonathon made it back to his place in Georgetown. It had been a condo development twenty years earlier. Now they were called Domiciles. He threw his jacket on the chair in the living room, told his domitoid to hang it up, and gave Sarge, his two-year-old Bernese Mountain dog, who came charging across the room to him, a vigorous scratch behind the ears.

He changed into his jogging togs, got the dog's leash from the closet, and the two of them set out on the three-mile run. Something Jonathon tried to do every night he returned from the Hill.

When he got back from his run, he mopped the sweat from his face, and went into the second bedroom, which served as his home office. He let Sarge into the room and locked the door.

He ordered the lights on. "Dimmer, five degrees." He looked at the ceiling and said, "Deploy."

Sarge moseyed to a spot in front of a small sofa, circled a few times, as if trying to find the exact spot on the rug that would be the most comfortable, and then settled in.

Before Jonathon moved in, Saratoga operatives disguised as interior designers had installed a security system comprised of nano-drones that permeated the space in this room and emitted screens of waves to block any attempted electronic intrusion. He could do or say anything in this room without sharing the experience with Mother. It had been installed so he could communicate with Agnes or Ashley.

He moved across the room, to a framed picture by Fredrick Remington of a cowboy sitting on his horse atop a bluff somewhere in the American Southwest, and said, "This is Jonathon. One-zero-zero-seven-seven-seven."

The picture swung outward. Jonathon reached into the safe and removed his alternative iDevice. "Ashley," he said as he headed to his desk and sat. It took a few moments before she appeared, buttoning the front of a blouse. Her hair was wet and plastered to the sides of her head. She appeared to be blushing. "You caught me just coming out of the shower."

"It's eight o'clock there. What are you doing taking a shower?"

"Just back from a trek up the mountain," she answered. "It was glorious here today. I couldn't resist."

"I have to see you," he said.

"What? You want your own girlie show?"

"No. I mean see you. I miss you, terribly. Where can we meet? Somewhere in the state so the trip looks constituent-driven?"

"Not here," she said.

The sound of an ambulance screamed by the window. Then another.

"Another shooting?" she asked.

"I don't know," he answered. "Where? We need privacy, and a bed."

"Cool down, cowboy," she said. "Do you know Ojai?"

"Sure. It's where they filmed that old classic Shangri La. Gorgeous, but a lot of celebrities there. Too public."

"About forty miles due north of Ojai is a small outpost community with a smattering of wooden cabins. It's called Camp Sheideck. Very rustic, very private—"

"I like it. I can be there day after tomorrow. You?"

"I'll be waiting for you at the country store at 6:00 p.m. You will need to get out of LA without drone surveillance."

"I know the drill," he replied.

"Does this mean I'm going to be sleeping with a United States Senator?"

"That would be a patriotic thing to do." Jonathon smiled.

What Jonathon hadn't counted on was the TSA agent attaching a nano-tracker on his briefcase as he passed through airport security at Reagan National. Nano-drones, so small they could not be seen without a microscope, were monitored by ultra-sensitive wave detection equipment and were reasonably new.

So were the countermeasures. Jonathon had one of the new nano-detection screening devices at home and one at the office. He did not have the portable version.

Senator Carr's travel schedule was public record. Traveling

to California was a normal occurrence. That he was leaving in the middle of the week and would miss a key vote on the president's nominee for the Supreme Court, was unusual, though it was well known she had enough Senate votes for confirmation. Jonathon's vote would have been a matter of political cosmetics, but it would have added a Progressive feather in his cap.

Oscar Schmidt had arranged for Senator Carr's travel schedule to be sent encrypted, to him daily. When Schmidt opened his computer the Senator's Wednesday morning flight to Los Angeles hit his screen. He stroked his goatee, and then arranged for the placement of the nano-tracker when Carr passed through security.

Schmidt knew the Senator would have no way of knowing his movements were being tracked unless he decided to run a personal screening in Los Angeles that included his briefcase. If he did find the tracker, it could not be traced back to DHS. The liability was that Carr would know he was being followed, and the primary source of this he would know was DHS. For Jonathon Carr, DHS meant Oscar Schmidt.

###

Sheideck, California looked like an outpost Jonathon might have stumbled upon trekking through the Blue Ridge Mountains of Kentucky in the Nineteenth Century. There was an old country store and a couple of dozen rustic cabins situated on either side of Reyes Creek, a lazy stream ambling through the community. The setting was tucked into the Cuyama Valley at about four thousand feet in the Los Padres National Forrest.

Ashley stood on the porch of the general store, wearing Levi's, hiking boots, and a smile. She waved him to follow her down toward the creek and pointed to a spot in front of a cabin that had two sets of deer antlers hanging from the front door. The fern-lined creek meandered along the back side of it.

The cabin had a wood-burning stove that had easily seen four score and ten years, a sink with running water from a nearby mountain spring, and a double bed with a thin mattress set on coiled box springs. The outhouse was a short walk, but a shower stall provided water from the nearby spring, which promised a bracing "Good morning."

Ashley had come prepared with two baskets of banned commodities. Venison jerky, organic corn, snap peas, cherries, oranges, and plums. She had breakfast items as well. All food products were now required to have been grown using genetically created seeds, to reduce the energy required to grow them naturally.

Ashley had also purchased three bottles of locally produced wine, two of Cabernet Sauvignon, one Merlot.

They ate and drank and made love all night.

Jonathon awoke to the smell of bacon, eggs, and coffee, and thought for a moment he was a kid again, living with his parents in the Valley.

"Good morning, Cowboy," Ashley said.

She was cooking the bacon and eggs on the wood burner, wearing her bra and panties, and she looked so sexy Jonathon almost charged from the bed.

"How much time have you got, Ash?"

She looked over her shoulder at him. "Let's eat first."

He walked across the cabin floor naked and into the shower stall. He stepped in, turned the handle, and let out a scream like a wolf caught in a bear trap. After a minute he soaped up, washed it off, and toweled dry.

He threw on some pants, socks, and a tee-shirt. Ashley put the two plates of bacon and eggs on the small, wooden table, threw some clothes on, and sat down to eat with him.

When they were done, they took their coffee to the back porch, dangled their feet over the edge, and watched in silence as the creek bubbled by on its cryptic journey down the valley.

"What are we going to do?" he asked.

"About us? Or the condition of the country?"

"Us. I love you, Ash. I don't want to have to sneak off to see you every two or three months. Let's get married."

She leaned over and kissed him on the cheek. "I love you too, Jonathon, but we've had this conversation—"

"We are working on the same team now. We have the same goal. You could move to D.C.—"

"Jonathon, the DHS would have me in leg-irons in a heartbeat. You know that."

He looked back down at the creek and back at her. "It's killing me, Ash."

She put her head on his shoulder. "I'm yours," she said. "You know, if we actually pull this off you can commute any sentence that could result from my earlier acts of 'terrorism.'"

"I will commute your sentence, but it will cost you."

He picked her up and carried her back to bed, where they spent the rest of the morning engaged in their own brand of sexual entertainment. A little after noon they got up and shared the ice-cold shower, which they had taken to calling Siberia Falls, wrapped in each other's arms. Fresh and shivering, they dressed and walked out of the cabin into brilliant, afternoon sun.

They strolled hand-in-hand down the dirt road that ran out of town. They found a cluster of majestic pines and sat on the carpet of pine needles beneath them. Ashley had a bag of fruit and nuts, and they snacked and talked about the future.

When they were about to return to their cars and go their separate ways, Ashley told him Agnes had been able to place a

Saratoga operative inside DHS headquarters in Washington. "She has one unconfirmed report that someone at DHS is monitoring legislators. You watch your back, Jonathon."

Chapter Forty-Two – Sheideck
March 14, 2039, Washington, D.C.

"I thought you said he was going to California for a fundraiser," Schmidt said.

"That's right," Monica replied.

"Then what the fuck is he doing in the Los Padres National Forest?"

"The what?"

"I put a nano-tracker on his briefcase," Schmidt declared. "He drove a couple of hours out of LA to a bump-in-the-road in the Los Padres National Forest called Sheideck. What would he be doing there?"

"I have no idea," Monica said.

"Why the fuck not?" Schmidt yelled.

"Because I am not his scheduler or his appointment secretary or in charge of his fundraising." She had an edge in her voice. "You wanted to know his legislative priorities. I am his Chief Legislative aide."

Schmidt disconnected the conversation and summoned Maya Contreras.

Maya, palms sweating, took two steps into Schmidt's office and stood trying not to shake. He seemed to have an ever-present lecherous aura about him.

"I want all video feeds for the last forty-eight hours," he said, "with or without facial recognition programming, from a small community north of Los Angeles called Sheideck. Sheideck, California. Also, all drone and satellite imagery."

"Yes, Dr. Schmidt."

"I want it ASAP."

"We will need an authorization from the Pentagon to access the satellite feeds from the Air Force, Dr. Schmidt," she said. "Shall I prepare the request for your signature?"

"That will take fucking forever," he responded. "Don't you know anyone over there? Tell them it is a matter of national security."

"Yes, sir."

"If anyone has any questions, you tell them this is coming from my office and involves a possible act of terrorism against the Homeland."

"Yes, sir."

A hellacious blizzard had ripped through the nation's capital during the night, causing the traffic inching across the Theodore Roosevelt Bridge into an endless, snow-bound caterpillar.

Maya Contreras tried to keep her nerves under control, knowing Schmidt would be livid when she arrived late. He would accept no excuses for her not having the reports he had requested by 8:30 a.m. He had taken the alarmingly unusual step of iDevicing her at home last night for an update, of which there had been none.

"I want it first thing, Ms. Contreras, understood?"

"Yes, Dr. Schmidt."

It was 9:15 when she knocked on his office door. She clenched her teeth, prepared for an angry dressing-down, but he was so anxious to get his hands on the reports he grabbed them from her without saying a word.

Paper reports were rare, but Schmidt had specifically asked they not be sent to his iDevice.

She had reached the door, on the way out, when he spoke. "What the fuck is this?"

"I'm sorry, Dr. Schmidt?" She had not read the reports.

"This report from the FBI says there are no video feeds from Sheideck, California." He continued reading as she stood there. "It says there is only one commercial establishment in Sheideck, California, a general store, and they maintain no security cameras of any kind."

"Yes, sir," she said, as if she had read the report.

Schmidt put the FBI report to the side and read the next one. "What the fuck?" he asked again.

"Sir?"

"The Air Force claims to have no satellite surveillance of Sheideck, California," he said. "According to their records, the town has a total of seventeen permanent residents. They don't waste resources on it. What about drone surveillance?"

Maya Contreras swallowed. "There is no drone surveillance in the area Dr. Schmidt."

"Fuck!" he screamed and threw the reports on the floor. "Get me two terrorism investigators. I want every fucking person in that hole interrogated personally. You understand? It's a matter of national security. Have HR get me investigative personnel immediately."

"Yes, sir." She trembled as she walked back to her desk and told her iDevice to contact the Director of Human Resources for the Department of Homeland Security.

Chapter Forty-Three – An Inconvenient Truth
March 14, 2039, Brentwood, California

The aging film star hosting the fundraiser answered the door personally. She wore a sheer blouse, no bra, and was pulling on a hash pipe.

She had a house full of celebrity friends who had forked over five thousand credits each to nosh on sushi and sip sake with the Senator. Jonathon kissed cheeks, shook hands, and stood for photo ops with starlets.

He talked tax policy with studio execs, sang a karaoke duet with a country recording artist, politely bowed out on an invitation to spend the night with a porn star, and caught the 8:00 a.m. American flight to Reagan National.

Here he was, he thought, sipping his coffee on the 1,500 mph flight home, with access to some of the most watched and listened to people in the country, in the world, and he could not talk to them about what really mattered.

They fawned over his work for environmental justice, and despite four decades of cooling global temperatures, a director had given him a script for a remake of An Inconvenient Truth. The script brushed over the inconvenient truth that virtually all of Al Gore's predictions of environmental Armageddon had never materialized.

It drove him crazy not to talk about what really mattered.

The Saratoga strategy has to work, he thought, or I will have wound up forwarding the cause of Constitutional destruction.

Shortly after 9 a.m. the following morning, Monica gave a couple of light knocks on Jonathon's door. Again she didn't wait for an invitation and entered the office. This time it backfired. Jonathon was in a conversation with someone on his iDevice and the holographic function was enabled. He was speaking to the Majority Leader.

Jonathon gazed at her with a scowl.

"Oh. Pardon me, Senator," she said, and turned and walked out, her face flushed with embarrassment.

An hour later the receptionist, Cynthia Blackwood, told her she could see the Senator now. This time she knocked and waited for him to answer.

"Come on in, Monica."

When she sat down, he said, "Look, there is a lot going on in this office, as you know." Monica nodded. "Scheduling around here is somewhat new to all of us, so until further notice I've made a policy that Cynthia will handle my in-office staff scheduling. You can just check with her in the future as to my availability. Make sense?"

Monica nodded again.

"Okay," he remarked. "What have you got for me?"

"The terms of the IMF loan proposal."

"Okay," he said. "Let's do it."

Monica deployed a holographic image of a document with the heading Term Sheet.

The first item was a seventeen-paragraph plan, written in the elegance of international finance legalese, regarding the regulation of U.S. tax policy.

Jonathon opened a drawer and pulled out a lined legal pad. Monica looked at the pad then to Jonathon and back to the pad as if he had made a horrid mistake.

"Some of us are dinosaurs," he said, and started diagraming the progression of conditions set forth in the agreement with boxes and arrows. He had filled two pages with diagrams, charts, and lines before he put his pen down, sat back in his chair, and looked at her. "This ultimately gives them control over our tax policy."

"They can't set policy," she said, as if giving him a way to defend the provision.

"No," he replied, "but they can reject any tax provision they disagree with. Which, in the final analysis, gives them control."

He sounded opposed, but she couldn't tell for sure. Schmidt would want to know what he thought. "What's your take, Senator?"

"It would be a pivotal step," he remarked. "What would the political fallout be?"

"The public deserves the help," she said.

"Come on, Monica. That is not the question I asked."

"The national iDevice polls," she offered, "show the public continues to be disgusted with Congress to a point bordering on rage, but close to half are opposed to trying to let the IMF meddle in domestic affairs. A like number are in favor. Fifteen percent are undecided."

Jonathon made some notes on his legal pad. "What's next?"

"A one thousand-credit penalty per child to be imposed on any couple with more than one child," she answered.

Jonathon made another note. "The dependents deduction was eliminated, what...five years ago?"

"Seven years ago now, Senator, and the funding for family planning must be increased annually at one hundred fifty percent of the rate of inflation," her reply.

Cynthia's voice came through his iDevice. "The delegation from the San Jose Environmental Forum is here, Senator."

"We'll finish this later," he said to Monica.

"Certainly," she said. "How did the fundraiser go Senator?"

"Excellent," he responded. He stood, rolled down and buttoned his sleeves and the top button of his shirt, then tightened his tie.

"Good to hear." She picked up her iDevice and left the office. Her attraction and admiration for Jonathon was growing, along with unexpressed sexual desires. There would be a right time. But now she had to put that aside, she had a job to get done.

The time was a little after 10:00 p.m. when Jonathon returned home. He settled in his den with his alt iDevice perched on a mahogany end-table. The holographic function was enabled and Agnes Morningcloud blossomed into the room.

"Ashley made it home safely," she said.

"Good."

"She seemed to glow," Agnes added.

Jonathon allowed himself a moment of recollection and smiled before he said, "I've got a legislative aide named Monica Ruiz."

"Yes, I know."

Someone came into Agnes's office and asked a question, which Jonathon couldn't hear. Agnes told them to come back in fifteen minutes. "Is there a problem with Monica?" she then asked.

"She flashed me a bunch of thigh the other night," he replied. "Clear invitation."

"If you didn't look like a young Leonardo Di Caprio you wouldn't have those problems," she said.

He got the tease. "Leo is sixty-five."

"Leo? You're comrades?"

"He's a committed environmentalist. We've talked. But that's not the point."

Sarge stood up, put his paws out in front of himself, and stretched. He ambled over to Jonathon and put his head on his lap, hinting for a scratch behind the ears. Jonathon complied.

"I know," she agreed. "Look. We checked her out when she joined the campaign. Background checked. Biometric ID valid. Eyebrow raising IQ. Passed the polygraph. Initial review found no enemy connections. She's clean. At least she was."

"Okay. Okay," he said. "More importantly, I have to figure out how to kill this IMF loan without showing my colors. The loan terms turn the country over to them, gives them control over our tax policy, and it implements enhanced population control. There's more, but those are key."

"When's the vote?" she asked.

"We just have a few days."

Not far from Jonathon's residence, Robin Delgado's apartment, rented under her cover name Monica Ruiz, was not as fancy as Senator Carr's, but her alt iDevice was hooked into the DHS's fiber optic system, which was instant.

"How is he going to vote on the IMF terms?" Schmidt asked.

"I don't know yet," she said. "I get the sense he is opposed, but he hasn't said that."

"I don't need your 'sense.' I need to know what he's going to do."

"He's been noncommittal so far."

"Why don't you get him in bed and fuck his brains out and see if he talks," he said.

"I've made entrees. No joy." She added, "I think I'd enjoy it."

"Did he talk about his trip?"

"Just that the fundraiser was 'excellent.'"

"He didn't talk about anything else? Any mention of Sheideck?"

"No."

"I've got two investigators on their way there now," Schmidt said. "We'll find out just what he was doing there and who he met with and why. He was not a progressive then and his political masquerade now is only for fools to believe. His political views are extreme and antipathetic to the best interests of this country. I'm going to prove it and then I'm going to lock him up."

Chapter Forty-Four – DHS Odd Couple
March 17, 2039, Sheideck, California

There was no agency drone transportation to Sheideck from LAX. Nor could iDrives operate on the dirt roads of the Los Padres National Forest.

Mohammed Abboud had reptilian eyes and the full beard of Muslim manhood and his partner, Farah Kashani, a colorfully tattooed lesbian, styling a masculine coiffure and of Pakistani heritage, drove an electrically powered Hongqi, a car of Chinese manufacture, into the mountains North of Los Angeles.

They were an odd couple. Not because of their differing sexual orientation or the lands of their forefathers–the DHS, after all, held diversity to be the most valued doctrine of the department—but because Farah Kashani considered Senator Carr one of the most important political figures in decades, due to his vigorous prosecution of climate injustice. Mohammed, who considered himself an Islamically-centered patriot, thought Carr was a United Nations stooge who should be barred from holding public office and perhaps tried for treason.

These conflicting points of view surfaced on the couple's trip from the nation's capital and had erupted into a shouting match on the way up to the mountain. In a harsh and louder than normal tone Farah fired a question to Mohammed but sounded more like an assertive comment – "You don't think major investor-owned fossil energy companies around this beautiful planet carry significant responsibility for climate change?"

"You and your climate change pussies," Mohammed yelled back, "don't have and never will have substantial climate change evidence. It's just a fucking scam."

"Look you ignorant fool," Farah attacked, "you've been blinded by your radical conservative propagandist." This rancor carried on for a while and by the time they arrived at Sheideck they were not speaking.

Mohammed parked the Hongqi in front of the Reyes Creek Bar and Grill, blocking the hitching post where locals tied their horses. There were no horses to be seen, but several motorcycles stood uniformly aligned in front of the saloon, awaiting the twenty-first century cowboys inside.

Mohammed grabbed his iDevice, got out of the car without saying anything, and headed to the tavern. The bar also served as the general store. Farah followed.

The wooden building resembled an old man who was about to fall over. The walls consisted of aged one-inch by eight-inch unpainted slats. Mohammed peeked into a large window next to the front entrance before pushing the door open and marching through, Farah a couple of steps behind him.

The bartender was a huge man of maybe thirty-five, his gut pouring out of a white tee-shirt. He had long, stringy, brown hair and a mountain-man beard. He was leaning on the bar, talking to a younger woman in an immodest tank top.

The bartender looked up from his conversation with Tank Top and squinted at Mohammed, who had stopped after taking a few steps into the bar. His gaze drifted to Farah and back to Mohammed.

"Are you the owner?" Mohammed asked.

"Who wants to know?"

"The Department of Homeland Security."

"Who's the gender trender?" the bartender inquired.

"Department of Homeland Security," Farah said. "Division of Domestic Terrorism. Here to arrest the Pillsbury Doughboy."

"The fuck you want?" the bartender demanded.

Mohammed walked over to the bar and called up the picture of Jonathon Carr on his iDevice.

"This man was here last week," Mohammed said.

"If you say so," Bartender replied.

"I do say so."

Pillsbury eyeballed Mohammed and offered nothing.

"Who was he with?" Farah asked.

Four guys in grease-laden Levi's and jean vests with the skeleton head and trailing feathered emblem of the Hell's Angels put their pool cues down on the pool table at the far end of the bar and sauntered toward the door.

"You guys see this guy here last week?" Mohammed asked, motioning at the hologram.

"We're just passing through," a beer-gutted Angel with an eye patch answered. "Ain't seen no one."

One of the group let out an "Oink" as they passed through the door.

The only ones left in the bar now were Fatso, Tank Top, Mohammed and Farah.

Farah walked over to the bar and sat down next to Tank Top. "How about you, Sweet Lips, you see this guy last week?" An unexpected hand landed on her thigh.

"Get your fucking hand off my thigh, bitch. I only bat from one side of the plate and it ain't yours," she said.

"It's your loss sweetie," Farah said. "What about the guy?"

"Never seen the guy," Tank Top replied, and then looked at the picture again. "Wait a minute, isn't he a movie star or something?"

"Nothing here," Mohammed gesturing to Farah to leave.

They walked out of the bar and decided to go house to house, or cabin to cabin. It only took one door. The occupant was a sixty-something woman with dirty, gray hair and several teeth missing.

"What did he do?" she asked and brought forth a cough that started from deep in her lungs. She hacked phlegm onto the dirt next to Mohammed.

"We're just checking on some things," he said.

"You one of them Muslims?" she asked.

"I am," he replied. "Did you see this man?" He motioned to the holographic image again.

"Was he with the blonde?" the woman asked.

"What blonde?" from Farah.

Thelma Severtson explained that there had been a tall, blonde woman, an out-of-towner, in the general store last week buying food. She hadn't seen a man with her.

Mohammed and Farah went back to visit Mr. Pillsbury. Mohammed approached the bar.

"Had a tall blonde woman, late twenties to early thirties, out of towner, come by the store last week?" he asked.

"She sure was pretty," Pillsbury answered. "You don't have women up in these parts looking like that. Rented one of the cabins for a night."

"What was her name?" Mohammed queried.

"I don't know," Pillsbury replied.

"She must have given you an iDevice account to charge."

Fatso took a pull on his beer and then shook his head. "Don't use that electronic money up here," he said. "She paid cash."

"That's against the law," stated Farah.

"So is the sexual harassment you laid on my lady, so fuck off."

They got the key and headed down the dusty road to the cabin with two sets of antlers on the door. Some rudimentary housekeeping had been done, but it did not take them long to find several strands of long, blonde hair on the floor of the shower stall.

They scanned the strands of hair with the forensic function on Mohammed's iDevice, capturing its molecular structure, and sent it to the DHS's forensic lab in D.C.

Seventeen minutes later they received an analysis from the lab. The hair belonged to one Ashley Lawford, a fugitive. She was wanted for having assaulted a TSA officer and escaping from a Behavioral Education Center in 2025. She had been sent to the behavioral center after engaging in acts of terrorism at Barack Obama High School in Thousand Oaks, California.

According to the report she had not been heard of since her escape over thirteen years ago, but if located she should be considered dangerous, apprehended, and committed to a level-three behavioral facility for domestic terrorists.

Chapter Forty-Five – The Hack
March 20, 2039, Washington, D.C.

Sarge poised like a boot camp recruit, sitting at attention, immobile with ears erect, eyes laser-focused on Jonathon, who was cooking a steak on one burner and sautéing mushrooms on another. Both activities, eating animal protein and cooking with gas, were frowned upon but had yet to be legally banned. They were, however, viewed as predictive indicators of future anti-government activity.

The iDevice droned through the terms of the IMF loan agreement over the sound of the sizzling steak. Jonathon had promised his constituents that he would read every page of legislation he voted on. In retrospect he regretted the promise but felt he had to keep it, and he didn't think listening to the language as opposed to reading it violated his commitment.

For entertainment he used the male voice on the iDevice with a Texas accent, though one could select a female or what was designated "no genetic orientation" voice.

As he slid the mushrooms from the frying pan onto his plate, the iDevice hiccupped, was silent for a second, and then carried on. Jonathon put the plate down and glanced over at the device, sitting on the counter. He went to the machine and told it to pause, backup fifteen seconds, and come forward. He watched the text as the iDevice complied. When it came to the end of section 301.48 on page 1738, it paused for a moment and then skipped forward to section 301.50.

###

At 9:17 the following morning, Jonathon summoned Monica to his office and asked her to take a seat. "Pull up page seventeen thirty-eight of the IMF loan agreement on your iDevice."

She placed her iDevice on his desk, enabled hologram, and called for the page. "Yes, Senator?"

"What does section 301.49 say?"

She manually scrolled down the page. Her brow furrowed. She scrolled back up and then down the page again. "It seems the agreement has been incorrectly numbered," she replied. "It skips from 301.48 to 301.50."

"Check with someone in Senator Horowitz's office next door," Jonathon said. "See if their version is also numbered in this way. If there is a section 301.49, please get me the wording."

"Yes, Senator." She stood and walked to the door. "It should just take a minute." She gave him her most demure smile and left.

Ten minutes later Monica knocked, stuck her head in the door when acknowledged, and said, "There is no section 301.49. Jeremy, Senator Horowitz's Chief of Staff, hadn't read it, but when he pulled his copy up, he said it simply looked like a misprint."

"Okay, Monica. Thank you."

Jonathon grabbed his coat and told Cynthia he would be out for a while but she could message him if needful. He walked down the hall to the office of Senator Elizabeth Ferguson and asked the receptionist if she was in. The young woman pressed a button and said, "Senator Carr is here to see you." She gave him her one thousand-watt smile. "Go right in, Senator."

They were both freshmen, and though from different parties had taken a strong liking to each other. Lizzie was older and always seemed to have a beautiful smile on her face. She reminded Jonathon of his mother.

He pretended to disagree with her on matters of policy, but in truth they were very politically aligned, and somehow she seemed to sense it.

"Now, what's a young, good-looking Progressive doing in my office?" she asked. "You want to convince me how wonderful this IMF loan is?"

"Have you read it?" he inquired.

"It's twenty-six hundred pages long and the vote on the loan terms isn't for a week yet. You're lobbying for this thing already?"

"Not really," he replied. "Can I ask you a favor?"

"Sure," she said, "as long as it's not for my support of it."

"No. Can you call up your copy of the agreement? Page seventeen thirty-eight."

"Hmm, okay," she responded with a quizzical expression on her face.

Jonathon watched Lizzie, not the agreement. "Can you tell me what your copy of the agreement says at section 301.49?"

Lizzie asked her iDevice for the section. She peered at her screen, glanced up and down the page. "That section is missing."

The old, brick building on North Capital Avenue still had Government Printing Office engraved above the front door, but the name had been changed to the Government Publishing

Office in 2014 to recognize the ascendancy of digital publishing. Whatever the name, it was here that all federal government documents were printed or published.

The Director, a gray-haired Filipino woman named Victoria Santos, rose from behind her desk when he entered. She walked around it and shook his hand. At five feet one inch she stood just shy of a full foot shorter than Jonathon.

"What in the world brings the junior Senator from California down from the Pantheon of the Capitol to our humble abode?" she asked.

"Thank you for seeing me, Director Santos," he said. "I have a question I am hoping you can help me with."

"We are at your service," she offered. "Please have a seat."

Jonathon sat, activated his iDevice, and called up page 1738 of the IMF loan agreement. He asked Victoria Santos to read the page. As she got to the bottom of the page, she squinted. "Perhaps your iDevice—"

"The section is also missing in Senator Horowitz's and Senator Ferguson's copies," Jonathon said. "My question is, was it a numbering mistake, or has the section been omitted?"

She told her secretary to have the Chief of Operations come to her office. Mitchell Sanders came in wiping ink from his hands with a tattered rag. The Director introduced Senator Carr and then showed Sanders the omitted section. "The section is also missing from other Senators' copies. Is it a numbering error?"

Sanders, a heavy-set man with a handlebar mustache, stated, "Absolutely not." He appeared indignant. "There is a section 301.49."

"How do you know?"

"Because I read it."

"You read the entire agreement?" Jonathon asked.

"Every page."

Without asking permission, Sanders left the office. He returned three minutes later with the GPO's master iDevice. He placed it on the Director's desk and called up page 1738 of the IMF loan agreement.

Section 301.49 was titled LOAN COLLATERAL. Showing several paragraphs long.

"Like I said. There's section 301.49."

The Director quickly scanned the section and then gave the iDevice to Jonathon. He began reading the section out loud. His eyes were riveted. "Borrower hereby grants the International Monetary Fund, to secure the payment and performance in full of all of the Obligations, a continuing security interest in, and pledges to the Fund, the Collateral, wherever located, whether now owned or hereafter acquired or arising, and all proceeds and products thereof. Borrower represents, warrants, and covenants that the security interest granted herein shall be a first priority."

With a sense of foreboding he continued reading.

When he finished, Sanders asked to see the agreement displayed on Jonathon's iDevice, sitting on the Director's desk. He studied it for a moment. "Someone must have tampered with the wording before the legislators received it."

"Tampered?" Victoria Santos asked.

"We've been hacked," Sanders chimed in. "Someone deleted the section."

Victoria looked at Jonathon waiting for him to say something. Silence permeated the room. He had an idea of who was behind this but how to expose it and when.

Chapter Forty-Six – The Leak
March 21, 2039, DHS Headquarters, Washington, D.C.

Oscar Schmidt's dome-shaped pate glistened as he paced back and forth in front of State TSA Directors, packed into a stuffy conference room. The group was a palette of the social and sexually diverse. Government hiring regulations mandated that federal employees maintain quotas for all minority populations including the obese, the mentally challenged, dwarfs and all segments of LGBTQ, black, brown, red, and yellow.

"She is a violent domestic terrorist and a fugitive from justice," he barked. "I want this picture sent to every agent in the country. I want it programmed into all facial recognition systems and uploaded to all drone patrols. I want her found!"

He held up a picture of Ashley Lawford as a fifteen-year-old patient of the Covina Behavioral Education Center. It had been enhanced by a genetic programming algorithm that added fifteen years to her features and several inches to her hair.

The TSA had evolved from its earliest operations in airports following 9/11, which had been enshrined into a national day of mourning, to trains, buses, and cabs, then to all federally funded highways, toll roads, educational campuses, and all public buildings. There were now more than eight hundred fifty thousand TSOs, or Transportation Security Officers, who were Mother's human tentacles into society.

###

In the evening Agnes and Ashley sat on the trunk of a fallen redwood, dangling their legs over a quietly bubbling creek like a couple of kids on a wilderness hike. A gray fox moved cautiously to the edge of the creek, dipped its head, and lapped some water. Its head jerked up and he stood motionless, surveying the other side of the creek. Apparently seeing nothing of immediate import, it trotted off beneath a canopy of swordtail ferns.

"They know you were at Sheideck," Agnes said.

"What? Who?" Ashley asked.

"DHS. Our agent inside was at a meeting yesterday of all State TSA Directors. Schmidt showed an enhanced version of your high school picture to everyone. It's not perfect, but it's close enough to be dangerous. It's going out on the entire DHS iDevice network, the facial recognition system, and drone programs."

"Over thirteen years," she said. "All gone." She stiffened. "My God, what about Jonathon? Do they know he was with me?"

"They must have tracked him to Sheideck," Agnes replied. "That would be how they got the lead on you. Maybe a nano-tracker. He wasn't mentioned at the meeting but we have to assume they know. A plus is they have no idea where you are based. Stay at the top camp, no trips to town. Let me know if you need anything."

###

Despite the fact Jonathon paid his neighbor's teenage

daughter to take Sarge to the park and have him chase down tennis balls on weekdays, the dog always wagged his tail furiously and danced around in circles while Jonathon changed into his running clothes.

The night carried a biting chill, but the sidewalks were still busy with GW students, and despite the grueling economy, cherry-blossom tourists were beginning to arrive in town. Jonathon and Sarge jogged through and around the crowds down Wisconsin Avenue to the dead-end at the water park, and then took the Capital Crescent Trail along the Potomac.

Jonathon caught sound bites from several of the jumbo digital news screens as they ran, which talked of little else but the pending vote on the five trillion loan from the IMF and the devastating effects a rejection of the loan would have on those in need. At a news conference earlier in the day, the President had made it clear that the loan would relieve the intense economic stress being experienced by so many Americans. "Once the country is back on its feet," he had promised, "we will repay the loan."

The current administration, Progressive to the core, was engaged in a full-court press, along with the media, to persuade the public to contact its representatives in Washington to support the agreement, unless they wanted to experience several more years of economic hardship.

The political truth was that if the loan agreement was not approved, the current administration could pack its bags after the next election, a fate worse than death for a politician.

The night air was bracing, and Jonathon picked up the pace as they ran beside the river. They ran up the pedestrian walkway to the Key Bridge and across the river to Arlington. When they reached the other side, he reversed course and they ran home.

Jonathon was pouring sweat and Sarge was happy but still

panting hard. He put a bowl of fresh water down for the dog and jumped into the shower. Towel-dried and dressed in sweats and a Cal Bears tee-shirt, he grabbed a bag of trail mix and a bottle of fresh water and made for the den. Sarge followed.

Jonathon accessed his alternative iDevice and connected with Agnes, who seemed troubled.

"We have to discuss this loan agreement," Jonathon said, "but you look like you have something on your mind."

"The DHS knows Ashley was in Sheideck. My guess is that they nano-tracked you. They have issued a warrant for her arrest."

Jonathon blanched. "Do they know where she is?"

"No."

Jonathon sat back and thought for a minute. Sarge got up from his spot in the corner and walked over to his master and put his head on his lap. Jonathon scratched him behind his ears and said to Agnes, "I screened everything here before I left, but they could have tagged me on the way through security."

"They are watching you, Jonathon," she warned.

"Schmidt?"

"Schmidt."

"Is she safe?"

"Depends on whether a DHS investigative team swings through Santa Cruz. She's encamped at the top of the mountain. I've told her to stay put. If they come to town, somebody is likely to ID her."

"Can you get her out of the country?" he asked.

"Good luck with that," she replied.

Jonathon threw his pen across the room. It hit the far wall and bounced to the floor. "I should have never asked her to meet me."

"What's done is done. She just needs to stay completely out of sight for now," Agnes said.

Jonathon put his head in his hands and sat that way for a good two minutes. Agnes said nothing. Sarge laying at his feet. A thought haunted him now. Will I lose her again? No, I can't let that happen. I don't know what I would do if I lost her again. Guilt flowed through his veins like a whitewater rush. Then a spark of hope consumed him. I know she'll be ok. She's too smart to be caught.

When he raised his head, Agnes said, "Meanwhile, we're expanding. Saratoga is expanding. People are being placed. We can do this, Jonathon."

He felt exhausted but he gathered himself, sat back up.

"I have to figure out what to do to kill this IMF loan agreement," he said. "The five trillion dollar loan would never be repaid and the collateral for the loan includes the natural resources of the entire country. It is a bloodless coup."

"What do you mean?" she asked.

He told her about his visit to the GPO, how the legislative file had been hacked. and that the section on the collateral had been covertly removed.

"What does it say?"

"Section 301.49 says..." Jonathon quoting from memory. "Borrower hereby grants The International Monetary Fund, to secure the payment and performance in full of all of the Obligations, a continuing security interest in, and pledges to the Fund, the Collateral, wherever located, whether now owned or hereafter acquired or arising, and all proceeds and products thereof. Borrower represents, warrants, and covenants that the security interest granted herein shall be a first priority . . ."

"Okay, okay. What is the collateral?" Agnes asked.

"All public land and all resources thereon and therein owned by the government of the United States of America."

"That's insane."

Jonathon continued.

"All forests and timber thereon, parks, recreational facilities; all agriculture products of any kind produced on the public land of the government of the United States of America—"

"These people are mad," she interrupted. "Who knows about this?"

"Right now, the management of the Government Publications Office and yours truly. That will all change tomorrow because the corrected version is going to be securely sent to the iDevices of all of the legislators by noon."

"Not a lot of time," Agnes stated, "and not a lot of wiggle room. If you oppose the loan, you show your colors."

"If I vote in favor of it I couldn't live with myself. But I have an idea."

Jonathon heard Max bark. Sarge's ears shot up. He stood and looked toward the iDevice.

"Give me a minute," Agnes said. "Someone's at the door." She disappeared from the hologram.

Sarge remained focused on the iDevice until Agnes retuned to the holographic image and resumed speaking. "Messenger," she said. "You were saying?"

"The collateral section was obviously omitted because those pushing the loan think public disclosure of these terms could stop it. I think an explosive exposure of the hacking of this section might defeat the legislation."

"The terms of the agreement are supposed to be confidential," she voiced. "Only members of Congress have access. If you publicize it they'll come after you regardless of the language."

"Exactly," he responded. "That's why I want you to do it."

"Me?" she queried. "Oh, you want me to leak it." She thought a moment. "I know just the person."

"Someone in the network?" he asked.

"Yes and no. You'd be surprised at the number of broadcasters who are just waiting for us to launch, but this guy is different. I have a contact at the Times. He doesn't know who I am but he takes my information and runs with it. I'll suggest he contact Director Santos for verification. She won't confirm it, but she won't deny it, either. With the new versions hitting every legislator on the Hill, the source of the leak will not be identifiable."

"Tell him," Jonathon said, "imply very strongly that the IMF itself, wanting to own and control our natural resources, hid the section. The truth is it was either them or the administration."

"Once the Times article is published, the very moment, I will commence an attack on the IMF." He thought a moment. "How they are trying to steal our resources right out from under our noses and are committing felonies in doing so."

"They'll deny it," she countered with a smile in her voice. "Vehemently."

"Exactly," he said, "and a denial in D.C. means you're guilty. Besides, there's nothing more Progressive than attacking a bank. How is the administration going to oppose that?"

"Brilliant," she said. "If the administration did it, and I wouldn't put it past this pathetic president to do something like this in order to hold onto his presidency and re-election, they will probably join the attack to deflect attention from their crime."

"It's good in theory," Jonathon added, "but if the source of the leak gets traced back to me, my political career is over. The whole game is over."

Chapter Forty-Seven – Not On My Watch
March 30, 2039, National Press Club,
Washington, D.C.

The headline of Jonathon's press release had the conference room at the National Press Club, where virtually every news organization on the planet had an office or a representative, packed by 9:00 a.m.

All the tables were full, and reporters from the less prestigious news services lined the rear of the room, iDevices on audio-video record mode and held high.

"Leave it to a cabal of rapacious foreign bankers to try to steal our national resources like a thief in the night," Jonathon proclaimed, holding up a fist full of papers, his voice rising. "They tried to steal our oil, our gas, our gold, our silver, our forests, trees, and parks, our—"

"Aren't the terms of the loan agreement confidential, Senator?" Skyler, a Washington Post journalist interrupts.

"They are," Jonathon replied. "What I hold in my hand is the article published in the Times this morning, quoting the Chief of Operations at the GPO. It explains the hack and the subterfuge, and it contains the collateral section, which had been deleted. That's a crime."

The reporter for the Times, apparently unable to reach the Director, had found his way to Mitchell Sanders, who considered that a crime had been committed on a branch of the United States Government, since the GPO was the publishing arm of the U.S. Congress, and he felt duty-bound to report it. That, and he was quite determined not to be the scapegoat for the missing collateral section.

Part of Agnes's deal with the reporter was that she get a copy of the article before it was published, as long as she promised not to disclose it before 9:00 a.m., when it would hit the iDevice wire.

When Jonathon finished his talk, the room exploded. Half the reporters bolted to their offices down the hall to write their stories. The other half mobbed Jonathon when he left the podium.

"What does this mean to the IMF loan, Senator?" Eleanor, a Daily Tribune reporter asked.

"Are we to borrow money from thieves?" Jonathon replied. "From European bankers who have apparently committed a felony on the government of the United States, in a secret scheme to abscond with the assets of everyday Americans? I don't think so."

"What about the unemployed and the elderly and—"

He cut the reporter off. "There is more than one way to skin a cat, Eleanor. We will not leave our nation nor our most disadvantaged to be covertly plundered by the banking vultures from the IMF. The decent, deserving citizens of the United States will not be crucified on the cross of international banking. Not on my watch."

He said the last sentence with such force and finality, for a few moments the room went silent. Then it exploded again.

A Progressive Senator opposing the IMF bailout alone was blood in the political waters to the media sharks. But he was attacking Big Banking, the traditional foil of Progressives. Which made it all right, didn't it?

The media didn't really care. It was controversy. A David and Goliath, and they feasted.

Overnight, Senator Jonathon Carr, the Hollywoodesque-handsome junior Senator from California, was all anyone could talk about.

The jumbo digital media screens that dominated every major population center in the country ran his post-press conference interview again and again.

"Not on my watch!" took on a life of its own. The phrase screamed through the iDevice universe and became the most-repeated line on all social media channels. The hottest-selling items at Amazon.com were tee-shirts and baseball hats with "Not on my watch!" stenciled on them.

Jonathon Carr had gone from a political personage scarcely known outside California to a national brand. He had touched a nerve.

Oscar Schmidt sat in his glass-walled living space in Arlington, Virginia. Glorix26, his cyborg mate de jour, sat next to him, her head on his lap. She wore no clothes. He stroked her head and back as if she were a pet dog.

Schmidt was watching late-night television when the host introduced "The junior Senator from California, Not-on-my-watch Jonathon Carr." The audience clapped, cheered, whistled, and hooted.

Schmidt shoved Glorix26 off his lap. She slammed her head on the marble floor and howled like a wounded dog. Schmidt screamed at her to shut up. Glorix26 got to her feet, a blood type liquid, almost like human blood, dripping from her scalp. She touched her hand to the injury, saw the blood, and did something forbidden to all cyborgs. She dove at Schmidt and tore at his face with her fingernails, drawing blood herself. Stunned, it took Schmidt a moment to understand what had occurred. He kicked her in the stomach. Glorix26 staggered back several steps.

He ran to his bedroom, got his laser pistol, and returned. She was standing next to the couch, naked, bleeding from the head, her face a mask of fury. He shot her in the left breast and then the head. She dropped to the floor, spasmed for a moment, and terminated.

Schmidt left her lying there. He would call the cyborg removal detail in the morning. There would be paperwork, but nothing of concern for Dr. Schmidt.

He returned to the sofa and watched the rest of the interview on his wall screen. When it was over, he pulled Monica up on his iDevice.

"Your boy is a celebrity," he said.

"I know. The staff is spending half of its time handling reach-out from the press."

"What's he up to?"

"I don't know, but he's been meeting with leadership," she replied.

"What are they discussing?"

"I don't know. Not yet."

"Well, fucking find out. You're his legislative aide for Christ's sake."

Monica didn't respond. She was perturbed but he couldn't tell from the expression on her face.

He doubled down. "I also need you to see if there is any reference in his office to an Ashley Lawford. Any mention at all."

"Who is she?" Monica asked.

Was that a note of jealousy he detected? Schmidt thought.

"She is a convicted terrorist and a fugitive," he bellowed, "and it was she who he went to see before that fundraiser in Los Angeles."

"Can we prove it?" she asked.

"Not yet, but I will be able to soon," Schmidt declared. "We are investigating leads as to her whereabouts. When we get her, I assure you she will talk about Jonathon Carr."

Chapter Forty-Eight – The Profile
April 4, 2039, Washington, D.C.

The fanfare and the celebrity lasted less than a week.

Guesting on a Sunday morning political talk show, the host asked, "It's a great slogan, Senator, if we aren't going to get the money from the IMF and the Fed is not a source, how do you propose to help the millions of disadvantaged Americans out there?"

Jonathon had been thinking of nothing else since the press conference. "I have some proposals I am working on with some of my colleagues," he replied. "That is all I can say right now, Brian, but stay tuned."

Brian let him skate with that, but patty-cake wouldn't last long. He was now a brand, a political celebrity, which meant meat for feasting. The media whores would poke and pry and dig to find any little crack in the glowing armor currently blanketing the golden boy from California if it meant increased webNet news sales and ratings.

His new status opened doors to possibilities he hadn't contemplated opening for years. It also brought new responsibilities and dangers.

Lena Bullock, the gravel-voiced senior Senator from New York, was the Senate Majority Leader. Behind her back she was known as the Old Junkyard Dog. She knew this, of course, and pretended to be angered by its use, but secretly cultivated the image. The Progressives controlled the Senate and Lena ruled her domain like a Mafia Don. She demanded and rewarded party loyalty and punished deviation therefrom.

The American Conservative Party, the re-branded incarnation of the Republican Party, controlled the House.

It only made sense, Jonathon thought, to start on his home turf and within his own party. If he could marshal the Majority Leader's support he would have a towering stack of chips with which to bargain with the Speaker of the House.

The Majority Leader's office was all polished mahogany, silver trays, and leather chairs. She took a pack of cigarettes out of her top desk drawer, lit one, and offered a smoke to Jonathon, who declined.

"Well, Senator," she said, "I don't know how exactly, but you seem to have turned the entire country against the one thing that could save them. You've managed to box us into a nasty corner politically."

She took a pull on the cigarette and blew the smoke in his direction. "You breathe a word about this to the press, you will never see a committee assignment in this body."

Jonathon held both hands up in a mock sign of submission. Everyone knew she smoked but he wasn't going to burst her bubble. "The IMF loan is actually not the only thing that can save them, Madame Majority Leader."

"The Fed shut us down," she declared. "Where else are we going to get that kind of money?"

"It would take some work," he replied, "but here is what we could do…"

###

At the same time Jonathon was explaining his plan to the Majority Leader, a DHS immigration agent named Martino Mastrelli entered the lavish offices of Dubinova, one of Manhattan's most prestigious modeling agencies. The lobby, a three-story glass atrium, brilliant in an afternoon sun, blazed with color. Classical music floated through the atmosphere. Pictures of some of the most stunning models in the world lined the walls.

Mastrelli had recently been promoted at the DHS and now carried a rather large stick. He approached the receptionist, a startlingly beautiful girl with white-blonde hair and ice-blue eyes.

"I am here to speak with Elena Dubinova," he announced, and flashed his DHS shield. This was his favorite mode of introduction and usually established his dominance in a conversation instantly.

The receptionist looked at the badge and back to Mastrelli with the bare fraction of a smile. "I'll see if she is in, Mr. Mastrelli. Do you have an appointment?"

"I am with the immigration enforcement branch of the Department of Homeland Security."

"How nice for you," she said. "May I tell her what this is regarding?"

"Immigration enforcement," he replied, feeling agitated as his face started to redden.

"Yes, of course," she responded and pressed a button. "Please have a seat. I'll try to locate her."

"You do that," he said, and walked over to a luxurious sofa and sat down.

After fifteen minutes, "Ms. Dubinova can see you now. Take the elevator to the penthouse and she will meet with you there."

Elena Dubinova was a well-preserved and sculpted fifty-four-year-old Russian-born American with the bearing of a czarina. She offered Mastrelli a cup of Siberian tea, which he accepted.

The woman had some serious political connections. Having spent hours scouring through DHS immigration records and identifying infractions by Dubinova models, he had some leverage, but he had to proceed so as to avoid attracting attention to his personally driven investigation or else she would call her lawyer and the interview would be concluded before it started.

No, he thought, he would give her friendly and polite.

"And what can I do for the Department of Homeland Security?" Elena Dubinova asked.

Mastrelli took a sip of his tea and carefully placed it back on the saucer. "From time to time we perform routine checks on businesses employing a large number of foreign-born as an extra protection from terrorists."

"How dreadfully boring," she commented.

"Yes, well, someone has to do it."

Ms. Dubinova forced a tight smile and said nothing.

"It seems," he said, after realizing she was waiting for him to continue, "that some of your models have irregularities in their immigration status."

"Impossible," she remarked. "Our HR department is scrupulous in verifying that all of our models are in strict compliance with U.S. immigration laws."

"Not according to our records." He activated his iDevice. "A man named Rene Pardue, a French national, and a woman named Aamino Ali Farah from Somalia have immigration infractions, according to my records."

"Rene Pardue hasn't been a client here for six months," Elena replied. "I'm sure your records are equally incorrect regarding the status of Aamino."

Mastrelli made an adjustment to his iDevice, removing Rene Pardue as a Dubinova client.

"I wonder if I may speak to Ms. Ali Farah. Perhaps we can clear the matter up."

Mastrelli had no intention of clearing anything up. His intention was to inflict some damage to Elena Dubinova and her agency for ruining his relationship with his fiancée. Aamino Ali Farah was one of the most sought-after and highly paid models in New York. He planned to ship her back to Somalia.

"She's on a shoot," Elena Dubinova said.

Their negotiations resulted in an agreement that Mastrelli could interview Aamino in the conference room at Dubinova when her current photo shoot was over, in two days.

Though he had seen pictures of the model, Mastrelli was struck by how tall and dynamic the woman was. A balding, pin-striped man with a chrome-plated iDevice and a brief-case accompanied Aamino into the conference room.

In attendance were Mastrelli, Dubinova's Director of HR, Aamino, and her attorney.

Mastrelli commenced after the introductions. "Ms. Ali Farah, you were granted a resident card, permanent resident status, a little more than ten years ago. Is that correct?"

Aamino turned to her attorney. He glanced at his iDevice and nodded.

"Yes," she replied.

"Did you know that a permanent-resident card holder has to renew their card every ten years?"

Again the attorney. Again the nod.

"Yes," she repeated.

"Well, Ms. Aamino, I must inform you that you are in violation of U.S. immigration laws. You did not file your ten-year extension." He managed to suppress his smile.

The lawyer took over. "You people need to get your house in order. I personally filed Ms. Ali Farah's ten-year extension at the end of last year. Take a look. You will see your department's certification of the document a full three months prior to the ten-year anniversary date." The attorney pressed a button on his iDevice that forwarded Aamino Ali Farah's resident-card extension to Mastrelli's.

Mastrelli looked at his iDevice. He squinted, clenched his jaw, and swallowed. "I see. There must have been a mistake." He offered no apology.

"If that is all, Mr. Mastrelli, we'll be going," the attorney said.

Aamino and the attorney both stood.

"At least I didn't have to call my good friend Senator Carr," she laughed.

"You know the Senator?" the HR Director asked.

"Many years ago, when I was a grad student at UC Santa Cruz, I was waiting tables. He came in one night with a lovely, young, blonde woman. I served them and we bantered. Nice couple."

Being disappointed that his plan backfired he excused himself and left the room. As he got out of the elevator an urgent dispatch from HQ hit his iDevice, activating a flashing red light. Mastrelli wasn't paying attention to where he stopped to glance at his iDevice and got bumped several times by people coming in and out of the elevator. What he saw was a picture of a troubled, young woman in institutional clothing. It was an urgent BE ON THE LOOK OUT. Below the picture was the name Ashley Lawford with several digital transitional aging profiles of her and a text reading "May have been seen in the company of Senator Jonathon Carr."

Mastrelli ran back to the elevator, pushed the up button. Just as Aamino and her attorney walked out of the office and into the hall his elevator door opened. He approached Aamino. "What was the name of the woman Senator Carr was with?"

"I have no idea," she answered. "This was ten years ago in a small restaurant in Santa Cruz, California."

"Would any of these be her?" he asked and showed her the pictures of Ashley.

Aamino looked at the pictures for some moments.

"You don't have to answer that," her attorney offered.

Aamino shrugged. "It could be. Like I said, this was ten years ago, but that could be her," pointing to one of the profiles.

Chapter Forty-Nine – Badlands
April 5, 2039, Washington, D.C.

Jerimiah Carter, a six-foot, nine-inch African-American, had been a six-time NBA all-star power forward for the Golden State Warriors and been inducted into the basketball Hall of Fame. An NBA icon, he retired from a storied career with a nine-figure bank account from his Nike endorsement deals and a decade of multi-million-dollar paychecks.

JC, as he was called, jumped from the world of hoops to politics and played that game just as well. He ascended from the mayor of Berkeley to the California Assembly and then to Congress in less than a decade. It took him another ten years, but he was now the Speaker of the House of Representatives and the third most powerful political figure in the United States.

JC had been a masterful student of the opposition on the court. He could think two, sometimes three moves ahead of the player who was guarding him, or whom he was guarding. It would seem as though he would leave his body and view the game from above and then return to the court and act. He found this ability served him admirably in politics as well. As Speaker and the leader of the Conservatives in the House, he was not about to meet with the Progressive Party's reigning poster boy. At least not in public.

Jerimiah refused Jonathon's invitation to dinner at the Four Seasons. At the same time, he was intrigued by Senator Carr's invitation to sit down privately, no aides, no recording devices, no media, to discuss a possible alternative solution to the IMF loan proposal.

There had been intense pressure from the public on both parties to take the loan from the IMF to relieve the grueling economic stress, until Carr's press conference. Economic conditions had not improved but the only apparent solution to the growing crisis had been taken off the table.

Jonathon got a call from Peggy Blackstone, the Speaker's Chief of Staff. "Do you know McCormick & Rutter's on K Street?"

"Sure," he replied.

"The restaurant has a back door that leads in through the kitchen, and there are small, closed-door dining rooms in the back reserved for private dinners."

"Yes," Jonathon said. "I know where they are."

"The Speaker will be having dinner in the room closest to the kitchen at six tomorrow night," she said. "No staff. iDevices deactivated. Please do not discuss the meeting with your staff."

"I understand," Jonathon confirmed, and hung up.

At 5:30 the following afternoon, Jonathon, wrapped in a black, Burberry raincoat, left his office and caught a cab to McCormick & Rutter. Cynthia, the receptionist, left a few minutes later, calling out to Monica that she was the last one in the office and to lock up.

Jonathon exited the cab a block from the restaurant. He flipped up his coat collar to partially cover his face. A hat with the bill pulled down covered his forehead and eyes. Most of the people on the street were looking at the sidewalk to keep their faces out of the rain. It was unlikely that anyone would recognize him on the short walk to the rear of the restaurant.

He went quietly in the back door and straight to the closed dining room next to the kitchen. He went in without knocking and quickly closed the door behind him.

"Come on in, Senator," JC said. "You can hang your things there on the coat rack."

Jonathon removed his coat, shook the rain off, and hung it. He tossed his hat on another peg and walked to the Speaker and shook his hand. "I appreciate your taking the meeting, Mr. Speaker."

"What do you say we keep it to first names?" JC asked. "No one here but you and me. No fucking iDevices, no aides, no press. Just a couple of old jock-straps. I understand you used to wrestle?"

"Perfect," Jonathon replied. "Yes, I used to wrestle, but an NCAA wrestling crown and the Basketball Hall of Fame are different universes." He sat.

JC shrugged. "Have some of these bacon-wrapped water chestnuts. The waiter will be here in a moment. Shall we get right to it?"

Jonathon slid his chair a little closer to the table and said, "Here's my idea."

Oscar Schmidt read the report on his iDevice a second time. He almost couldn't believe his eyes. Overwhelmed by excitement, as if he had hit pay dirt. His suspicion of Jonathon was warranted.

He took a couple of yoga deep breaths to calm himself down

and called the person who had sent the report, an immigration officer named Martino Mastrelli.

"Yes, Dr. Smith," Mastrelli said. He had heard the rumors about how to address the director.

"It's Schmidt not Smith..."

He didn't give Masterelli time to recover or apologize.

"This Somali woman," Schmidt said. "She positively identified Ashley Lawford?"

"Absolutely," Mastrelli lied. It didn't really matter. Aamino hadn't been entirely positive because Schmidt would launch DHS SWAT to find the woman in any case. He sought to capture a toehold on a commendation for providing the lead to the fugitive.

"Santa Cruz, California?" Schmidt asked, to confirm what was on the screen.

"Yes," Mastrelli responded. "The woman was waiting tables while doing graduate work at UC Santa Cruz. You see, the University of California is the senior public educational system in the state and there are campuses at..."

"For Christ's sakes, Mastrelli, I taught law at Boalt Hall on the Berkeley campus. I know the UC system. It's in my bio on the agency's website. Do your fucking homework on DHS management," he said gruffly and disconnected the call.

The manhunt began the following morning, led by black-jacketed DHS SWAT teams with bullet- and laser-resistant clothing, laser-powered pistols, and long-range firearms.

They marched through downtown Santa Cruz in six-man squads as if they were in enemy territory. Black, bulletproof shields covered their faces and nano-sized dots on their jaws carried communication feeds on a dedicated iDevice channel.

They had the digital transition pictures of Ashley on their

iDevice screens. The SWAT troops stormed into every store, barked at the owners or managers, and bullied every pedestrian, townie or tourist. Fascist behavior in the search for a domestic terrorist was no vice.

No one recognized Ashley until one SWAT-team member approached a surfer coming up from the ocean, carrying a surfboard.

"You know this woman?" SWAT asked, showing him the different digital pictures.

The surfer, clenching to his surfboard and with curious eyes, studied them for a moment. "I don't know her, but I used to see her around. She's a Troll."

"A what?"

"Bunch of off-grid people who live up in the mountains," the surfer said.

"What do you mean used to see her around? When was the last time you saw her?"

"I don't know. Maybe a few weeks ago down at the beach."

"Where in the mountains?" SWAT demanded.

"I don't really know man. Is that all? Can I go now?"

In thirty minutes the mountains above Santa Cruz were crawling with DHS SWAT troopers and the air was filled with drones that could identify human bodies at great distance with infrared imaging.

Two communities existed in the mountains above Santa Cruz. One was an off-grid group living off the land, growing organic vegetables, which was against the law, as Fed statue 746iGMO authorized only genetically modified crops. Although illegal, it was rarely prosecuted. The group also forbade any electronic contact with the outside world. The community was called by the pretentious name Eden and had three to four dozen inhabitants at any given time. There were a limited number of old-fashioned, semi-automatic handguns at Eden, but members primarily hunted with crossbows.

Marijuana use, harvested from their own crop, was common. Wine was plentiful. Cigarettes were forbidden. Eden was governed by an elected council that assigned community duties and administered the group's own, rather mild code of justice. A certain amount of sexual freedom was permitted, but seducing and having sexual involvement with another's husband, wife, or committed mate was punishable by banishment.

Ashley lived in Eden to the extent of sleeping and eating breakfast there before returning down the mountain to work with Agnes at her cabin.

Badlands was farther up the mountain, with about two dozen inhabitants. All of them were militant, anti-government activists. Many of the Badlands members were former military servicemen, and the encampment was heavily armed. Though not Saratoga members, on occasion Ashley would head up the mountain and, in the course of a conversation with a Badlands member with whom she had made an acquaintance, she would drop some intelligence that Agnes wanted spread to DHS.

The mountains were now crawling with DHS SWAT teams and the skies were abuzz with human-seeking Drones all in search of the domestic terrorist, Ashley Lawford.

This would be her last trip up the mountain.

Chapter Fifty – The Secret Meeting
April 6, 2039, Washington, D.C.

Jonathon returned from a hurried lunch in the Senate dining room with two things on his mind. First, how could he reconcile the competing demands of the Majority Leader and the Speaker? Second, despite repeated attempts over several hours last night, he had not been able to reach Agnes. He wanted to get her feedback on his proposed strategy following his meetings with the congressional leaders.

When he hadn't been able to reach Agnes, he had tried Ashley. No joy. He was concerned. He walked straight by Cynthia without a word and into his office. He rolled back in his chair, put both hands, clenched, on top of his head, shut his eyes closed and suspended in that position for a few minutes.

The afternoon went downhill from there. A call came from the Speaker's office. Cynthia, thinking it was good news, passed it through to his iDevice.

"I had you figured wrong, Senator," JC stated flatly. "You seemed like the kind of guy who kept his word."

"What makes you think I'm not?" Jonathon asked, a bit more edge to his voice than he intended.

"My Chief of Staff says The Post is running with a column in this afternoon's iDevice feed that you and I met for an important discussion."

"Wait a minute, JC," Jonathon said, confused by what he just heard. "I told no one about our meeting. Your Chief of Staff asked for confidentiality and I honored that."

"This gives me some serious problems with my caucus, Senator. Did you discuss our meeting with any of your staff?" the Speaker asked.

"I repeat, I honored your request. I discussed it with no one," Jonathon reaffirmed.

"We have a very tight relationship with The Post," the Speaker continued, "and our contact there tells us this information came from your office. He wouldn't say who, but from your office. I can't do business with someone who can't keep a confidence when it is needed."

"Why would I do that, JC?" Jonathon asked. "It makes no sense to leak anything about this until our deal is done."

"I don't know. Maybe you enjoy all the media attention you've been getting lately."

Jonathon bit his tongue. "Come on, JC, you know better than that. There's something else at play here because I told no one in my office about the meeting. No one. It must have been one of the staff at McCormick & Rutter."

"Our contact at The Post was quite specific as to the source of the story."

Jonathon glanced at a handwritten note he had made to himself on a pad when talking to the Speaker's Chief of Staff yesterday. "Stay with me on this, JC," he urged. "Let me look into the matter here. But know this. I don't play that kind of game."

The Speaker grunted and hung up.

###

After Cynthia had left yesterday, Monica had gone to the receptionist's always-organized desk. Having casually watched Cynthia login one morning, she found the code to the Senator's office in Cynthia's computer and killed the recording equipment in his office. She went in and quickly closed the door, walked over to his desk, and started rummaging through his drawers. She knew, of course, he kept the information on his iDevice, but was desperate to uncover a clue as to his intentions on the IMF loan agreement. Otherwise Schmidt would eat her alive.

When she stood to leave, she saw the note on the pad. She looked at it long enough to memorize it and then left the office.

Returning to Cynthia's desk, she reengaged the locks and the recording equipment and rushed home to call Dr. Schmidt.

He didn't bother with a greeting. "Have you pinned down his stance on the IMF loan terms?"

"No, Doctor Schmidt, but I found something that might be of interest," she said, and told him about the note.

"What did they meet about?" he asked.

"All I have is what was on the notepad," she replied.

Schmidt fell quiet for some time. Then, "What if you leaked that they had a secret meeting?"

When she didn't respond immediately, he explained. "Look, we've got him. He had that meeting in California with a woman who, it turns out, is a fugitive and a domestic terrorist. We will have her in custody shortly. When we do, Senator Jonathon Carr will be facing serious prison time. The meeting was supposed to be confidential. Leak it to the press. It will disrupt whatever they were working on."

"But he'll suspect it was me who leaked it," she stated.

"Here's what you do," Schmidt said and told her his plan.

Schmidt also had a contact at The Post who was well appreciative of being first to get news that hadn't hit the street yet. "Call Roger at The Post. His number is 202-555-7656. He will be expecting your call and tell him there was a secret meeting with Carr and the Speaker. He will be able to fill in the rest."

Chapter Fifty-One – The Attack
April 8, 2039, Santa Cruz Mountain, California

The SWAT team crossed the footbridge and moved up the path to Agnes's cabin without making a sound. They listened. Heard nothing. One of the team members launched a mini infrared scope drone to circle the cabin. It sent digital images back to a receiver. No human or animal read inside. He turned around and looked at the team leader, who was crouched behind a redwood, and shook his head, "No."

The leader signaled two other team members. They swung out into the underbrush and circled around the cabin, one in front, the other in back. The leader whispered "Launch" into his mic. Each team member tossed an ultra-wave grenade through the windows.

The grenades threw the desk across the room, where it came to rest against the back wall under a picture of Thomas Paine, the Revolution-era author of Common Sense. Lamps, chairs, and other furniture was scattered around the space as if the living room had been put through a blender.

The leader counted to five in his head and commanded, "Go, go, go."

Masks down, weapons leveled, they stormed into the cabin,

lusting for the opportunity to laser-fry a terrorist. One team member spit at the picture of Paine as he moved past it into the bedroom.

When they determined the cabin was empty and contained no useful intelligence, not even clues about who had lived there, the team moved on.

The organic farm at Eden was fried with drone-based lasers. It looked like a red beet lightning storm. You could hear the cry outs and scuffles from different quarters. After the dust settled, with no fatalities and minimal injuries, members submissively surrendered, except for one woman, pregnant with her third child in violation of federal law, who broke and ran for the forest. She was slammed across her back with a bolt from a wireless electronic taser and crumbled to the ground, where she miscarried the fetus on the spot.

The other members were rounded up, loaded into a column of multi-passenger DHS drones that looked like a conga line of pregnant elephants. One elderly man stopped and refused to move. "Where are you taking us?" he demanded. Several others stopped and supported the elder man by yelling out, "Where are you taking us?" A taser gun was triggered and one of the men who had stopped fell to his knees. The others were then shoved back into the column and forced into the drones.

When all the members were loaded there was a loud echoing voice from an iMegaphone, "You are all being sent to the Behavioral Re-Education Center in the high desert north of Las Vegas for violation of DHS Terrorist Code: TA 6458-3i."

Badlands was another story. Team leader Johnson's intel showed taking Badlands would not be a walk in the park. "SWAT Green Team leader," Johnson radioed. "Compound is heavily armed with the latest weaponry. Caution on approach."

Word had gotten back to Badlands that five miles of mountain radius was under siege by the DHS. The patriots viewed the stand-off as America's Last Alamo.

"Blue Team leader," Johnson transmitted through his HTs transceiver. "I need infrared point positions, building count, room count and body count and location. Get the MAV drones up now and report data back immediately." SWAT teams were on hold until tactical data was received from the Micro Air Vehicles.

The compound was now surrounded from a distance of one thousand feet. SWAT teams were camouflaged by a Quantum Stealth, a light bending technology that provides active camouflage to the user and mimics the surrounding environment. A voice echoed through the sprawling woods. "My name is Johnson. I am with the DHS Special Forces and your compound is surrounded. We have reports of terrorist activities in the area and want everyone in your compound to come out with hands behind the head and to the ground on their knees."

Before Johnson could get out the last of his order, blasts of artillery from the patriots rang through the mountain range.

"Orange Team leader," Johnson ordered. "Fire the XM25 Counter Defeliades, 180 degree positional launch. Then move in five hundred feet for damage assessment."

The XM25 Counter Defilade Target Engagement System is a semi-automatic long-range airburst grenade launcher with a laser rangefinder system. Its gas explosives cause hard hit mental disorientation, defusing any artillery attacks quickly.

"Blue Team leader what do you see?" Johnson inquired.

"Nothing sir, it's quiet." Eyes pinned to his high-powered binoculars. "Wait, some men are running out from the far quarter of the compound firing Kriss Vectors." A Kriss Vector is a compact submachine gun, an extremely capable and flexible weapon.

"Ok hit squad," Johnson ordered with his radio. "Send in the Drones, toast the motherfuckers and let's end this quickly."

The drones flash-fried about half the patriots in their bunkers before the others decided prison would be better than being scorched alive by the airborne killer robots. The compound looked like 100 Indian tribes sending out smoke signals.

"Secure the area. Nice work men," Johnson announced through his iMegaphone.

Agnes's escape up the mountain wasn't by chance. Twenty-four hours before the attack she received a telecom from Jung Kim.

"Agnes, we've been compromised, DHS troops are heading your way," Jung Kim had relayed. He was one of her most talented hackers who was based at the Saratoga enclave outside of Washington, D.C. and had hacked into the alternate DHS iDevice system making Agnes's decamp occur without incident.

It was the De Anza Trail that Agnes followed through the mountains from Santa Cruz to the Saratoga outpost in Big Sur, just south of Carmel.

Agnes, always calm and collected with any dire situation at hand, was now feeling uneasy and perturbed, not knowing if Ashley had escaped or was now in custody, a catastrophe for Saratoga's plans with Jonathon Carr, to say nothing of Ashley herself. Agnes had repeatedly tried to reach her, but Ashley had gone up the mountain to Badlands and not responded to any of her messages.

Ashley had had a meeting with Wilbur Reboine, her Badlands buddy, and had started back down when the ultra-wave grenade explosions echoed up the mountain. She stopped and listened closely. She wasn't sure what she heard, but it didn't sound friendly. She was about to resume her descent when she caught the incessant buzzing sound of military drones in the distance. It was difficult to distinguish the sound of drones from a northern wind that blew through the redwoods, but the buzzing hiss was discernable and moving in her direction.

Ashley took off in a sprint through the underbrush, seeking a spot that would shield her from the human-seeking radar the drones deployed when on the hunt for criminals. She sprinted west across a ridge and then down toward an outcropping of granite that projected from the mountain like a duck's bill. She had rested there a month earlier when returning from a trek.

Fifty yards from the opening, she stumbled on a tree root and fell headlong into some chaparral. One of the sharp-ended branches pierced her jacket and buried itself into her upper arm.

Ashley screamed. She looked at her arm, impaled on the branch. She bit her lower lip and yanked herself free despite searing pain. Weak and dizzy, she stood for several seconds and regained her orientation. She could feel blood running down her arm as she jogged to the base of the cliff.

She tucked herself under the lip of stone and lay down, bleeding badly. Sitting up, she removed her jacket and tee-shirt. With teeth clawed in the fabric, she tore the tee-shirt in half, and fashioned a tourniquet. Winding it around her upper arm, she tightened it as best she could with her teeth and free hand, and then put her jacket back on over her bra.

Her eyes closed, she laid against the wall of the enclosure, intending a short rest. The sound of gunfire and laser exchange at the Badlands woke her some minutes later. She listened to the firefight rage for more than an hour and then heard the killer drones attack. It sounded like firebombs exploding, and artillery rounds rapidly firing, but did not last long. The forest turned quiet.

She'd begun to think she had escaped when she heard a dog bark and saw a DHS trooper and his dog coming up the mountain. The large Belgian Malinois had her scent and was dragging the soldier up the slope. The soldier carried a laser rifle in one hand and was trying to hang onto the leash with the other.

She quietly moved back into the cavern and breathed as delicately as possible, but the dog was driven by scent not sound. There was little she could do as the dog charged right toward her.

They were less than twenty yards from the lip of the cavern, moving fast, when the dog stopped, looked up, and started barking viciously.

Like the dog, the mountain lion must have been attracted by the scent of her blood. She saw its fury underbelly as it leaped from the outcropping above her and landed on the dog with bared claws. The Malinois gave out a loud screeching yelp. It tried to defend itself, but hopelessly. The cougar must have weighed three times as much as the dog, all muscle and easily held the Malinois down on its back while tearing at its face. It snarled savagely and swiped a paw across the dog's throat, blood gushing, and the canine was done.

The soldier, taken completely off guard, stumbled back and fell. His helmet was shaken loose and rolled to the side. The mountain lion straddled the dog, preparing to feast, looked at the soldier, and growled. He slowly pushed himself backward on his butt a few yards, and then stood and ran.

The mountain lion looked down at the dog, turned his head, stared at Ashley and growled. He turned back to his prey, bit into the dog, and dragged it from the open expanse in front of the cavern.

Ashley slid down the rock embankment and stood in the clearing. The mountain lion had disappeared into the underbrush with the dog. There was no sign of the soldier.

She knew he would connect up with his unit any minute and they would be back. Ashley felt weak and cold from loss of blood. She tightened the tourniquet and started back up the mountain. The storm that had been threatening introduced itself with a crashing of thunder and commenced a downpour.

The good news was, drones did not do well in turbulent weather. The bad news was, rain did not inhibit the ground troops. They would return to the hunt shortly, if they weren't already moving up the mountain.

Chapter Fifty-Two – The Spying Game
April 8, 2039, Washington, D.C.

It was shirtsleeve weather—the sky cloudless blue, and cherry blossoms bloomed along the Potomac.

Inside Jonathon Carr's office, the atmosphere was not so bon vivant. His entire staff sat before him. The phones had been programmed to auto-answer, and a sign reading "We will be back shortly" had been placed on the public door to the office.

"I presume all of you have seen today's iDevice feed about the confidential meeting I had with the Speaker of the House yesterday," he said.

Heads nodded.

"That meeting was confidential. Meaning it was between the Speaker and myself." He scanned around the room to see if there were any giveaways. He paid particular attention to Monica. Noticing nothing, he carried on.

"It turns out the leak originated from this office," he proclaimed. "The Speaker is less than pleased."

Feet shuffled, butts shifted in chairs, and eyes went to the floor.

His tone was measured. "There will be a no-recrimination confession from the person responsible. Whoever had leaked the meeting," he continued, "can notify me on my iDevice and we will talk about the matter privately." He then excused them.

Monica hung back. When all of the others had left the room, she quietly closed the door.

"You have something to tell me?" he asked.

"I do, Senator," she replied. "I feel a little awkward discussing it, but I must tell you that, eh, I have personally witnessed Cynthia listening in on your calls."

"Cynthia? Really?"

"Yes, sir."

"You couldn't have heard the conversation," Jonathon stated. "How do you know she was listening to my calls?"

"Because one time as I came out of my office she was listening to something and she muted her mic and whispered, 'He's talking to the White House.'"

"I see," he replied. "Thank you very much."

She stood there, seeming to expect more from him.

"Is there anything else?" he asked.

"No, Senator," she claimed, and departed.

Jonathon left his coat on the back of his chair and stepped out of his office telling Cynthia he was going to get some fresh air. He walked out of the Hart building and over to the mini-park outside the building at the corner of 2nd and C Streets, where he sat down on one of the polished, wooden benches.

A couple of young women, Congressional staffers, were having lunch on the bench next to his. They wore colorful spring dresses and smiled at him when he sat down. He smiled in return and then tilted his head back, closed his eyes, and thought.

It was hard to believe Cynthia was the leak, but she was the only one with the code to his office and it was she who had passed the call. He wasn't sure whether or not to believe Monica. Cynthia had the means and opportunity, but the motive? Jonathon didn't think so.

He had come to Washington driven by an inner purpose to fix a broken government. No, to derail the police state that had become the driving force of the federal government since 9/11. It was a passion that, if he was honest with himself, bordered on obsession.

In his mind he railed against the destructive policies of Progressives, but in his quiet moments there was a deep sense of guilt about where things stood. The march to Mordor had started with the Patriot Act almost four decades ago. The nation had then been marched, step by step, into a never-ending War on Terror that had migrated from the Middle East to the American heartland. It was like the frog in the beaker of water, the temperature of which was slowly increased to the point that the frog was cooked and never knew what happened.

The media had been complicit as the handmaiden that forwarded the message, but the core agenda was being driven by an increasingly fascist Department of Homeland Security.

He had fashioned a solution to the financial crisis around Article 1, Section 8 of the Constitution. It was radical, but if he could keep his little coalition patched together, it would stabilize not only the financial crisis but him as a national political figure and then he could get the job done.

After returning to his office he asked Cynthia to have her desk covered for a few minutes and join him.

Sitting behind his desk, he loosened his tie. Cynthia sat down in one of the visitor's chairs, knees together, hands folded in her lap. Clearly nervous, she picked at her nail polish.

Jonathon asked if she wanted anything to drink. She declined.

"Cynthia, you transferred the Speaker's call to me yesterday afternoon," he said.

"Yes, Senator," she replied.

"Did you tell anyone about that call? If you did, it's okay, we'll work it out."

"No, Senator. No one," she said. "I swear to God, I told no one."

"Okay, Cynthia, I believe you. Back to work," he responded with a smile.

Sarge was chewing on his hindquarters in the corner when Jonathon finally reached Agnes on the alt network in his den.

"I was worried," he confessed. "I couldn't reach you."

"You had reason to be worried," she said. "I have good news and bad news. Let me get the bad news out of the way. The DHS stormed Santa Cruz. Ashley is missing."

The conversation went silent. "Jonathon are you there?" Agnes queried.

"Did you hear what I just said?" she asked.

Jonathon swallowed, took a deep breath and wiped the wet from his brow. His facial color returning.

"What? How? Where?"

"Somehow they knew she was on the mountain," Agnes replied. "Probably somebody in town. Ash had gone up country to visit someone in the patriot group. When I received word the attack was coming, I tried to reach her repeatedly through patriot contacts up there, but I couldn't raise anyone. I barely escaped with the other members of my Santa Cruz team."

"They must have gotten her," Jonathon said.

"No. They don't have her. Not yet. That's the good news. One of my hackers was able to crack into the DHS alter-net feed.

We can now monitor all of their traffic. It's a huge breakthrough. They're still looking for her."

"Christ, Agnes. Can't we send a team up to rescue her?"

"I can and I will when the time is right," she responded. "The mountain is swarming with these guys right now. Sending a team there at this point would be suicide."

Jonathon stood and began to pace, running his hand through his hair, trying to think. Sarge got up and followed him as he paced.

"One more thing," she stated. "You were right."

"About what?"

"Monica," she said. "Her real name is Robin Delgado. She is an undercover operative for the DEA on loan, according to my report, to the Director of Domestic Intelligence for the DHS."

"Schmidt," he announced.

"Yes."

"Son of a bitch. Confirms my suspicion."

"And she is the source of the leak about your meeting with the Speaker," Agnes continued. "Our earlier background check didn't catch her because all of her documents were official government issue."

"We should leave her in place," he said. "I know what to do with her and she will regret ever having gotten involved in this spying game. You let me know as soon as there is any word on Ash, good or bad."

"Absolutely," Agnes agreed.

Chapter Fifty-Three – The Capture
April 8, 2039, Washington, D.C.

Ashley fashioned a cane out of a broken tree branch and began hobbling up the mountain trail like an old woman with arthritic knees. The rain had turned the trail into a muddy slush, forcing her to walk along the underbrush to the side when it wasn't too dense. Her left arm throbbed, but the blood-soaked tourniquet had stopped the bleeding.

She reached a rise and could see a clearing, and beyond that the De Anza trail about fifty yards in front of her, but the sun was fast leaving the Pacific sky. She would never be able to negotiate her way down the trail in the dark. She was shaking, weak from loss of blood and lack of nutrition.

Fashioning a camp site would attract the lions, and perhaps bears. The grizzlies were long gone from these mountains, but not black bears, of which there were often sightings. She had no way to start a fire. The ground cover was soaked.

Looking for a place she might rest, Ashley limped down the rise. She had started across the clearing when she heard the drone. It descended faster than her ability to make it across the field and came to a halt twenty yards in front of her, a single-person drone.

The cyborg exited the vehicle, laser pistol drawn. "You are Ashley Lawford, fugitive terrorist number 764558," it announced. "Get on the ground. Put your face to the ground. Do it now or I will eliminate you for non-compliance with a DHS anti-terrorism order."

Ashley let her cane drop, knelt on the ground, and then fell face forward onto the muddy turf. She lay there spent, exhausted, and now captured, after a nearly fourteen-year odyssey of concealment.

The cyborg had taken up a position behind her, about to administer the electronic cuffs, when she heard a vicious growl, followed by the cyborg's scream. The struggle raged behind her. She grabbed the cyborg's laser pistol which had fallen next to her head and struggled to belly-crawl across the field. Her movement was determined, but slow. She looked back to see how much distance she made... not much... and saw a two-person drone swoop down into the clearing. She thought they must have heard the cyborg's screams through the network and she tried with all the strength she had left to crawl faster. She even got up on her feet for a moment and then dropped to the ground defeated. She laid in a fetus position, tears running down her cheeks.

The drone's occupants let the mountain lion continue to feast, picked up Ashley and put her inside, and ascended straight up. They advised headquarters that the terrorist fugitive Ashley Lawford was in custody.

Jonathon decided to take the leak head on. He called the Speaker.

JC continued to make his displeasure known by having his Chief of Staff take the call but make Jonathon wait several minutes before passing it on. "Hello, Senator," he stated flatly, back to formal titles. No apology for the wait.

"Look, JC, let's not do this," Jonathon said. "Let's not roll back into these political straitjackets. I found the source of the leak. It came from my office, so I'm responsible. Not only will this person be relieved, but hell will have to freeze over before this traitor will be able to work in DC again. I sincerely apologize, but we've got a solution that can get the nation back on its feet. I think you can see that."

"I'm dealing with a shit-storm here with my own caucus after our highly publicized secret meeting," the Speaker responded. "I need to get it under control before trying to sell your plan. Check back with me in a week. I'll see where we stand at that time."

"You still on board?" Jonathon asked.

"Check with me next week," JC replied, and the line went dead.

It didn't take a week for the tables to turn. The lid finally came off the economic stress that was grinding the nation into the dust.

"The protests started in San Francisco on Thursday," the newscaster reported, "and are now spreading throughout the major cities." Behind the reporter's studio desk a big screen showed hundreds of people taking to the streets, signs waving and crowds yelling "we want economic stability," signs reading, we pay taxes, you pay the bills.

"It appears the pot had boiled over," the reporter continued, "when it was discovered an elderly couple who had lost their Social Security income had starved to death and were found in a death-embrace under the Golden Gate Bridge."

By Friday, civil unrest had spread across the country like a raging prairie fire. In Chicago, government buildings were stormed and then burned. Citizens in Indianapolis formed lines and laid down across all major freeway systems. In Charleston, the headquarters of the Bank of America was raided by mobs of unemployed men and women in broad daylight, while a flash-mob of the Medicare crowd pillaged Manhattan's diamond district on 47th Street, carrying off handfuls of precious stones they hoped to trade for food and drink.

Law enforcement was inadequate to handle most of the crowds, and in many cities they stood in sympathy with the rioters.

The riots in Baltimore were particularly intense.

With their roles reversed, JC called Jonathon. "Can you set up a meeting with the Majority Leader? If we don't get ahead of this, they will be storming the Capital next."

"Let me call her. I'll get back to you," Jonathon responded.

They met in a private room at Old Ebbit Grill on 15th Street, walking distance from the White House. Established in the middle of the nineteenth century, it was the oldest watering hole in the nation's capital and had been patronized for nearly two centuries by presidents, the political elite, and anyone else who loved crab cakes.

Besides Jonathon, the participants included the Senate Majority Leader and her number two, the Majority Whip, the Senate Minority Leader and his Whip. JC was there with his Chief of Staff and his Whip, as well as the House Minority leader and her Whip.

The Whips had to be there. They were second in command in their respective bodies, but, even more important, they rounded up the votes.

The meeting got off to a rocky start, as the legal and functional changes to U.S. law they had to consider were momentous. There was an instant jockeying for position and authority. With the Senate always the more august body, Lena sought to impose her seniority, though the Speaker of the House was actually senior to the Senate Pro-Tem in the line of succession to the White House. More to the point of the meeting, the legislation they had to craft dealt with matters of finance, and the House had the Constitutional power of the purse. The bickering continued. Like an Olympic hockey game, players slamming each other against the boards despite Jonathon's admonition. They were politicians. It was in their blood.

Jonathon finally had enough. "We are not on the floor of the House or the Senate. There is no media here. Our nation is crumbling in front of our eyes under the burden of decades of debt. We have a potential solution on the table. If you cannot set partisanship and political power aside, I will go directly to the public with this plan."

He let this hang. When there was no response he said, "Make up your mind. The nation isn't waiting."

Chapter Fifty-Four – Interrogation
April 9, 2039, Washington, D.C.

Schmidt turned the DHS press aide lose with the story. The media celebrated the daring capture of a leading domestic terrorist who had been on the run from authorities for well over a decade. Ashley's wild good looks didn't hurt.

The stories gushed from the media iDevice newsfeeds and the new government channel, USA1. Video footage of Ashley in custody, wounded, defiant, unrepentant, became the top featured news footage for the day.

She had been captured during the raid on a clandestine terrorist cell by a crack, anti-terrorist DHS SWAT team in the mountains above Santa Cruz, the anchor had said.

Cut to an interview with one Jose Mendoza, of the SWAT team that had stormed the mountain. Jose described the bloody shootout with the armed so-called anti-government patriots who had been fortified in a secluded, massively armed encampment deep in the Santa Cruz Mountains. Lawford, he said, had been captured miles from the patriot encampment. She was alone, having apparently been wounded in the battle.

Ashley was taken to the San Francisco County jail, a

facility that looked like an off-planet asteroid prison, and booked on charges of terrorism against the United States of America. Her arm was stitched, and she was dressed in a standard-issue prison-orange jumpsuit that reminded her of the institutional uniform from the Behavioral Education Center. She was locked in a solitary cell. Toilet, bed, table. All smooth edges.

A call came in from the DHS to Sheriff Carter. "I want her interrogated within an inch of her life," Schmidt demanded. "What is her relationship with Jonathon Carr? What are they up to? Do what you have to do short of killing her. No visible bruises. Keep it quiet, keep it secure. I don't want the press all over our asses on this. Once I know what Carr is doing I can get it to the press in a way to bury him."

"I got your back, Oscar," Carter said.

Schmidt and Carter go way back, high school romp days and each have stayed close and followed the other's career. Not the least of which is that they were both scumbags back then and now.

Carter knew he couldn't physically abuse her or even consider what Schmidt was inferring to get her to talk but he could scare the crap out of her.

He opened the cell and dragged a stool across to and in front of where Ashley was sitting on her bunk.

"Sweetheart let me make this easy for you," Carter began. "You are in a lot of trouble. I would say deep shit of trouble, but if you cooperate, I can make this go much easier for you."

Ashley stared with no emotional response. Inside she could feel her heart racing.

"We have an iDig recording of you and Senator Jonathon Carr up in those mountains where you were apprehended. What were you doing up there and what is your relationship with the Senator?"

"I don't know what you're talking about. I don't know of the Senator you are referring to nor for that matter any Senator. I live up there and have done nothing wrong."

"You are a fugitive," the sheriff said. "And you will come straight with me, I will make sure of that. Now, are you going to cooperate?"

"I've done nothing!" Ashley yelled out.

"You will cooperate. I will see to it," and he angrily scurried out of the cell.

She laid down on the cot and wept.

The manager at Old Ebbit Grill came into the private conference room at 2:00 a.m., closing time, and with all the deference he could muster, asked the ladies and gentlemen if there was anything else he could do for them before they closed for the evening.

Fourteen hours later they had hammered out the basics of an agreement.

"Will the President agree?" JC asked.

"We will announce this as a bipartisan solution," Lena replied, "and the only solution that will save the country. If he dares to contemplate opposition, they'll storm the White House. Besides, we might even have the makings of a veto-proof majority here."

She put her hand up and JC high-fived her.

Jonathon left Old Ebbits on a high, which lasted until he got in the cab. The USA1 iDevice newsfeed was playing in the back seat. He watched as Ashley was frog-marched from a law enforcement drone into the space opera-looking San Francisco jail.

His head was spinning when he walked into his domicile. Sarge danced around in circles, anticipating a run. Jonathon scratched him behind the ears absentmindedly and went into the den. Sarge followed.

"Did they shoot her?" Jonathon asked on connecting with Agnes.

"No. She fell down or something," Agnes said. "I don't have all of the information yet. I have the best criminal defense attorney in California on the way to the jail now."

"Who's paying him?"

"She's being paid by a human rights group based in Singapore," Agnes replied.

"What's she charged with?"

"I don't know yet."

"Why not?" Jonathon asked.

"Easy, Jonathon. She hasn't even been arraigned yet."

"Sorry. Let me know as soon as you hear anything. Oh, almost forgot. Senate and House leadership are agreed on the plan. We are going to draft the legislation in the next twenty-four hours and then hold a joint press conference."

"Get me on the first available flight to San Francisco," Oscar Schmidt said to Maya Contreras, "and have a department drone pick me up at the airport and fly me into the city."

Schmidt contacted his liaison at the FBI, a guy named Newberry, and told him to ensure Ashley Lawford was not arraigned until he arrived and questioned her.

"You've got a couple of days, Schmidt," Newberry said.

"It's Doctor Schmidt, Agent Newberry," Schmidt stated rudely, "and don't give me that 'couple of days' bullshit. This woman is a domestic terrorist."

"It's Special Agent Newberry, Schmidt, and there's a little thing called the Sixth Amendment. We cannot hold her for long without an arraignment. You know that."

"Fuck the Sixth Amendment," Schmidt bellowed. "She had better still be in custody when I get there or I'll have your fucking job."

Oscar Schmidt was still pissed off when he met with Stephanie Darling, the special agent in charge of the San Francisco Field Office of the FBI. She was Newberry's superior. Stephanie had joined the FBI after graduating from San Jose State with a degree in criminal justice. After two divorces and the third one in the making, she had the social demeanor of a worn-out razor.

"We are planning to arraign her tomorrow, Doctor Schmidt," she said.

"On what charges?" Schmidt asked.

"We have a memo from your office that the suspect violated Eighteen U.S.C. twenty-three thirty-two B, the federal terrorism act. Specifically, she attempted to kill officers and employees of the United States."

"That's right," he confirmed.

"And this occurred when?" she asked.

"You saw that she was part of the terrorist cell in the Santa Cruz Mountains."

"No," she responded. "The newsfeed I saw showed her captured miles from a DHS raid that was carried out above

Santa Cruz. Nothing tied her to the bubbas in that mountain encampment."

"There's no question she's part of that group," Schmidt proclaimed. "She's also an escaped fugitive, having previously committed multiple acts of terrorism. You keep her in custody so I can question her. That's an order."

Stephanie Darling shifted her weight from one foot to another.

The bindi, the dot between Indira Prashad's eyebrows, was a deep purple and it scrunched together as she listened, in the grimy, attorney-client interview room, to Ashley's story of her capture.

"Were you read your rights?" Indira asked.

Ashley thought back to her capture. "I was pretty wiped out, but I don't recall having my rights read to me."

"When did you escape from the BEC in Covina?" Indira asked.

"Let's see, I was fifteen at the time, so . . . fourteen years ago, give or take."

"You have been off the radar since then?" Indira asked.

"Completely," Ashley said.

The door to the interview room opened and Oscar Schmidt and Stephanie Darling entered.

Chapter Fifty-Five – A Real Winner
April 10, 2039, Washington, D.C.

JC towered over the Majority Leader at the joint press conference, but she looked regal today. They held the presser in room 325 of the Russell Senate Office Building, famous for the Watergate hearings of decades earlier. Renamed after the assassination of JFK, The Kennedy Caucus Room had held a number of historic hearings and was often used for high-profile press conferences, as it was today.

The Speaker and the Senate Majority Leader stood side by side at the podium, Jonathon just to the left of Senator Bullock. Floor-to-ceiling, twenty-foot, red velour curtains hung behind them; chandeliers the size of Volkswagens hung from the ceiling. The speakers were arranged like an electronic floral display behind a polished, walnut podium at the front of the room.

A sense of history filled the air, and the press, hundreds of them, could smell it, taste it. It wouldn't matter what was said today. Whether the legislation was good for the country or bad they would find flaws, attack it, inflame passions, and generate controversy. It's what they did and they were not ashamed of it.

The legislators, of course, knew this to be the case.

The Majority Leader stepped closer to the mic. "Thank

you all for coming. Over the last few days, the leadership of the House and the Senate have worked hard, on a bipartisan basis, to craft a solution to the defining issue of our time, the state of our economy and its ravaging impact on our citizens."

"When Senator Carr," she turned her head briefly to Jonathon and nodded, "exposed the covert attempt by the IMF to confiscate our natural resources, we went to work on a solution. And we have one, optimum for our citizens, our country. We believe it is a real winner."

The Majority Leader stepped aside and the Speaker took the mic.

"While the legislation we are about to enact is historic in the extreme, perhaps even more so has been the unique engagement between Progressives and Conservatives from both the House and the Senate to craft a solution for the American people. My sincere thanks to the Majority Leader for her leadership."

Lena smiled.

JC went on. "I, too, would like to acknowledge Senator Carr in particular for his leadership in crafting this legislation that brings great relief to a suffering nation." At this point JC turned toward Jonathon and nodded. Jonathon returned it.

"Never let it be said," JC continued, "when a problem of momentous import faces our nation, that the elected officials cannot solve it. We can and we have."

Reporters started shouting questions.

JC held up both hands. "We will take questions when we are done setting forth our plan, not before."

"This legislation has two major segments. It is a revolutionary approach to a problem we have created ourselves, and we are going to solve it ourselves, not some international bank, and not a private bank owned by special interests. The buck stops with Congress."

Again, shouts rose from the press corps.

Again, JC raised his hands and shook his head "no."

He turned to Jonathon. "Senator Carr will now give you the broad outlines of the legislation we will be enacting." Turning to Jonathon, he stated, "Senator, the floor is yours."

Chapter Fifty-Six – Confrontation
April 10, 2039, San Francisco, California

"Ms. Prashad, this is Oscar Schmidt, Director of DHS Intelligence," Stephanie said. "He has some questions for Ms. Lawford."

"Before you ask my client any questions," Indira replied, "I have a couple for the both of you."

"What's that, Ms. Prashad?" Schmidt inquired.

"With what charges, exactly, do you intend to charge my client?"

"Violation of Eighteen U.S.C. twenty-three thirty-two B, the Federal Terrorism Act," Schmidt stated, matter-of-factly, and took a step farther into the room so Stephanie could close the door behind him.

"What is the exact violation, and when is this violation supposed to have occurred?" Indira asked calmly.

Stephanie glanced over at Ashley, who sat at the table, staring at Schmidt as if he was some fecal matter she had stepped in.

Stephanie Darling was a sharp cookie. Rather than challenge Schmidt earlier and risk her pension, she had played passive. She knew Indira well and decided to let her slap Oscar around.

"She was caught participating in a violent attack on federal officers yesterday," he replied.

"Really?" Indira asked. "That's odd, because one of your own jack-booted goons told the news media that she was found miles away from the incident you described. Would you like to see this videoed DHS SWAT team member's statement to the press?" She lifted her iDevice.

Schmidt said nothing. A few beads of sweat broke out on the top of his head.

"In fact," Indira continued, "my client often hikes those mountain trails, and in this case she tripped on a tree root and fell into a bush with a sharp, protruding branch and punctured her arm. There is no way you can tie her to that skirmish because she wasn't there."

Schmidt's bald headed dome took on a wet sheen. "Your client is a domestic terrorist and a fugitive," he insisted, and mopped his brow. "I have some questions for her about a recent trip she took to Sheideck, California."

Ashley hadn't mentioned her meeting with Jonathon to Indira, but the attorney didn't miss a beat. "Do you mean when she escaped from the brainwashing clinic in Covina at the age of fifteen because one of the psychiatrists tried to rape her? That act of terrorism, Director Schmidt?"

"Surely you know that psychiatrist was later convicted of sexually assaulting several underage girls in that spin bin?" she asked. "Surely you and Ms. Darling are not going to try to label a fifteen-year-old's escape from a DHS pedophile mill as an act of terrorism, Mr. Schmidt?"

"It's Doctor Schmidt," he corrected her. He took a handkerchief from his back pocket and mopped his head again. As he did so, Indira cast a quick glance at Stephanie Darling, whose mouth was pushed together to suppress her smile.

Indira suddenly tilted her head and looked at him with a repugnant expression. "Wait a minute," she said. "Doctor Oscar Schmidt?"

"Yes!"

"I know you," she stated. "I was at Berkeley when they busted you for sex with a minor. You thought you were having sex with a cyborg, and it was some teenager, and now you want to accuse my client of terrorism for running from a DHS sexual predator?"

Indira looked at Stephanie for a split second and noticed she was suppressing a smile and then over at Ashley who gave her, a way to go girl, smile.

"I don't think this will play very well in front of Judge Milne in the morning. She's death on vice cases. She doesn't like child-molesters."

Schmidt started to take a swing at her, but Stephanie yelled, "Doctor Schmidt!"

"You think you're a smart attorney, but not so smart defending a terrorist. Do you know the power of my authority? Obviously, you don't. Your client will be found guilty of terrorist acts and if I find that you are connected to her acts in any way not only will you be disbarred but you will be arrested and tried for aiding and abetting a terrorist."

Ashley's confidence and composure turned to a haunting fear across her face. She wanted to explode but her fear held her back.

He spun around and opened the door to leave. Before walking out he turned to Indira. "There will be no arraignment tomorrow. I'll see to it."

"You know very well that is a violation of my client's Constitutional rights," she said.

"Fuck your client's Constitutional rights!" he yelled and slammed the door so viciously the room shook.

Chapter Fifty-Seven – The Bank Of The United States
April 10, 2039, Washington, D.C.

"Good morning, ladies and gentlemen," Jonathon opened. "As the Speaker mentioned, there are two major sections of this legislation. They work in tandem."

The room was silent.

"We pay one-point-two trillion a year in interest on the national debt. It is now the largest item in the federal budget. It diverts critical funds from some of our most important social programs, as well as defense," Jonathon continued as he sought to carefully walk both sides of the aisle.

"This money is paid to a private bank, the Federal Reserve, whose stock is owned by other banks. It is not paid to the United States government. The Fed does return some of it, but they keep tens of billions in profit."

Murmurs could now be heard throughout the room.

"When, in our questionable wisdom, we overspend," Jonathon said, "which we do every year, we issue IOUs called Treasury Bills and Bonds. The Fed, among others, buys these bonds. However, the Fed buys them with a mere click of a mouse, sending zeros and ones to our bank account and creating money out of thin air. As a result, we pay interest on money we received for those bonds, which, to repeat, the Federal Reserve created out of whole cloth. We are paying interest on money–" he raised his hands and made quotation signs, "–that was created out of thin air."

"It was Wright Patman, a former Chairman of the House Banking Committee for twelve years, who famously said, 'I have never yet had anyone who could, through the use of logic and reason, justify the Federal Government borrowing the use of its own money. I believe the time will come in this country when they will actually blame you and me and everyone else connected with the Congress for sitting idly by and permitting such an idiotic system to continue.'"

"The Federal Reserve Act was passed on December twenty-third, nineteen-thirteen. One hundred and twenty-six years later we are finally going to follow Chairman Patman's advice. Our legislation will terminate that Act and re—"

He didn't get the words "replace it" out of his mouth before pandemonium broke. Reporters bolted to their feet and began shouting questions. Some screamed, "No!"

Jonathon with a hand gesture motioned the attendees back to their seats. When the shouting had subsided sufficiently to make himself heard, he continued, "We will take questions after I lay out what we are going to do. Many of your questions will be answered. We will then answer those that aren't."

"But, Senator!" A reporter from USA2, who had frizzy, red hair, stood and shouted above the din, "The Fed controls the money supply. You can't—"

"We can, Rhoda. Let me explain how and why," Jonathon said. "We will create our own bank within the organizational structure of the Treasury. The Bank of the United States will carry out all of the functions the Federal Reserve does today, except we will not have to pay interest on the money we create, saving trillions for future generations. That is money that could be going to our most deserving. Do you want to deny that to them?"

Frizzy shook her head, "No, but that's not legal."

"Oh, but it is. The Constitution and well-established Supreme Court decisions make clear Congress has this authority," he stated. "In fact, in 1861 Congress authorized Abraham Lincoln to print government money to finance the North's efforts during the Civil War, when New York bankers wanted to charge twenty-four to thirty-six percent interest. They called those notes greenbacks."

The bedlam of questions had now risen to hurricane force. The Senate Majority Leader joined Jonathon at the podium and said in a very soft voice, "We will take questions now, but one at a time."

The crowd turned instantly quiet, trying to hear what she had said. She stepped into the breach and took the first question.

"Who will appoint the Chairman of the Bank?" a network reporter asked.

"We will use the same procedure that has been in place for the Federal Reserve," she replied. "The President will appoint the chairman, the Senate will confirm, or not. That will also hold true for most of the bank's functions. We will examine those procedures, but in general they will not change for now."

"What about the trillions owed to the Fed?" This came from a reporter for the Financial Times of London.

JC stepped to the mic. "The Majority Leader and I will select a bipartisan team from Congress to work out a payment plan with the Fed, bearing in mind they did not pay for the bonds with legal tender of any kind. They paid for the bonds with Monopoly money."

"So you're defaulting on government debt?" the Brit shouted.

"Not at all," JC said calmly. "All Treasury securities held by sovereign governments, local governments, banks, insurance companies, mutual funds, private individuals, pension plans, retirement accounts, et cetera, et cetera, will be honored exactly per the terms upon which they were purchased. We will, however, have a discussion with the Fed on how we retire the debt they hold."

The din subsided again as the crowd digested this development. Some reporters felt they had had enough and bolted for the exit to file their stories.

JC decided to get ahead of the key question that had yet to be asked. "The Majority Leader and I are currently working on regulations for the new bank to put the nation on a more sound financial footing. We have agreed that no deficit can exceed that of the current fiscal year and we are crafting a path that reduces the budget deficit every year going forward until the budget is balanced."

"This will not happen overnight, but we have agreed to stop the bleeding, and to stop paying interest on debt to a bank that acquired that debt without really paying for it."

The press conference lasted another hour, as questions were hurled at the three of them nonstop. The room became uncomfortably hot, and as news deadlines approached people began to leave.

The Majority Leader stepped back to the mic. "You will be hearing more about this in the days ahead. In closing, we have undertaken this course for the benefit of the American people. Understand what the Federal Reserve refused to do for our government we can do for ourselves, and much more inexpensively."

The Fed and the New York banks were not without their media connections. Attacks on the plan– "Congress to default on U.S. debt"—had begun to scream from every iDevice channel before Jonathon made it back to his office.

Cynthia flagged him down as soon as he walked in. "There's an urgent message from the White House, Senator. The President's Chief of Staff … less than pleasant."

This was no surprise to Jonathon. He suspected the President was the wizard behind the curtains, the poster boy for the IMF loan, and his plan would have repercussions with the White House. What was not made public by the mainstream media was the President's family ties to the head honchoes at IMF. Not only would the debt loan get the President out of the burning goals of a financial catastrophe, no matter the consequences to the country, but give him high points with the wealthiest men on the planet. People had disappeared, found dead with blood splattered suicide notes lying next to their bodies. But these were never linked back to the IMF.

Jonathon was well aware of the danger. He could be a missing person. But he had a plan.

Chapter Fifty-Eight – Arraignment
April 11, 2039, San Francisco, California

Stephanie Darling took a tentative sip of her latte and jerked her head back when it burned her lips. "Damn!" Her eyes watered. She blinked the tears away and opened the office door. She did not have far to walk.

Neither did Sam Rock, the Assistant U.S. Attorney. The FBI's San Francisco Field Office and the U.S. Attorney's office were both located in the federal building in San Francisco on Golden Gate Avenue, which was named after the long-dead California Congressman Phillip Burton.

She met Rock on the way to the courtroom to answer Indira's motion to have Ashley arraigned.

"The fuck's the matter with this guy, Schmidt?" he asked as they walked to the courtroom.

"He's got some hard-on for this chick," Stephanie replied. "I don't know exactly what it is, but he's obsessed with wanting to question her."

"I could give a shit," Rock said. "We have to arraign her and I don't even see grounds to charge her. Doesn't he know the statute of limitations on terrorism is eight years?"

"Indira reminded him last night," she stated simply.

Rock smiled. "I'll bet that was fun... so this woman escaped from some sicko shrink at one of those behavioral centers when she was a kid?"

"Right," Stephanie confirmed.

"Any evidence she was connected with the patriot group involved in the shootout in Santa Cruz?"

Stephanie shook her head.

They entered the courtroom. Stephanie scanned around. Oscar Schmidt sat in the back row on the plaintiff's side of the room. Indira Prashad was taking papers out of her briefcase and placing them on the defense table. Ashley sat to her left, clad in neon orange.

Stephanie took a seat behind the prosecution table.

Sam walked through the gate and over to Indira. "Counselor," he said in greeting.

"Good morning, Sam," she replied.

"Can I speak with you outside for a moment?" he asked. They had five minutes before the hearing was to begin. They returned just as the judge was taking the bench.

"All rise," instructed the clerk.

Before the proceedings commenced, Sam Rock said, "May we approach, Your Honor?"

Judge Joseph Burke nodded, his face flushed from what looked like a recent trip to a cocaine vial, and hound-dog bags under his weary eyes.

Oscar Schmidt scooted to the front edge of his chair and leaned as far forward as he could, trying to hear what was being said.

After the two attorneys and the judge conferred for a couple of minutes, the judge looked at Sam and said something. Schmidt could not hear the conversation. The Assistant AG nodded in the affirmative.

"Case dismissed," Judge Burke declared.

"No!" Schmidt shouted.

"Order!" Burke commanded.

"You can't dismiss this case," Schmidt nearly screamed. "I am Doctor Oscar Schmidt from the Department of Homeland Security. The woman is a terrorist."

"Any more from you, Doctor Schmidt, and you will be held in contempt," Judge Burke advised.

Schmidt's face flushed. He sat back down.

Indira and Ashley were pushing the door open to exit the courtroom when Schmidt stood and stepped in behind Ashley. With his face a few inches from her ear, he whispered, "This is not over, Ms. Lawford. I am going to expose your relationship with Senator Carr and find out what you two are up to."

Ashley stopped and turned around. "Oscar," she said, "I know a couple of fourteen-year-old heroine junkies I can fix you up with. Give me a call."

On their way out of the building Indira told her, "That slug is not going to let this go."

"I know," Ashley responded.

Chapter Fifty-Nine – Junkyard Dog
April 11, 2039, The White House

Jonathon sat on a white sofa, crossed his legs, and looked across the room at a portrait of Abraham Lincoln, who appeared to stare back at him with a profound sense of sadness.

He glanced to his right. There, George Washington – dignified, noble, but warrior like – gazed into the distance, dressed in his full military attire, in a portrait that hung over the fireplace.

Jonathon experienced an overwhelming sense of déjà vu. He had a strong sense he had been here before. He knew he hadn't, but felt he had. He had never been in the Oval Office. He was sure of that. However, he vividly recalled standing in front of that picture of Lincoln wondering what was on the great president's mind, and at the same time experiencing a deep sense of guilt, shame, and betrayal of the American people. He felt it now as if it were yesterday. A chill ran through his body, as if he was drowning in ice water. His memory was haunting. For a moment it felt like he had lived another life at another time but in the same surroundings.

He was yanked to the present when Stanford B. Jones, the Progressive President of the United States, entered the room.

Jonathon stood, as did the Speaker and Majority Leader.

There couldn't be more differences between the two African-American politicians than there was between the Speaker and the President, JC hard right, the President hard left. While both were coming up through the political ranks their discourse over the years showed it. Their relationship reminded those who could remember of the bloody wars of decades past between the LA street gangs, the Crips and the Bloods. The President was cordial in his greeting but you didn't need a thermometer to feel the suppressed resentment.

He gave Lena a hug after shaking JC's hand, and turned to Jonathon. "Well, Senator, you've certainly been making some waves. Let's hope we can surf them, and not drown in the undercurrent." He gave Jonathon a sarcastic smile.

He asked everyone to sit back down, pulled up an armchair at the head of the two sofas, and joined them.

"Let's put our cards on the table," the President said. "We certainly cannot remove the Federal Reserve System."

"Not the system, Mr. President," Lena offered. "The Federal Reserve Bank. Much of the system, many of the functions anyway, will be transferred to the Bank of the United States. We simply won't be paying interest on our own currency."

It was an odd situation, and no surprise the Speaker had not discussed the bill with the White House, but Lena Bullock was, at least nominally, the President's strongest ally in Congress. Yet she had worked a deal with the Speaker instead of coming to him.

Media reports had claimed the President was "furious" at the Junkyard Dog, but Lena had become increasingly angered by the President's virtual total disregard of Congress. The effort to expand the power of the Executive Branch by use of Executive Orders had started in earnest nearly three decades earlier when the current Secretary General of the United Nations, then President Barack Obama, regularly sought to bypass a politically opposed Congress with countless Executive Orders.

In many cases these orders were invalidated by the Supreme Court, but their impact was felt on the nation for the year or more it took for the question of their Constitutionality to be decided by the Court. In a couple of cases the orders had held. Since Obama, the tendency to govern by executive decree, when dealing with a Congress dominated by the opposing party, had grown.

In this case, the President's own party controlled the Senate but he had done everything he could to govern around them.

Things had changed. The President's approval numbers rested in single digits. More to the point, he was boxed into a political corner with this legislation. Polls showed overwhelming support for the radical restructuring of the country's monetary policy and Stanford B. Jones had no leverage in the situation except one. He could veto the bill when it hit his desk. He didn't lead with that salvo, however.

It was an open secret that despite the President's liberal credentials and rhetoric, he had massive financial support from New York City banks. In fact, a rumor had been leaked months earlier that Jones had already been offered a position on the Board of J.P. Morgan, once he completed his term in the White House, which came with millions in stock options.

The New York City mega-banks that owned the Federal Reserve Bank of New York also owned Stanford B. Jones.

"The Fed has been steadfast in supporting our economy for over a hundred years," the President proclaimed.

"Due respect, Mister President," Jonathon said, "but we are fifty-eight trillion in debt and the economy is a dead man walking."

"It will recover," the President stated flatly.

JC had had enough. "In case you hadn't noticed, Mister President, there are one hundred seventy-five million Americans out of work and riots rule our cities. Your precious Fed bears no small part of the responsibility for this mess."

"Oh and Congress doesn't?" the President quipped.

"We do, and we are doing something about it," JC countered.

"Not if I have anything to say about it." The President stood. The meeting was over.

Chapter Sixty – Tease Schmidt
April 11, 2039, San Francisco, California

Ashley stopped at the bottom of the Burton building steps and, hands on her hips in a touch of free-spirited defiance, looked out at the city. She squirmed for a second feeling the pain from her injured arm but smiled for the first time in days. She no longer needed to hide her face in public. It gave her a sense of freedom she hadn't felt in many years.

She and Indira walked to Indira's iDrive and got in. Indira opened her briefcase and took out two miniaturized iDevices. She handed them to Ashley.

"These were dropped off in my room last night with a note to give them to you. The note said one is registered in your name, the other is registered to an untraceable identity. Of course, that is in violation of federal law and so I assume that was either a false statement or a joke."

"Clearly a joke," Ashley said.

"Both carry five thousand credits," Indira told her.

Ashley put the iDevice registered to her on her arm and tucked the other into a pocket in her jeans. "You saved my butt in there."

"Schmidt hasn't given up, you know. He seems to see you as

a channel to something else," Indira said.

"Yes. I know." Ashley leaned over, gave Indira a hug.

"Where are you off to?" Indira asked.

"The airport," Ashley replied.

"No need. I live in Menlo Park. It's on the way."

Ashley was free to walk the streets, but she couldn't contact Mrs. Wilson across the bay, or any of the Saratoga team or outposts, or the man she loved. At this time, her new freedom came with limits.

She knew Schmidt would try to follow her. Did he think she was going to now go flying into Jonathon's arms? She couldn't contact him, but she decided to tease Schmidt.

Ashley got out of Indira's iDrive in front of the United terminal at San Francisco International. She went to the kiosk and bought a roundtrip ticket to Washington's Dulles airport on the 1:55 p.m. flight with her iDevice and headed to a Starbucks for a fix.

Oscar Schmidt had promised Amanda Campos, Chief of TSA Operations at SFO, an increase in grade and pay if she was able to help bring Ashley Lawford to justice. She jumped on Schmidt's offer without a thought.

Changed out of her uniform, she sat at an oxygen bar in tan slacks, a blue jacket, and a grey-and-gold silk Hermes scarf, with her eye on Ashley. A brushed-chrome tube ran from a tank under the bar to an oxygen-infusion patch pasted on her neck over her jugular vein.

The digital light on her iDevice turned green. She put her patch on a holding tray on the bar and told the attendant that she would be right back.

"Yes, sir," she said to Oscar Schmidt.

"You on her?" Schmidt asked.

"Like a rug," Amanda replied. "She just purchased a round trip ticket to DC, Dulles."

"I can read her fucking iDevice feed," he said, berating her. "Stay with her. You placed the bag with her name on it on the plane?"

"I personally handed it to a baggage handler and watched him place it on the baggage cart," she replied. "I placed the weapons in the luggage myself."

"Do not lose her. I'll want you to take her into custody when she lands at Dulles, for violation of the firearms statutes."

"Yes, sir."

Ashley took the exit aisle seat for the two-and-a-half hour flight to Washington. The woman in the Hermes scarf who had watched her purchase her ticket walked by her heading toward the rear of the plane, studiously avoiding eye contact.

The scarfed woman had moisture on her upper lip. One of Schmidt's, Ash thought, as the seatbelt automatically strapped her in and the pilot announced the take off.

Ashley was halfway through the crossword puzzle in the in-flight magazine when the pilot announced the need for an emergency landing. "Ladies and gentlemen, a passenger in the first-class cabin has experienced a medical event and we have to make an unscheduled landing. We have been cleared to land at Salt Lake International Airport. We'll be on the ground in twenty minutes."

By the time they landed and the medics took the passenger off in a stretcher, Ashley was nearly done with the crossword puzzle. "What's a five-letter word for 'subterfuge' that ends in 'e'?" she asked the college student covered in body-art sitting next to her.

"Guile," the kid offered without looking up from his iDevice.

"Right," she said. "Thanks."

No response from the human canvas.

The captain returned to the airwaves. "Unfortunately, ladies and gentlemen, due to our unscheduled stop and the air traffic here, we will need to remain on the ground for another two hours before we resume our flight to Washington, Dulles."

Groans rose from the passengers.

"That being the case, you can disembark for restrooms or snacks for an hour and a half, but please keep your iDevices with you at all times."

The seat belts unfastened. Ashley stood and scrambled around passengers who were getting to their feet. She was the third person out the door. As she exited, she glanced back down the aisle. Hermes Scarf was fighting her way through the crowded aisle, literally climbing over people, but she was coming from the far rear of the plane.

Once out the door, Ashley walked as fast as she could toward the terminal exit without calling attention to herself. She stripped the iDevice off her arm and dropped it in a baby stroller heading in the opposite direction without the wireless earbud-wearing mother noticing.

She strapped the other iDevice to her arm. It bore the name of Meridith Devore.

Outside, she stood in line and waited her turn for an iCab. While she waited she found the address of a theater arts store in downtown Salt Lake. She gave the address to the computer operating the cab and sat back and closed her eyes while the cab negotiated its way downtown.

At the Wardrobe Connection she bought a black wig, brown contact lenses, and a set of false teeth. She paid with Meridith Devore's iDevice, and then searched for and found a tattoo parlor six blocks away. Black hair flying behind her in a brisk wind, Ashley hurried to Beautiful Body Art.

The studio was located in a rundown duplex with psychedelic posters serving as wallpaper. The artist, a Norwegian man with watery eyes and a glazed mind, asked Ashley what she wanted. Using her airplane seatmate as a model, she had a Japanese opera tattooed around her neck, up her cheeks, and across her forehead. It can be lasered off later, she thought.

With wig, teeth, and tattoos, Ashley Lawford was no more. Meridith Devore looked like something out of a low-grade horror movie.

Even though she had slipped Schmidt's agent, he would still think she was headed to D.C. to see Jonathon. Meridith Devore rented a car and headed west out of Salt Lake on Interstate 80, with constant attention to the sky for drones.

Chapter Sixty-One – Intelligence "Seven"
April 12, 2039

Korea was recognized for having the finest military cyborgs on the planet, Japan for cyborgs for domestic help, and Germany's worker-borgs were the envy of the industrialized world. The Bahamas is where the ultra skin-sensitive sex partner and porno-borgs were produced.

Jason Lawrence, a former operative of Britain's MI-6, sat at a leather-topped table in the plush parlor of a fifty-foot yacht, quietly cruising Chesapeake Bay outside of Baltimore. Lawrence was employed by a private intelligence group based out of Grand Cayman Island. The little-known organization, simply called Seven, employed former operatives from Russia's FSB, Israel's Mossad, the Chinese Ministry of State Security, the CIA, the FBI, the German BND, and Britain's MI-6.

Seven was exclusive and eye-wateringly expensive. Potential clients were screened at three different levels before there was any personal contact with them. The client in this case was represented by a quietly powerful international law firm based in Havana, a metropolis that had flourished following U.S. recognition in 2015 and the deaths of the Castro brothers a few years later.

Seven never knew that the client was an Estonian-based corporation, the owner of whose stock was a Cook Island trust funded by J.P. Morgan Chase, Citibank, and Goldman Sachs.

Across the table from Jason Lawrence sat Oscar Schmidt. They had engaged in meaningless small-talk for thirty minutes. Schmidt was now eating some prawns served by a female cyborg, who captured much more of his attention than Lawrence did.

"So here's the deal, Dr. Schmidt," Jason said. He slid a picture across the table, of a stylish home set among palm trees and banana leaf fronds, atop a knoll overlooking the Caribbean.

"Two of Bahama's highest priced sexual cyborgs maintain this home and its owner." He had Oscar Schmidt's attention now. He slowly slid the deed across the leather-topped table, along with a video clip of two stunning cyborgs engaged in an act of intense sexual foreplay.

Some drool escaped from the corner of Oscar Schmidt's mouth. He picked up the deed and studied the first page and then the second. The deed transferred ownership to a Belize corporation.

"The shares of the corporation are bearer shares," Jason continued. "Whoever holds the shares owns the corporation. There are no names involved." He returned his attention to the video clip.

"What—" Schmidt's voice was so thick he took a sip of wine and tried again. "What is it you want?" Schmidt inquired.

"There is legislation moving through Congress that will eliminate the Federal Reserve Bank," Jason said.

"Yes," Schmidt offered.

"The President is going to veto it," Jason stated, matter-of-factly.

"So I have heard," Schmidt replied.

"Leadership of the House and the Senate are strategizing

how to overcome the President's veto."

Schmidt stared at him, waiting for the penny to drop.

"It will be a disaster for the nation if the Federal Reserve Bank, which has been monitoring monetary policy for more than a century, is removed from the economic life of the nation," Jason said.

"And . . . ?" Schmidt asked.

"If someone could monitor the iDevice messages and conversations of House and Senate leadership and the chairmen of the key committees, then steps could be taken to defeat the veto override," he suggested.

Schmidt continued to stare at him, waiting for the rest.

Silence.

"Is that all?" Schmidt asked.

Jason Lawrence shrugged, both hands out in front of him, palms up. "That's it," he remarked. "We would need to know what was being discussed, of course."

Oscar Schmidt picked up the deed to the house and the video clip. "And so you shall."

What Jason didn't tell Schmidt is, the cyborgs were programed assassins.

Chapter Sixty-Two – Spying Revealed
April 12, 2039, Washington, D.C.

It could have been a meeting of a Mafia crime family except the Senate Majority Leader sat at the head of the table. She sipped a glass of expensive Cabernet Sauvignon, her pinky extended as if she was dining with the Queen. Her Chief of Staff, a ruggedly handsome man, sat to her right. JC and his aide, a former linebacker for the 49ers with a twenty-inch neck, and Jonathon made up the rest of the group.

They sat in a private dining alcove at Charlie Parker's Steakhouse a few blocks from the U.S. Capitol Building and had just finished a discussion of strategy on how to defeat the president's veto over lobster tails and white wine. The food was very good, the atmosphere not so much.

"Something rather odd today," JC said, and paused to take a sip of wine. "The Chairman of the Ways and Means Committee told me he's received a sudden influx of constituent pressure in opposition to our bill."

Jonathon replied, "I thought you said the normal route for that bill in the House was through the Financial Services Committee. How would the public know we were planning to go through Ways and Means?"

"Exactly," JC declared. "I think we've got a leak." He peered curiously at Jonathon, his eyes tightening.

"Hey, hey, hey," Jonathon deflected the inference. "I haven't discussed this strategy with a soul, no one, in or out of my office."

"I'm just saying," JC shrugged, and turned away.

The meeting broke up a few minutes later on this less-than-positive note.

Jonathon was thinking of blowing off his run, but Sarge would not permit it. By the time he got back to the house and made it into the den, barefoot, tee-shirt drenched, it was 8:00 p.m., only 5:00 on the West Coast.

"How goes the legislation?" Agnes asked when he called.

"We need to talk," he stated.

"Aren't we doing that. But before we jump in, I have some news, some good and some great."

"I could use some good news about now ... lay it on me," he requested.

"Jonathon—?"

"Ash? Ash, is that you?" he asked.

"Alive and well, babe," she replied. "It's a very long story. I'll give you the blow by blow next time I see you. I made it to our outpost in Big Sur. I'll be working here with Agnes for the time being. I'm fine and I love you."

"Enough kissy-face," Agnes chimed in. "Here's the good news. I told you our guy in D.C. had hacked into the DHS alt iDevice network."

"Yes," Jonathon said.

"Schmidt is spying on the Speaker, the Majority Leader, and several committee chairmen in both bodies."

"What?" Jonathon felt incredulous.

"He has tapped into their personal iDevice accounts," she continued.

"Are you sure?"

"Here are audio recordings of some conversations from the accounts of both leaders and some others."

Jonathon's iDevice received them instantly.

"Give me a minute." He listened to recordings of both leaders and several others. Much of the communication was about legislative strategy, but personal conversations were recorded as well, some of them highly compromising.

He glanced at Sarge as he listened. Sarge lifted his head and looked at Jonathon expectantly. When Jonathon continued to listen to the recordings, Sarge put his head back down on his paws and closed his eyes.

"This is unbelievable," Jonathon was astonished. "It's a violation of Federal law, to say nothing of a massive abuse of the Fourth Amendment."

"I'm not sure what had prompted Schmidt to take such a risk," Agnes said, "but it seemed tied to the Federal Reserve legislation. We'll stay on it and keep you posted."

They were back in the Majority Leader's office, all five of them, though getting JC there was a little like extracting a molar. Once seated Jonathon asked them all to disconnect their iDevices.

"We don't need theatrics," JC asserted.

"Turn them off," Jonathon repeated. "If after five minutes you don't see a need to have them off, turn them back on."

They did so.

"You may find what I am about to tell you hard to believe," Jonathon began, "but please hear me out. I have proof of what I'm about to tell you. You remember the leak of my meeting with

JC?"

Everyone nodded except JC, who just listened.

"I retained an investigative firm to track it down. A good one. Turns out it was my Legislative Aide, Monica Ruiz. Except her name isn't Monica Ruiz, it's Robin Delgado."

Lena leaned forward on her elbows.

"Robin Delgado is an employee of the DEA who works as an undercover narcotics agent. She is currently on loan to the Department of Homeland Security. Oscar Schmidt, the Director of Domestic Intelligence at DHS, planted Miss Delgado in my office. She sends him reports concerning my political activities."

JC's aide twisted his head as if he was trying to get a kink out of his neck.

"Conservatives trying to keep track of you since your newfound popularity," Lena said.

"It's a violation of Federal law," JC countered. "Not my style."

"Right," Lena commented. The sarcasm wasn't muted.

"Hold on, you two. There's more. It's not just me," Jonathon said.

He told them about the DHS surveillance on the committee chairmen, and then sprung the fact that DHS was spying on each of them as well.

"Did they spy on me?" blurted out Red, Lena's aide. In this day and age for a homosexual to hide the fact he was gay was unusual, but for reasons of his own Red did so, despite the fact everyone knew this to be the case.

"I don't know," Jonathon replied.

"Damn it!" Red exclaimed.

The room remained silent for a few moments, after which Red said, "Sorry."

JC declared, "This is bullshit, Jonathon."

"I wish it were bullshit, JC." He had his iDevice play a clip of JC talking to the Chairman of the Rules Committee.

"Play that again," JC requested. He cocked his head to the side, like a dog listening to something in the distance. When the audio finished, he asked, "How did you get this?"

"The investigators were able capture the unauthorized iDevice surveillance from an alternate iDevice network, JC. There are hours of it." He summoned his iDevice to play some more.

After listening to a dozen recordings, Lena sat back in her chair. "That dickhead in the White House has gone too far this time."

"Due respect, Madame Majority Leader, I'm not sure that's the case," Jonathon offered. "Perhaps, but what we know for certain at this point is that Oscar Schmidt is driving this train."

"Jonathon, why are the DHS and Schmidt even interested in this legislation," Lena asked. "Someone else or a group must be involved. You're not sure the President isn't involved but I am."

"I don't know but before this is over I will be," Jonathon declared.

"The President is his boss," JC pointed out. "This is executive power run amuck. Does he think he is running the Stasi? The man took an oath to uphold the Constitution of the United States for God's sake."

"So help me, God," uttered Jonathon. He had no idea where that came from. Everyone looked at him for a moment and then carried on.

"We need to impeach him," declared JC.

"First, our legislation," Jonathon said. "Let me suggest a strategy."

Chapter Sixty-Three – The Veto
April 12, 2039, Washington, D.C.

"What do you mean, you lost her?" Schmidt screamed at his iDevice.

Amanda Campos could feel the perspiration running from her armpits and down the sides of her ribcage and propped her body against a wall as she spoke. In her rush to change clothes in order to follow Ashley, she had neglected to stuff her heroin into her purse and was now so weak from the onset of withdrawal she slid down the wall and came to rest on a trash receptacle.

The iDevice remained engaged.

"There was an emergency landing in Salt Lake and—"

"I don't give a shit about an emergency landing. You fucking lost her," Schmidt, nearly shouting.

"But—"

"If you want that promotion, you find her," Schmidt ordered. He signed out of the conversation and threw his iDevice across the room.

###

Monica Ruiz hadn't spoken to the Senator in several days and was considering telling Schmidt she suspected the Senator had discovered she was operating in his office at the behest of DHS.

When Cynthia told her the Senator wanted to see her, she jumped out of her seat so fast she slammed her knee into a corner of her desk, sending a searing pain shooting down her shin bone. "Shit!" She winced, rubbed her knee, took a deep breath, and walked through the office lobby to the Senator's door, and knocked.

"Come on in," Jonathon said, and had her take a seat.

"Sorry I've been out of touch," he offered. "Endless meetings on this Fed legislation."

"I understand completely, Senator."

"To compound my felony, I need to have you go through the draft legislation tonight and get back to me first thing in the morning with any comments," he said.

"Yes, Senator."

"I am sending the final draft of the bill to you now. I'd like you to read it. The Majority Leader and the Speaker will be running with it the day after tomorrow. The good news is, we have the votes to override a veto." He smiled.

"Great," she responded with a plastic smile.

"This is strictly confidential. I'd just like another set of eyeballs on this to see if we missed anything."

"I'll get right on it, Sir."

"It's going to be a late night for you, Monica. It's lengthy," he added.

"No problem," she replied.

###

Monica was pumped, having finally obtained some confidential information from Senator Carr.

Schmidt's iDevice engaged.

"I hope you have something good to tell me, I'm in no mood for fucking excuses," Schmidt barked.

"I got a copy of the final draft of the bill from the Senator," excitement in her voice. "He wants me to look it over to see if anything was missed. I'm sending the draft to you now." With some hesitation she continued, "But I must tell you, if this leaks before it is taken up in Congress, my usefulness would be over." They disconnected.

"Finally something useful," he voiced to himself, "I got that son of a bitch now."

He then encrypted the draft legislation and forwarded it to the blind iDevice address Jason had given him.

Jason immediately forwarded the encrypted file to his superior at Seven. From Seven it was flashed to the senior partner at the law firm in Havana, who in turn sent it to the address for the client in Tallinn, Estonia.

The server for the Los Trés, a reference to the three amigos whose attorneys were joint trustees of the Cook Island Trust that held the bearer shares to the Estonian corporation, forwarded the now well-traveled digital file to Max Putter, senior partner at Putter, Sandborn & Chavetz. Putter-Sandborn was an elite, up-market, D.C. law firm with a deep roster of well-connected attorneys. They represented the mega-rich, both personal and corporate. The Putter firm was one of the few on K Street that did not lobby. They consulted. They advised but did not overtly seek to influence legislation.

Max Putter, a suspendered, silver-haired German, having read the time-sensitive nature of the file, removed his coat, told his secretary, an "M Class" Korean cyborg he called PK, to bring him some coffee, and added that he was not to be disturbed.

After spending four eye-squinting hours poring through the provisions of the eighty-nine pages of proposed legislation, he sat back in his chair and smiled. He told PK to arrange a conference call with the three attorneys whose names he gave her. When she had them connected he commenced the call.

"Good afternoon, gentlemen. Please pardon the insistence on a prompt teleconference," he said, viewing the three life-sized holographic figures projected in front of his desk. "As always, of course, this conversation is attorney-client privileged."

The three grunted their assent, anxious to get to the meat of the call.

"I have just finished reading the final draft of the Federal Reserve legislation that will be voted on tomorrow," he declared, and held up the printed draft of the bill. "This draft was procured in a confidential manner and its terms cannot be disseminated before the bill is voted on."

"Don't they have to post the legislation?" the attorney for J.P. Morgan asked. The other two attorneys on the call, one representing Goldman Sachs and the other Citibank, confirmed that was the case.

"That is the rule," Max said, "but it is disregarded with regularity. In fact, it is supposed to be available for public review for a minimum of forty-eight hours before the vote. But Congress often violates its own rules and the public does not hold its feet to the fire. I am sending each of you a copy, but let me give you the bottom line, the good news and the bad news."

"Bad first," remarked Murray Gould, the Goldman attorney.

"The bad news is that they have the votes to override a veto," Max said.

"Shit!"

"And the good news," the attorney from Citibank chimed in.

"The good news," Max offered, "is, the President doesn't need to veto it. Look at what is buried on page eighty-four, section seventeen-oh-one, first paragraph."

Silence reigned for five minutes while each of the attorneys read and then re-read the paragraph.

"Is this power nullified anywhere else in the legislation?" Gould asked.

"It is not. I have been through this draft with a fine-tooth comb," Max stated. "They have given the President this power unilaterally. If, after consulting with the Secretary of the Treasury, he feels the removal of the Federal Reserve Bank will put the country at risk for an act of financial terrorism on the homeland, he can prevent its removal, or if removed, have it reinstated."

"Why would they do this?" Goldman Sachs asked.

"Terrorism is the ultimate 'go' button, Murray," Max responded.

They all nodded in agreement. "It is that," Murray concurred.

The conference ended with a sense of great relief on the parts of all.

A superior at Seven gave the go ahead for Max to communicate to the Secretary of the Treasury, the former CEO of Citibank and a vehement opponent of the legislation, to meet with the president this evening and give him the good news. He would not have to veto the legislation and suffer the humiliation of the veto being overridden because the legislation carried a specific provision enabling him to maintain the Fed at his sole discretion.

He could sign the bill and be a hero.

Some kind of loan agreement would have to be worked out with the Fed at some point, but in the meantime his poll numbers would soar.

Chapter Sixty-Four – BAT BIG
April 13, 2039, The White House

Maxwell Mendoza, a hairless, Princeton-educated albino with multiple sclerosis, had been President Stanford Jones's Chief of Staff through his two terms as governor of New Mexico and the two years of his presidency.

He opened the door to the Oval Office and rolled his wheelchair to the President's desk. Maxwell could actually walk normally but milked the diagnosis he had been given in college by a cyborg medical assistant for every advantage he could.

"Here it is," he said, placing the bill on the desk. "Are you sure you don't want a signing ceremony?"

"There isn't time," the President replied. What he didn't say was he wanted to appear to be moving as fast as Congress in addressing the escalating economic crisis. They had gotten out in front of him. The press was fawning over certain Congress members. He didn't like it.

The House had passed the Better Approach to Banking in Government Act, BAT BIG, at 10:00 a.m. It was through the Senate by noon. He would sign the bill and it would become law before dinner was served.

Having been briefed by the Treasury Secretary last night,

he took from its holder the old quill pen given to him by his grandmother, dipped it in the inkwell, and signed.

The bill was now law.

Maxwell Mendoza would see to the wide distribution of the video of the President signing the bill on all major iDevice channels.

Of course the bill the President signed had only a passing resemblance to the draft legislation that Monica Ruiz had passed to Oscar Schmidt. Omitted was the provision enabling him to maintain the Fed at his sole discretion.

The majority leader had decided to let JC take the lead on the Federal Reserve legislation. She would follow and Jonathon would finish.

"The prior legislation was child's play compared to trying to do the right thing for the American people at a time like this," JC stated, "but with the help of our friends in the Senate, the Majority Leader and Senator Carr, we have crafted a solution, not only for the immediate financial needs of the government, but for a long-term restructuring of our nation's financial operations."

"This legislation does three things. First, it repeals the Federal Reserve Act and eliminates the Federal Reserve Bank. If and when the government borrows, and we have set limits to the borrowing, it can do so without having to pay what is now over a trillion a year in interest."

JC went over several additional details of the bill and then passed the podium to the Majority Leader.

"Secondly," she said, "this Act creates the Bank of the United States inside the Department of the Treasury. The Bank of the United States will carry out many of the functions that have been conducted by the Federal Reserve Bank."

She provided more detail on how the bank itself would operate and decided to take head-on the objections she knew would be coming. "If you are concerned because you think the Federal Reserve System, which is supposed to control the economy, will be gone, I invite you all to look around at the results of their control. Look at Cleveland and Chicago. Look at Los Angeles, Tampa, and Seattle. Look outside your window at home."

###

President Jones's stomach started to turn sour as he watched the press conference with Maxwell on a floor-to-ceiling video screen in the Oval Office. The acid-stomach and the heartburn that followed was always a harbinger of evil tidings to come. He asked Maxwell to get him a copy of the legislation he had signed and some antacid tablets.

###

Jonathon wore a dark suit, a solid yellow tie, and carried a leather file-folder to the podium, which he opened deliberately before he started to speak.

"Good evening, ladies and gentlemen. I'm sure it is clear to all of you that the bipartisan, bicameral cooperation displayed in Congress in the creation of this legislation is nothing short of historic. I am honored to have been part of it."

The universally negative press corps did something no one could remember having occurred. They broke into applause.

Jonathon waited for it to subside and then picked up his narrative. "In the course of House and Senate leadership crafting this bill, a situation arose outside the financial sphere that also demanded a legislative solution."

The mood in the room changed. This was new. Unexpected. The crowd's attention was now riveted.

With a sense of history he felt to his core, he commenced his presentation. "Almost everyone in this room remembers nine-eleven," he said. "It was a watershed event in American history for a number of reasons. It changed the way we traveled and how we lived. Some of those changes were necessary, but the legislative solution spawned a surveillance leviathan that dismantled our time-honored Constitutional safeguards."

"The USA Patriot Act and its progeny turned the nation's intelligence services, and eventually our law enforcement agencies, into handmaidens of an Orwellian surveillance state. Those of you who have studied your twentieth-century American history will recall the so-called Cold War, and with it the tyranny of the East German Stasi."

Murmurs rustled through the crowd. Senator Carr, a rising Progressive star, was speaking in tongues, the tongue of a Constitutional Conservative.

"Government surveillance," he asserted, "has obliterated the privacy protections of the Fourth Amendment. It is officially out of control. How out of control is evidenced by the case in point that was discovered as we worked through this legislation. Certain people in the Department of Homeland Security took it upon themselves to conduct unauthorized and illegal surveillance of leaders of the House, the Senate, and several key committee chairmen."

"Without probable cause and without warrants, they eavesdropped on at least twenty-three members of the House and Senate, including the Speaker and the Majority Leader. They even went so far as to infiltrate Congress and plant spies in

Congressional offices."

Mayhem. Every reporter in the room was on his or her feet, shouting questions.

"We will not provide any names at this point," he declared through the clamor, "as the matter has been referred to the Attorney General. I can tell you, however, that several federal laws have been broken and this sedition was orchestrated by the Department of Domestic Investigation in the Department of Homeland Security."

In a dim room with the shades drawn Oscar Schmidt, while chewing at his nails and stroking his glabrous shiny dome, could not believe what he is seeing and hearing. "I knew that son of a bitch was a fake – a liberal my ass. I'm not through with him, that fuck." Schmidt thrashed the top of his desk with his fists, sounding like a madman on the war path.

The information Jonathon shared regarding illegal surveillance was enough for several reporters to break from the room at a dead run. One woman tripped and went sprawling onto the lush, gold carpet. One of the celebrity news anchors rushed over and helped her to her feet. This brought the stampede to a halt.

Once people were back in their seats, he continued.

"So, in addition to fixing a broken and oppressive monetary system, we have done the same for our intelligence system. We are grateful to have the President's support of this very historic legislation."

In the oval office the President sat and watched in disbelief. "How could this have happened," he asked one of his aides.

"Mr. President this could be for the better. This could be a plus for your re-election."

"Yes, you could be right." The President responded meekly.

What was really going through his mind were the repercussions this would have with his relationship with the IMF authoritarians.

"To start, we have returned the structure of our intelligence services to their rightful roles. The Department of Homeland Security will confine itself to matters of immigration and transportation. As of today, the DHS Department of Domestic Intelligence has been defunded. Under this legislation, the CIA is again formally and quite specifically barred from conducting domestic intelligence operations, and the FBI will resume the prosecution of federal crimes."

"In no case will government surveillance be conducted without strict adherence to the Constitutional protections guaranteed by the Fourth Amendment. Any government surveillance, local, state, or federal, which is conducted without probable cause and a warrant, according to this Act, will itself be prosecuted to the fullest extent of the law."

"Finally, warrants sought for surveillance in matters of national security will no longer be presented to a secret judicial body but rather to federal judges, for which there will be proper review and oversight."

"With BAT BIG, we restructure the nation's monetary system and our intelligence system, bringing stability to the economy and returning privacy and security to our citizens."

Epilogue

Weeks after Senator Carr's presentation, President Jones suffered a massive stroke. He lived through it, but the right side of his body was paralyzed, and he was unable to speak. When efforts by several of the nation's leading physicians failed to restore his speech or mobility he abdicated his office.

The Vice President, a former Mixed Martial Arts champion named Gloria, pledged to do everything she could to carry forward with President Jones' legislative agenda, which included the implementation and execution of BAT BIG. Both programs had gotten off to successful starts.

Dr. Oscar Schmidt struck a deal with prosecutors and plead guilty to two Class Three felonies, for which he would do time in the Allenwood Federal Correctional Institution in Pennsylvania. Allenwood was a low-security institution in which Oscar Schmidt would serve five years. He was not overly concerned with the length of his stay, as he had fallen in love with a foreign national, a check-forger from Panama named Manuelito.

Jonathon continued to caucus with the Progressives but became widely admired in both Conservative and Independent circles. He was a frequent guest on iDevice channel shows.

In the fall Jonathon and Ashley got married and, with Sarge, moved into a larger home in Georgetown. There, over morning coffee on their deck a year later, Jonathon shared the news… "I need to talk to you about something."

There was a certain gravitas in his voice, so she put her book down, brushed the unruly strand of hair back from her face, and turned it brightly toward him.

"I've been approached by some people," he teased.

"A commodity of which Washington has no shortage," she stated.

He broke off a small piece of the strawberry he was eating and tossed it at her. She grabbed it in midair and offered it to Sarge, who licked it off her hand, leaving a fine deposit of dog slobber.

"People with a lot of money," Jonathon added.

"Often a good quality," she quipped.

"People," he continued, "who think the way I do, and you do."

"Yes?"

"They want me to run for President."

Ashley leaped out of her chair, rounded the glass-topped table, plopped into Jonathon's lap and kissed him deeply. "Now," she exclaimed with a mischievous smile, "we're talking. I'll call Agnes."

A feeling of redemption swept through his soul. His amends were complete.

Two Faces of a Patriot
Glossary

Abscond: leave hurriedly and secretly, typically to avoid detection of or arrest for an unlawful action such as theft.

Abdicate: to renounce or relinquish a throne, right, power, claim.

Admonish: warn or reprimand someone firmly.

Admonition: an act or action of admonishing; authoritative counsel or warning.

Agape: (of the mouth) wide open, especially with surprise or wonder.

Amble: (Noun) a stroll; (Verb) walk or move at a slow, relaxed pace.

Amped: full of nervous energy.

Antipathetic: showing or feeling a strong aversion.

Ardent: enthusiastic or passionate.

Array: display or arrange (things) in a particular way.

Askew: not in a straight or level position.

ATF: The Bureau of Alcohol, Tobacco, Firearms and Explosives (ATF) is a law enforcement agency responsible for examining violations of Federal laws within the jurisdiction of the United States Department of Justice.

August: respected and impressive.

Autocratic: relating to a ruler who has absolute power.

Axiomatic: self-evident or unquestionable.

Azalea: a deciduous flowering shrub of the heath family with clusters of brightly colored, sometimes fragrant flowers.

Balmy: (of the weather) pleasantly warm.

Banter: the playful and friendly exchange of teasing remarks.

Beaker: a lipped cylindrical glass container for laboratory use.

Beatific: blissfully happy.

Bicameral: of a legislative body having two branches or chambers.

Bill: during the 1940s, latex rubber became the stiffening material inside the hat and the modern baseball cap was born. The peak, also known in certain areas as the "bill" or "brim" was designed to protect a player's eyes from the sun.

Billed hat: a flat bill snapback hat. The bill being the part of the hat that protects the wearers face from the sun.

Bindi: a decorative mark worn in the middle of the forehead by Indian women.

Biometric: relating to or involving the application of statistical analysis to biological data.

Blanch: (of a person) grow pale from shock, fear, or a similar emotion.

Blitzkrieg: an intense military campaign intended to bring about a swift victory.

BND: abbreviation of Bundesnachrichtendienst, German "Federal Intelligence Service", foreign intelligence agency of the West German government. Its divisions were concerned with subversion, counter-intelligence, and foreign intelligence, and it was headquartered at Munich, West Germany.

Boff: have sexual intercourse with someone.

BOLO: a law enforcement code meaning be on the lookout. It's an order issued to fellow police officers based on specific criminal intelligence.

Bone marrow: a soft fatty substance in the cavities of bones, in which blood cells are produced (often taken as typifying strength and vitality). "To the marrow" can be used to show how strong someone's feelings or beliefs are.

Bonvivant: a person who enjoys a sociable and luxurious lifestyle.

Boofing: to have anal sex with someone, usually as the penetrative partner (possibly with negative connotations).

Book spine: the outer portion of a book which covers the actual binding. The spine usually faces outward when a book is placed on a shelf. Also known as the back.

Boorish: rough and bad-mannered; coarse.

Bot: a computer program that does automated tasks.

Bottlebrush Mustache: a short, bristly moustache.

Bracing: fresh and invigorating.

Buxom: (of a woman) plump, especially with large breasts.

BYU - Brigham Young University: a private, non-profit research university in Provo, Utah, USA completely owned by The Church of Jesus Christ of Latter-day Saints (LDS or Mormon Church) and run under the auspices of its Church Educational System.

Cabal: a secret political clique or faction.

Cache: a collection of items of the same type stored in a hidden or inaccessible place.

Cacophony: a harsh discordant mixture of sound.

Cadence: a modulation or inflection of the voice.

Cant: to set at an angle.

Catwalk: a platform along which models walk in a fashion show.

Cantilever: a long projecting beam or girder fixed at only one end, used chiefly in bridge construction.

Chaparral: vegetation consisting chiefly of tangled shrubs and thorny bushes.

Che: in other Hispanic American countries, the term Che can be used to refer to someone from Argentina. For example, the famous Argentine revolutionary Ernesto "Che" Guevara earned his nickname from his frequent use of the expression, which to his Cuban comrades in the Cuban Revolution was a curious feature of his idiolect.

Clad: clothed.

Cogent: of an argument or case, clear, logical and convincing.

Comer: a person who arrives somewhere.

Complicit: involved with others in an illegal activity or wrongdoing.

Complicity: the state of being involved with others in an illegal activity or wrongdoing.

Compost: decayed organic material used as a plant fertilizer.

Composter: a compost bin.

Conga Line: a novelty line dance that was derived from the Cuban carnival dance of the same name and became popular in the US in the 1930s and 1950s. The dancers form a long, processing line, which would usually turn into a circle.

Copious: abundant in supply or quantity.

Coiffure: a person's hairstyle, typically an elaborate one.

Cotton to: to get to know or understand something.

Covetous: having or showing a great desire to possess something, typically something belonging to someone else.

Crocked: slang word meaning drunk; intoxicated.

Cryptic: having a meaning that is mysterious or obscure.

Dally: act or move slowly.

Dead Fish: of all the types of handshakes, the 'dead fish' is the most infamous one. The hand has no energy, there is no shake, no squeeze, not even a pinch, and it gives the feeling you are holding a dead fish instead of a hand. This handshake is synonym to low self-esteem.

DARPA - Defense Advanced Research Projects Agency: an agency of the United States Department of Defense responsible for the development of emerging technologies for use for the development of emerging technologies for use by the military.

Debauchery: excessive indulgence in sensual pleasures.

Decamp: depart suddenly or secretly, especially to relocate one's business or household in another area.

Deference: humble submission and respect.

De jour: of or from the day, special to that day.

Deltoid: the deltoid muscle is a rounded, triangular muscle located on the uppermost part of the arm and the top of the shoulder. It is named after the Greek letter delta, which is shaped like an equilateral triangle.

Demagogue: a political leader who seeks support by appealing to popular desires and prejudices rather than by using rational argument.

Demure: (of a woman or her behavior) reserved, modest, and shy.

Denizen: an inhabitant or occupant of a particular place.

Derisive: expressing contempt or ridicule.

Despotism: the exercise of absolute power, especially in a cruel and oppressive way.

Deviant: departing from usual or accepted standards, especially in social or sexual behavior.

DHS - The United States Department of Homeland Security: is a federal agency designed to protect the US against threats. Its wide-ranging duties include aviation security, border control, emergency response and cybersecurity.

DIA: Defense Intelligence Agency (USA).

Digs: clothing.

Diminutive: extremely or unusually small.

Din: a loud, unpleasant and prolonged noise.

Dissonance: a tension or clash resulting from the combination of two disharmonious or unsuitable elements.

Disposition: the way in which something is placed or arranged, especially in relation to other things.

DOD - Department of Defense: the federal department responsible for safeguarding national security of the US; created in 1947.

Dome: slang for the head.

Domicile: a place of residence; abode; house or home.

Duplicity: deceitfulness; double-dealing.

Effigy: a roughly made model of a particular person, made in order to be damaged or destroyed as a protest or expression of anger.

Eidetic: relating to or denoting mental images having unusual vividness and details, as if actually visible.

Emancipated: free from legal, social, or political restrictions; liberated.

Enigmatic: difficult to interpret or understand; mysterious.

Enigmatically: difficult to interpret or understand; mysterious.

Epilogue: a section or speech at the end of a book or play that serves as a comment on or a conclusion to what has happened.

Estonian: Estonians are Finnic people who speak Estonian, which is closely related to Finnish. The ethnic breakdown is currently 69% Estonian, 25% Russian, 2% Ukrainian, 1% Belarusians, 0.8% Finns and 1.6% other.

Euphemism: a mild or indirect word or expression substituted for one considered to be too harsh or blunt when referring to something unpleasant or embarrassing.

Eavesdrop: secretly listen to a conversation.

Eviscerate: deprive (something) of its essential content.

Facilitate: make (an action or process) easy or easier.

Fashionista: a devoted follower of fashion.

Faux: not genuine; fake or false.

Fawning: displaying exaggerated flattery or affection; obsequious.

Federal Security Service (FSB): Russian Federalnaya Sluzhba Bezopasnosti, formerly (1994-95) Federal Counterintelligence Service, Russian internal security and counterintelligence service created in 1994 as one of the successor agencies of the Soviet-era KGB.

FEMA - Federal Emergency Management Agency: an agency of the United States Department of Homeland Security, initially created by Presidential Reorganization Plan No. 3 of 1978 and implemented by two Executive Orders on April 1, 1979.

FISC - The United States Foreign Intelligence Surveillance Court.

FISA Court: a U.S. federal court established and authorized under the Foreign Intelligence Surveillance Act of 1978 (FISA) to oversee requests for surveillance warrants against foreign spies inside the United States by federal law.

Fleck: a very small patch of color or light.

Flint lock: an old-fashioned type of gun fired by a spark from a flint.

Foil: a setback in an enterprise; a defeat.

Foreboding: fearful apprehension; a feeling that something bad will happen.

Four-minute mile: in the sport of athletics, a four-minute mile means completing a mile run (1,760 yard or 1,609.344 meters) in less than four minutes.

Frogmarch: force (someone) to walk forward by holding and pinning their arms from behind.

Frond: the leaf or leaflike part of a palm, fern or similar plant.

FSB: Federal Security Service (FSB), Russian Federalnaya Sluzhba Bezopasnosti, formerly (1994–95) Federal Counterintelligence Service, Russian internal security and counterintelligence service created in 1994 as one of the successor agencies of the Soviet-era KGB.

Gaunt: lean and haggard - grim or desolate in appearance.

Glabrous: (chiefly of the skin or a leaf) free from hair or down; smooth.

Glitterati: wealthy, famous, or glamorous people who attend fashionable events.

GPO - Group Purchasing Organization: in the United States, a group purchasing organization (GPO) is an entity that is created to leverage the purchasing power of a group of businesses to obtain discounts from the vendors based on the collective buying power of the GPO members.

Gravitas: dignity, seriousness, or solemnity of manner.

Grecian: relating to ancient Greece, especially its architecture.

Grimace: a grimace is a facial expression that usually suggests disgust or pain, but sometimes comic exaggeration. Picture someone wrinkling his nose, squeezing his eyes shut, and twisting his mouth and you'll have a pretty solid mental image of a grimace.

Gripe: express a complaint or grumble about something, especially something trivial.

Guardsman: (in the US) a member of the National Guard.

Guile: sly or cunning intelligence.

GW Sweatshirt: George Washington University sweatshirt.

Ham Hock: a bar to build up biceps - inferring big biceps.

Handmaid: a female servant; a subservient partner or element.

Harbinger: a person or thing that announces or signals the approach of another.

Hellacious: very great, bad, or overwhelming.

Hijab: an Arabic word meaning barrier or partition. In Islam, however, it has a broader meaning. It is the principle of modesty and includes behavior as well as dress for both males and females. The most visible form of Hijab is the head covering that many Muslim women wear. Hijab however goes beyond the head scarf.

Hoe: a long-handed gardening tool with a thin metal blade, used mainly for weeding and breaking up soil.

Hollywoodesque: Resembling some aspect of Hollywood.

Hydrochloric Acid: a strongly acidic solution of the gas hydrogen chloride in water.

Hyperbole: exaggerated statements or claims not meant to be taken literally.

Ideation: the formation of ideas or concepts.

IED: a simple bomb made and used by unofficial or unauthorized forces.

Immodest: lacking humility or decency.

Impale: pierce or transfix with a sharp instrument.

Incessant: (of something regarded as unpleasant) continuing without pause or interruption.

Indenture: any deed, written contract, or sealed agreement. A contract by which a person, as an apprentice, is bound to service.

Indignant: feeling or showing anger or annoyance at what is perceived as unfair treatment.

Insouciant: showing a casual lack of concern; indifferent.

Inspissate: thicken or congeal.

Intonation: the rise and fall of the voice in speaking.

Intransigent: unwilling or refusing to change one's views or to agree about something.

Ionosphere: the region of the earth's atmosphere between the stratosphere and the exosphere, consisting of several ionized layers and extending from about 50 to 250 miles (80 to 400 km) above the surface of the earth.

ISBN: International Standard Book Number.

ISP: an Internet service provider is a company that provides individuals and other companies access to the internet and other related services such as website building and virtual hosting.

Jarhead: a US Marine.

Jettison: to push to the side or toss away.

Labyrs: symmetrical double-bitted axe originally from Crete in Greece, one of the oldest symbols of Greek civilization.

Largesse: generosity in bestowing money or gifts upon others.

Lavish: sumptuously rich, elaborate, or luxurious.

Lascivious: (of a person, manner or gesture) feeling or revealing an overt and often offensive sexual desire.

Lecherous: having or showing excessive or offensive sexual desire.

Leviathan: a thing that is very large or powerful.

LGBT: stands for Lesbian, Gay, Bisexual and Transgender.

Lidded: having lids especially of a specified kind - used usually in combination i.e. heavy-lidded eyes.

Lilt: a characteristic rising and falling of the voice when speaking; a pleasant gentle accent.

Maelstrom: a situation or state of confused movement or violent turmoil.

Malinois - The Belgian Malinois (MAL-in-wah): a medium-size Belgian Shepherd Dog that at first glance resembles a German Shepherd Dog.

Mane: a person's long or thick hair; a growth of long hair on the neck of a horse, lion or other animal.

Mania: mental illness marked by periods of great excitement or euphoria, delusions, and overactivity.

Marginalized: of a person, group, or concept) treated as insignificant or peripheral.

Metastasis: the development of secondary malignant growths at a distance from a primary site of cancer. A metastatic growth.

Metastasize: (of a cancer) spread to other sites in the body by metastasis.

Mordor: in J.R.R. Tolkien's fictional universe of Middle-earth, Mordor is the dwelling place of Sauron, in the southeast of Middle-earth to the East of Anduin, the great river. Frodo and Sam went there to destroy the One Ring.

Multi-Spectral: A multi-spectral image is a collection of several monochrome images of the same scene, each of them taken with a different sensor. Each image is referred to as a band.

NAFTA - North American Free Trade Agreement: a treaty entered into by the US, Canada and Mexico; it went into effect on January 1, 1994 (Free trade had existed between the US and Canada since 1989; NAFTA broadened that arrangement.)

NCAA: NCAA stands for National Collegiate Athletic Association.

Neocon: (in politics) a person with neoconservative views.

Nominally: in name only; officially though perhaps not in reality.

NSA - The National Security Agency: a national-level intelligence agency of the United States.

Obsequious: obedient or attentive to an excessive or servile degree. They were served by obsequious waiters.

Odyssey: a long wondering and eventful journey.

Officious: assertive of authority in an annoyingly domineering way, especially with regard to petty or trivial matters.

Ominous: the impression something bad or unpleasant is going to happen; threatening; inauspicious.

Opine: hold or state as one's opinion.

Ostensible: stated or appearing to be true, but not necessarily so.

Oxblood: a color considered to be a dark shade of red. It resembles Burgundy but has more purple and dark brown hues.

Palette: a thin board or slab on which an artist lays and mixes colors.

Pandemonium: wild and noisy disorder or confusion; uproar.

Pallor: an unhealthy pale appearance.

Pansy: a timid man or boy considered childish or unassertive.

Pantheon: (especially in ancient Greece and Rome) a temple dedicated to all the gods.

Paralytic: relating to paralysis. Something causing paralysis.

Pate: a person's head.

Personage: a person (often used to express their significance, importance or elevated statue).

Peruse: examine carefully or at length.

Perturb: feeling or showing agitation; bothered, upset

Placate: make (someone) less angry or hostile.

Polymers: a substance that has a molecular structure consisting chiefly or entirely of a large number of similar units bonded together.

Pontificate: express one's opinions in a way considered annoyingly pompous and dogmatic (inclined to lay down principles as incontrovertibly true).

Portent: a sign or warning that something, especially something momentous or calamitous, is likely to happen.

Post-mortem: an examination of a dead body to determine the cause of death.

Pragmatic: dealing with things sensible and realistically in a way that is based on practical rather than theoretical considerations.

PRC: "People's Republic of China."

Preen: congratulate or pride oneself.

Pro tem: for the time being.

Proclivity: a tendency to choose or do something regularly; an inclination or predisposition toward a particular thing.

PTSD: Short for post-traumatic stress disorder.

Pugilistic: boxer appearance, especially a professional one.

Purport: appear or claim to be or do something, especially falsely; profess.

Rail: to complain bitterly or vehemently.

Rakish: having or displaying a dashing, jaunty or slightly disreputable quality or appearance.

Rancor: bitterness or resentfulness, especially when long-standing.

Rapacious: aggressively greedy or grasping.

Rarefied: distant from the lives and concerns of ordinary people.

Rebuff: reject (someone or something) in an abrupt or ungracious manner.

Reciprocate: respond to (a gesture or action) by making a corresponding one.

Recursive: characterized by recurrence or repetition, in particular.

Redress: remedy or set right (an undesirable or unfair situation).

Regent: a member of the governing body of a university or other academic institution.

Replete: filled or well-supplied with something.

Repugnant: intense disgust.

Rivulet: a very stream.

Roguish: playfully mischievous, especially in a way that is sexually attractive.

Rutted: having long deep tracks made by the repeated passage of the wheels of vehicles.

Sake: "alcohol" in Japanese.

Salvo: a sudden, vigorous, or aggressive act or series of acts.

Sans: without.

Saucy: bold and lively; smart-looking.

Saunter: walk in a slow, relaxed manner, without hurry or effort.

Sauvignon: a variety of wine grape. A wine made from the Sauvignon grape.

Scythe: a tool used for cutting crops such as grass or wheat, with a long curved blade at the end of a long pole attached to which are one or two short handles.

Sedition: conduct or speech inciting people to rebel against the authority of a state or monarch.

Searing: extremely hot or intense.

Semayne's Case Law: an old English common law case, which held that a right of a home-owner to defend his/her premises against intrusion should yield to those seeking to enter under lawful authority like to make an arrest.

Skew: suddenly change direction or position.

Smattering: a small amount of something.

Smoke eater: a device or piece of equipment designed to remove smoke from the air.

Sop: a thing given or done as a concession of no great value to appease someone whose main concerns or demands are not being met.

Spent: drained of energy or effectiveness: exhausted.

Squalid: (of a place) extremely dirty and unpleasant, especially as a result of poverty or neglect.

Stasi: official name Ministerium fur Staatssicherheit (German: Ministry for State Security) secret police agency of the German Democratic Republic (East Germany). The Stasi was one of the most hated and feared institutions of the East German communist government.

Step into the breach: replace someone who is suddenly unable to do a job or task.

Stoically: without showing one's feelings or complaining about pain or hardship.

Strain: a genetic variant or subtype of a microorganism (e.g. virus or bacterium or fungus). For example, a "flu strain" is a certain biological form of the influenza or "flu" virus.

Stultify: cause to lose enthusiasm and initiative, especially as a result of a tedious or restrictive routine.

Sublimate: especially in psychoanalytic theory to divert or modify (an instinctual impulse) into a culturally higher or socially more acceptable activity.

Subterfuge: deceit used in order to achieve one's goal.

Sumptuous: splendid and expensive-looking.

Surreptitiously: in a way that attempts to avoid notice or attention; secretively.

Sycophant: a person who acts obsequiously (obedient or attentive to an excessive or servile degree) towards someone important in order to gain advantage.

Talon: a claw, especially one belonging to a bird of prey.

Temple: Often called the arm, this is the piece of the frame that extends over the ear to help hold the sunglasses in place.

Tender: to present for acceptance.

Testicular Cancer: Testicular cancer occurs in the testicles (testes), which are located inside the scrotum, a loose bag of skin underneath the penis. The testicles produce male sex hormones and sperm for reproduction.

TIA - Total Information Awareness: a US DARPA program now called Terrorism Information Awareness.

Tog: clothes.

Tread: walk in a specified way.

Trek: go on a long arduous journey, typically on foot.

Triumvirate: (in ancient Rome) a group of three men holding power.

Troglodytes: a person who lived in a cave. A hermit. A person who is regarded as being deliberately ignorant or old-fashioned.
Trump: (in bridge, whist, and similar card games) a playing card of the suit chosen to rank above the others, which can win a trick where a card of a different suit has been led.

Unabated: without any reduction in intensity or strength.

Unceremoniously: with a lack of courtesy; roughly or abruptly.

Unflappable: having or showing calmness in a crisis.

Urbane: (of a person, especially a man) suave, courteous and refined in manner.

Verdant: (of countryside) green with grass or other rich vegetation.

Vigil: a period of keeping awake during the time usually spent asleep, especially to keep watch or pray.

Virulent: bitterly hostile.

Vociferous: (especially of a person or speech) vehement or clamorous.

Voyeurs: a person who enjoys seeing the pain or distress of others.

Watershed: an event or period marking a turning point in a course of action or state of affairs.

Whip: an official of a political party appointed to maintain discipline among its members in Congress or Parliament, especially so as to ensure attendance and voting in debates.

Whole Cloth: pure fabrication or fiction; a story invented with no basis in fact.

Writ of assistance: a written order (a writ) issued by a court instructing a law enforcement official, such as a sheriff or tax collector, to perform a certain task.